HILARY BAILEY was born in Kent in 1936. Educated at ten schools and Cambridge University, she worked for a time in publicity until marrying in 1962 and having three children. She has written many short stories and articles for magazines, and has reviewed fiction regularly for the *Guardian*. Her novels are *Polly Put The Kettle On* (1974), *Mrs Mulvaney* (1976) and *All The Days Of My Life* (1984). She lives in London, and is at present working on a new novel.

Hannie Richards Or The Intrepid Adventures Of A Restless Wife is a sharp and witty pastiche of the world of John Buchan, the story of a female buccaneer with a liberal conscience. Hannie Richards leads a double life – one as a wife and mother in a Devon manor house, the other as an international smuggler. Our heroine brings back cures for cancer from the Brazilian jungle, takes a small child across war-torn Chad and steals the vital papers which restore a Black family's rights to their Caribbean island. Between trips she recounts her adventures to her friends at the Hope Club, a notorious women-only version of the Garrick or the Reform.

Virtuous Hannie is not: she wants it all – luxury, excitement, love, security. Perhaps she pays a price for it, for something goes horribly wrong and Hannie loses her cool, with disastrous consequences.

Hannie Richards

or
The Intrepid Adventures
of a Restless Wife

Hilary Bailey

Published by Virago Press Limited 1985
41 William IV Street, London WC2N 4DB

British Library Cataloguing in Publication Data
Bailey, Hilary
    Hannie Richards: or the intrepid adventures
    of a restless wife.
    I. Title
    823'.914[F]   PR6052.A318/

    ISBN 0-86068-346-X
    ISBN 0-86068-351-6 Pbk

Typeset by Clerkenwell Graphics and
printed in Great Britain by Anchor Brendon
of Tiptree, Essex

For Diane Lambert and Meg McDonald – and Bill Webb and Ursula Owen, who dreamed up the whole idea

Contents

1. The Hope Club

The Hope Club in D'Arblay Street, London W1 is unlike any other club. Situated in the middle of Soho's network of narrow streets and alleys, its members are not cabinet ministers, merchant bankers or army generals snoozing in leather armchairs. Nor are they the pimps, prostitutes and gangsters who frequent the gambling and strip clubs and blue movie cinemas near by. Behind its façade the Hope Club offers the same facilities found in the grander gentlemen's clubs of Mayfair or Belgravia – a restaurant, comfortable sitting rooms, bedrooms, a bar. The Hope Club is different for one reason only: all its members are women.

The Hope Club was started during the war when a group of women friends decided to rent a flat where they could meet each other and talk or retreat from the pressures of the world outside, a flat where they could spend the night or meet a friend for a drink. The new club fulfilled a need and was an immediate success, attracting, over the years, an increasing number of members. Gradually it grew and had to move from the tatty two-room flat to a large building with many rooms. The outside remained oddly scruffy and the entrance was down one of those narrow, pitted alleys so frequently found in Soho, but inside the rooms were elegant and large, with comfortable furniture, open fireplaces and a well-stocked bar.

The members of the Hope Club each contributed one-sixth of their net income. This meant that some paid little or nothing, while others paid a great deal. Prospective members had to be sponsored by three actual members, and, similarly, any prospective member could be blackballed by three other members. Like all thriving clubs, the Hope Club flourished on a basis of friendships, connections and previous associations between the members. Decisions were made by consultation. The real managers were Mr and Mrs Knott, who paid the bills, kept the restaurant and ran the bar, called the plumber and hired the help. They ran it very smoothly.

These days the Hope Club is larger and grander than it was, but let us go back before recent renovations and visit the Club a few years ago.

Turning into the dark alley to enter 41 D'Arblay Street, we pass a fish shop with its big marble slab displaying magnificent fresh crabs and large baskets of oysters. Opening the front door with its peeling green paint, we find ourselves in a narrow, shabby passageway covered with linoleum so old it has lost all recognizable pattern. Continuing down, we come to a second door, not much smarter than the first, but beyond that lies the bright, freshly painted restaurant with a dozen tables covered with red gingham cloths. There are a few plants, including a daisy tree of which Mrs Knott is very fond, and a fish tank containing tropical fish, which is Mr Knott's pride and joy. In the restaurant breakfasts,

2

lunches and dinners are served.

To the left of the restaurant a curved, green-carpeted staircase with white wrought-iron banisters leads upstairs where, on the next floor, two small rooms have been knocked together to form a clubroom. On the floors above are bedrooms for overnight stays.

This is the Hope Club, a haven for women in the heart of London. And it is here in the clubroom, with its long bar, pale paint, comfortable chairs and sofas, that on a chilly summer evening some years ago, with a bright fire burning in the grate, we begin our tale.

'My big advantage,' said Hannie Richards, 'is that I can disguise myself as a woman, which, in most societies, means that no one notices you.'

She was wearing a slightly crushed pink linen suit and leaning back in a big, cream leather armchair. Her long, tanned legs were stretched out before her, and her bare feet, with their painted toenails, rested on the brass fender. She was a tall, attractive woman in her thirties with dark brown eyes and dark red hair. A pair of cream linen sandals lay beside her on the floor, next to two plastic bags one marked 'Portobello Health Stores', the other, 'Posh, Georgetown, Barbados'.

She added to her friend Elizabeth Lord who was sitting opposite, 'The last time I smuggled something, I was dressed practically all the time in something resembling a black plastic rubbish bag – like the ones you find clustered round lamp-posts when there's a dustmen's strike. No one noticed me as long as I kept my eyes on the ground. No one bothered to check what I had stuffed up my *burkha* either.'

'I know the feeling,' Elizabeth said. 'It's like that when my husband's colleagues come to dinner with their wives. The men don't expect us women to say much or offer opinions.' Elizabeth was a pale, pretty woman with anxious blue eyes and blonde hair which reached to her shoulders. She was wearing a raspberry-coloured woollen dress from Harvey Nichols. She added wryly, 'The last time I managed to cook a huge dinner one of the guests, a man from the Foreign Office, turned to me and said, "And what do you do?" I just started to sweat and said in panic, "Nicely, thank you, sir." Like a Victorian servant. I couldn't think of anything else to say. Then I burst into tears and cried so much that I had to leave the room. Anyway,' she continued, 'what did you have stuffed under your black draperies, Hannie?'

'Just a passport, tickets and a bit of money – and a spare *burkha* some of the time,' Hannie said. She paused.

Julie St Just, who was sitting on the rug in front of the fire, drew on her roll-up cigarette, grinned at Hannie and said instantly, 'You were smuggling another woman – right?' She was wearing a shiny blue trouser suit and her hair ended in matching beads of the same colour. She had a long, coffee-coloured face and her eyes looked tired. 'Come on,' she said, 'what was it all about?'

'A couple living in Cumberland rang,' explained Hannie. 'They'd been put on to me by a man I once did some work for. And they told me that their only daughter, a nurse, had suddenly got restless and shipped herself out to Saudi Arabia as a children's nanny to an Arab family. After a few months the parents lost contact with her. They weren't getting replies to any of their letters, and when they phoned they were always told that the girl was away somewhere with the children. They knew there was something wrong, but no one could help them unless the girl herself asked for help. They sent a man from the Foreign Office round and he saw her and said she was all right. She still didn't get in touch, and the parents went on worrying, but after the initial check the FO was unhelpful. The employer, needless to say, was from a big oil-owning family, and they didn't want to upset anybody. They even suggested the parents were being overprotective. When the parents decided to go out there themselves this old client of mine suggested it would be better if I went. He even helped them out with the money. So I went and found her. Guess where.'

Julie's eyes opened wide. 'In the wicked sheikh's harem, guarded by eunuchs with machine-guns,' she said.

'Nearly true,' Hannie laughed. 'They'd got the poor girl in custody and she was under heavy siege from the sheikh's eldest son. His mother was tearing up the letters from home and keeping off strangers. They had her passport and her bankbook. The young man from the Foreign Office had never seen her – just a girl they must have got to impersonate her. I got in by hiding in a deep freeze in the back of a truck – the driver was sympathetic and greedy. And we shuffled out with our knees sagging so's not to look too tall and also to try to persuade the menfolk that underneath we weren't young and beautiful. And back she went to her parents in Cumberland.'

'How wonderful!' exclaimed Elizabeth.

'I'm a public benefactor,' Hannie declared. 'No doubt about it.' She yawned. 'My goodness, I'm tired.'

'Jet lag?' observed Elizabeth.

Hannie shook her head. 'I've only been in Notting

Hill Gate,' she said wearily. 'It's the mothers.' She yawned. 'It's the mothers that did it.' She yawned again, shut her eyes and was, according to her usual habit, instantly asleep.

'Mothers? What's she going on about?' asked Julie. She foraged in the big red leather bag at her side and fished out her tobacco tin. As she rolled another cigarette she muttered, 'I need mine that's for sure, to look after me. I ought to go home to Mother – back to Barbados.'

'What's the matter?' asked Elizabeth.

Julie lit up the cigarette. 'Ah, man, I only got up at six o'clock, that's all, to do a make-up commercial. For the darker skin, of course. My manager tells me I owe him money for the last tour – like I always do. And I got this bill for unpaid tax he's supposed to have taken care of, only he didn't do it. After that there's a whole afternoon in the recording studio, but we never did anything, and while I'm there I get a call from my friend Leona, who takes care of the kids while I'm working, and she tells me my Thomas probably has the mumps, only the doctor's not sure about it and also she says that my son John is out on the street again with the boys who got him in trouble the last time. I have to call everyone to get him home. Now I'm waiting until ten and then I have to go on to the club and sing. That's the day,' she said, 'and like my mother used to say, "Oh, Lud – oh Jesus Chris! – I wish I never was born."' She paused, then grinned at Elizabeth. 'Well, that's the moaning over – I feel better. Maybe even Mother couldn't help me out of this one. How're things with you?'

Elizabeth's anxious face relaxed a little. 'My problems come from the other end to yours,' she said. 'With you

6

it's all movement and flashing lights. With me it's all static and solid grey. And what you need, Julie, is an accountant.' She spoke firmly.

Julie smiled wryly. 'I've got one of those. I got a lawyer, a manager, a bank manager and an accountant. Everywhere I look there's a white man in a suit saying I owe him money and telling me to go and get some more. And I can hardly pay my bills. I don't need any more white men. I'm thinking of running away, like a slave.'

'Well, then,' said Elizabeth. 'Why don't you get all the papers together – contracts, bank statements, manager's records – and bring them along to me. At least I could look at them for you.'

'You couldn't make any sense of it all,' Julie said, shaking her head. 'They can't and I can't and now I got the bailiffs breathing down my neck.'

'Bring all the papers along to me,' Elizabeth insisted. 'Please. You can't get much worse off. I'm a trained accountant. I don't need to understand your business to understand the accounts, and I'd like to help.'

'I'd be really pleased. Even if you can't help, I'd be pleased. You can have ten per cent of what you save me.'

'I'll do it for the fun,' Elizabeth said.

Julie grinned. 'Has your analyst told you to find an outlet, then?'

Elizabeth sighed. 'He thinks I have a deep problem. At the moment he just asks me if I think I'm coping better. He told me last week I should think about whether it was something to do with having two older brothers.' Her face took on lines of weariness and defeat. 'It's this idea of coping. What he really means is am I getting in a firm to clean the carpets or lying in bed all day, too weary to get up. I'm sure John wouldn't mind if I got a job. The children are old enough now. But he says – the analyst – that the problem is deep-seated.'

'That's a tiring word – coping,' Julie said. 'It makes me feel weak when I hear it.'

Elizabeth stared into the fire flickering in the grate. 'Women are expected to cope; men manage.'

'Coping just means keeping up,' said Julie.

Elizabeth nodded. 'No progress, no joy.'

'No satisfaction,' carolled Julie.

'No hope,' droned Elizabeth.

They looked at each other and laughed. 'I wouldn't let your analyst use that word to you no more,' suggested Julie. 'If he changes his vocabulary, maybe your deep-seated problems will get a lot shallower.'

'I'll pull them up like weeds,' Elizabeth said lightly, looking at her watch. 'It must be time for a drink.' Getting up, she went to the bar and poured herself a gin and tonic. 'What's yours?' she asked.

'Just a lager from the fridge,' Julie replied quietly, so as not to wake the sleeping Hannie.

Elizabeth made a note of the drinks on a pad on the bar counter and carried them back to the fireplace. She sat down, and the two women drank them quietly. The fire burned, the clock ticked. The noise of rush hour traffic subsided.

The door by the bar opened, and both Julie and Elizabeth hissed 'Shush' across the room as a tall woman entered and started to pour herself a whisky at the bar. Margaret Wilkinson glanced over at Hannie as she shot soda into her glass. 'Why isn't she in bed? She usually goes to bed when she's got jet lag.'

Elizabeth shrugged. 'She hasn't got jet lag,' she said.

'She told us she's only been to Notting Hill Gate.'

'I don't believe it,' replied Margaret as she joined them by the fire. 'That bag says Georgetown,' she added, pointing at the plastic bag near Hannie's chair. 'Anyway, look at that tan,' she added conclusively. She took a swig of Scotch. 'Phew,' she exclaimed, sinking back into the armchair. She smiled at Julie. 'What a day! I must say, you look very glossy.' In contrast to Julie St Just's shiny suit and dangling seahorse earring, Margaret was dressed in a shapeless oatmeal-coloured dress, which hung loosely on her spare figure. Though less than forty, her brown hair, piled bird's-nest style on top of her head, was heavily scattered with grey. She had a long, sharp nose, an authoritative manner and a great deal of energy. She was already getting up to pour herself another drink. 'I'll end up in the dock on a drunk and disorderly charge at this rate,' she muttered. 'You know, I was in court at Chelmsford today when my clerk rang and said he'd made a mistake and that I was, in fact, due to start a case at the Old Bailey instead. I had to put a junior in to cover for me. Then I sat and prayed that the jury would return soon – even if the verdict went against my client. When they came back in ten minutes and pronounced him guilty I almost cheered. That's a shocking thing for a barrister to do. Then, still in my wig and gown, I drove all the way to the Old Bailey for the other case. And I've spent the last two hours with a surgeon accused of malpractice. Not easy to sort out the facts, since he was drunk while I was talking to him. I'm cross-eyed now. I daren't go home until the steam's stopped coming out of my ears.' She noted down her second drink on the pad. 'I don't believe Sir Patrick Hastings used to fight a case, see his murderer walk forth a free man and then go straight home and take complaints about the tough roast beef.'

'No,' agreed Elizabeth. 'He probably went to his club, and all his friends said what a jolly fine chap he was and bought him drinks. Sir Margaret, will you allow me the honour of buying you a drink?'

'My dear fellow,' said Margaret, 'that's extremely generous of you! I accept with pleasure.'

'I wish my Thomas would become a lawyer,' brooded Julie. 'But he can't even read. His teacher says I don't read to him enough – but how can I when I'm working so much?'

'Can't your friend who looks after him read to him sometimes?' asked Margaret.

'Leona?' said Julie. 'I doubt it. I don't think she's that keen on reading. She never paid attention at school. The teachers don't expect much, especially if the kids are black.'

Hannie awoke. She looked round in confusion for a moment but then her face relaxed. 'I'm at the club,' she murmured in a satisfied tone. She stretched. 'Margaret, how are you?' she asked.

'I've been wondering what you were doing in Georgetown?' Margaret asked.

'I was in Notting Hill today,' Hannie said. 'Before that I was in the Caribbean. I must tell you one day.'

'You can tell us now,' Margaret said firmly.

At that moment the telephone rang. Margaret got up and answered it. After a brief conversation, she put down the receiver and went to the door. 'I must go down into the restaurant for a few minutes,' she said. 'A witness the solicitors have been trying to track down for two months has turned up at last. She's downstairs now. I've just got to run through the evidence with her – it won't take long.' She pointed a finger at Hannie. 'Don't you dare start until I return, Hannie. You're the only source of fantasy in my life.' With that, she was gone.

'Only source of fantasy, my foot,' said Elizabeth sceptically. 'She's got a thriving barrister's practice and a husband and a lover. You'd think with courtroom dramas and her private life she'd have enough excitement and fantasy to satisfy several women.'

'Everything gets down to a dull routine in the end, I guess,' said Julie.

'I'd give a lot to be jaded like that,' Elizabeth told her. 'I think I need romance.'

'Now you're getting excessive,' Hannie replied. 'There's not much of that about. Sex, yes. Love, yes. Thrills and spills – yes, if you know where to find them. But romance? That's rare.'

'Thank God,' said Julie. 'Because that's the worst drug they ever invented.' She looked very tired as she sat sipping her glass of lager in front of the fire.

'It's a Western luxury most people can't afford,' Hannie said, looking sympathetically at her friend. She said tactfully, 'Know where I was – want to hear about it?'

Julie said, 'You're going to tell me a story to take my mind off my problems.'

'That's right,' Hannie agreed. 'It's all about an island called Beauregard.'

Julie sat upright, suddenly alert. She began to laugh. 'That was you? That business on Beauregard?'

'That was me,' Hannie told her. In the quiet room, as the logs hissed and flickered and the light grew darker, she began her story, saying inconsequentially, 'I'll always think this really began with a visit to my mother in the nursing home in Streatham.'

2. The Adventure of the Little Coral Island

'I wish you'd ask them about the heating here. It's either too stuffy or too chilly. It can't be healthy,' said Mrs Edwards. 'I feel dreadful about complaining all the time and I don't think they pay any attention when I do. Really,' she concluded, 'it's most unsatisfactory.'

Hannie Richards looked at her mother, who sat, in her quilted violet robe, in an armchair. The room smelt of violets. She reflected absent-mindedly that you had to be English to show such profound satisfaction while able to declare, 'This is most unsatisfactory.' To her mother she said, 'Of course, I'll speak to them today.'

'Thank goodness,' said Mrs Edwards. 'I'm sure they'll pay more attention to you. I suppose I should ask your brother to do it really –' Her voice trailed away.

Hannie offered her mother some grapes from a blue-patterned plate and thought how much her own living, if not survival, depended on her being able to read, from gestures and intonations and clothing, exactly what people were like and what they were thinking about. How, she wondered, would she interpret her own mother, by just looking at her, if she came across her by chance?

Mrs Edwards' small, carefully made-up face was almost unlined, although she was fifty-five years old. The large dark blue eyes with their heavy, fragile lids were slightly drooped as though she were drugged all the time. Her pale brown hair was neatly cut, and her small hands, displaying a number of diamond and sapphire rings, were carefully manicured. Her little feet, shod in violet satin slippers, barely touched the ground. Behind those dazed eyes, Hannie knew, lay a thousand anxieties, and her mother had the pathetic appearance of an Indian child bride, heavily ornamented, made-up and drugged before being placed in a chair to receive the groom. It was probably the sleeping pills, Hannie thought. Her mother had been a user for as long as she could remember. In the suburb where she had grown up it had been regarded as a mark of distinction among the women to be in great need of sleeping pills and nerve pills. It had been a sign of sensitivity. Her mother had unfailingly come out ahead in these competitions: she always had enough prescribed drugs on hand to dope a racehorse.

'I got these shoes to go with the green coat I bought,' Hannie said brightly, pulling out the shoebox from a carrier bag.

Her mother looked at them for a few moments. 'How nice,' she murmured. 'They're just the right shade. But I do wish you'd try a higher heel. It improves the line from calf to ankle so much.'

Hannie's eye travelled over the main road on which the clinic stood, where the buses and cars went by on their way from this section of suburbia down to the declining main street of Brixton, with its boarded up shops and 'To Let' signs, on to central London and the stores, cinemas, theatres and air of prosperity. Opposite, on the other side of the street, a woman with a shopping bag came out of a supermarket lodged between a tall block of flats and the forecourt of a garage. She said, 'Big, tall women like me don't need high heels,' knowing that the reference to her own height would please her mother. Mrs Edwards loved to feel small and frail. 'Did they tell you when they'd finally have your old room ready for you again?' she went on. 'The view from here isn't too good.'

'Oh,' Mrs Edwards sighed. 'First it was the week before last – then last week – now next week. They say they're having difficulties with the plumbing. I long to be back in it. You're right – the view from here is depressing. I've always thought views so important.'

'Especially when you can't get out,' she agreed.

Her mother had been unwell for most of Hannie's childhood. There had been migraines on school sports days, faints before school plays and concerts, and bad backs liable to strike especially cruelly at birthdays and Christmases. Before, or sometimes during family holidays, Mrs Edwards had been able to produce, seemingly at will, a huge variety of symptoms from swollen ankles to laryngitis. Spectacularly, she had once gone blind on the train to Dover at the outset of a holiday in Brittany, so they had spent most of that summer in the environs of Harley Street. The blindness had cleared up by mid-September. All these ailments had been perfectly authentic. If Mrs Edwards said she had a migraine, she really had a migraine. If she began to whisper, any doctor could look down her throat and see that she had laryngitis. Because Hannie's father, a prosperous restaurant-owner and director of a mini-cab firm, could afford extra help in the house, and because his childless sister lived only half a mile from the family, neither Hannie nor her brother and sister suffered in any practical way from their mother's constant ill health. On the other hand, always feeling sorry for Mother was a strain. And they did notice that the mothers of other children, despite their bad nerves, were usually there to listen to the guitar solos at school concerts or go along to talk to the headmaster when they needed to. Later, of course, came the disillusion, when in adolescence they realized that their mother was not so much an invalid as a sufferer from hysterical illnesses. Once they had coped with that, and the fear that it might be hereditary, Hannie and her brother and sister continued to thrive, although Mrs Edwards' state might have had something to do with Hannie's decision to study biology at a university and her brother's successful career with a pharmaceuticals firm.

The sad part was that after Hannie's father's death, when the children were wondering whether widowhood would alter their mother's invalid habits, she was apparently struck by a genuine, severe illness, a degeneration of the spine which was likely to leave her bedridden in a few years' time. It was decided that she would shortly need full-time, professional care, and she had therefore gone into the clinic on Brixton Hill. Almost immediately the complaint had gone into abeyance. She did not seem unhappy, Hannie thought, but it was a pity that she had to be here. On the other hand, perhaps it was where she wanted to be. It was hard not to think sometimes that, faced with widowhood and change, her mother's mind had rallied for a final campaign and seized permanent control of her body, declaring that henceforth it would be in sole charge and would not tolerate any rebellion.

Looking for conversation, Hannie asked her mother who else had visited her recently.

'Kerry. Well, Catherine was here earlier, of course,' replied Mrs Edwards. 'And Kerry came in a few weeks ago. I asked Kerry to find me a nightdress while she was at Marks and Spencers, but she's not been back since,' she confessed bitterly. 'You'd think she'd pop in more often.'

'She's pretty busy,' Hannie said. 'She may be waiting for the end of term.'

'Kerry's only got one child,' replied Mrs Edwards. 'You'd think she could have managed. She could have posted it.'

'It's the school,' Hannie said again. It was a bold remark. Mrs Edwards disliked references to her daughter-in-law's job. Kerry was deputy headmistress of a large comprehensive school, but Mrs Edwards preferred not to think about it. Talking about Kerry's school was rather like reading pornography to the vicar – all right so long as you left out the really dirty bits, which could be done by somehow implying that Kerry was in charge of the fingerpaints at an infants' school.

It had been Kerry who had said to her, 'Your mother must be the last of the great Victorian invalids. Those women lying in darkened rooms weren't just getting out of all the boring things they'd have had to have done otherwise; they were a real status symbol for the family. It proved you could afford to keep someone in idleness. And what a wonderful focal point for love and sympathy – there were people starving to death under bridges, and you could work it all off carrying a *tisane* up to Aunt Fanny. They performed a real social function. I wonder

16

how your mother got the idea?'

'I should think Robert could bring the nightdress in,' Hannie said to her mother. 'After all, he's redundant now. He's got more time during the day than Kerry.'

Mrs Edwards looked quite faint. 'But poor Robert's got so many anxieties. I wouldn't want to trouble him. And men don't really like clinics and hospitals, do they?'

Encouraged not to, thought Hannie.

While the bad daughter spoke inwardly, the good daughter reached into her bag and produced an envelope. 'I brought some pictures of the twins on their new ponies. I thought you might like one for your wall when you get back into the old room.'

'Oh,' said Mrs Edwards, opening the envelope. 'Aren't they nice. I must get some framed. They'll be a wonderful addition to my wall.'

'I hoped you'd say that,' Hannie said, full of mingled maternal pride and secret horror at supplying yet another piece of documentation for what her mother called 'her wall', where pictures of the family hung in celebration of close blood ties and middle-class success. Hannie and her brother and sister held tennis rackets and university degrees. There were weddings where the bride wore a white dress and the groom held a top hat; Robert and Kerry sat in a gig in New Orleans, Hannie and Adam held hands by the pram containing their babies, their old house discreetly in the background. Hannie would not have minded the gallery of grins, sunshine and doing-very-nicely-thank-you if it had not been for blood-chilling moments when she almost literally saw the wall of pictures interspersed with big, grainy, blown-up newspaper pictures of her own arrest, trial and conviction – photographs of herself being hauled off between two sweaty policemen in tropical suits, being dragged into court with a newspaper held over her face, even standing against a background of big steel tubs in a prison laundry, wearing a sagging cotton dress and no make-up. The thought of what would happen to her mother if she ever made a mistake and got caught genuinely frightened Hannie. Mrs Edwards had controlled her own reality for so long that a sudden, brutal attack on it might lead to a complete mental or physical breakdown. She sometimes felt that she should make an effort to lead her mother in the direction of certain basic truths but knew she would never succeed. Mrs Edwards' way with unpleasant realities was ruthless. She would appear not to hear anything she did not wish to hear. And, as a last resort, she would have a dizzy spell or a menacing attack of breathlessness.

Even so, Hannie worried about the effect on her mother if she got caught. And, almost as bad, it would leave her husband Adam, her brother-in-law, and, now, Kerry, in charge of all the hospital fees. The whole burden would be carried then by son- and daughter-in-laws – not a desirable situation. As she chatted about her children and what was happening in Devon and talked to her mother about the other people in the nursing home, she prayed that she could stay out of trouble. Then she got up to leave. Normally, farewells in hospitals are painful as a fully-clad person, about to rejoin the great world outside, leaves behind someone in her pyjamas. But Hannie had spent the best part of her life leaving her mother in a chair or in bed. And Mother liked it.

As she got in the car she remembered her mother sitting in a sweet-smelling room full of flowers, a smile

18

on her painted face. The little feet in the violet slippers had been together, with only the tip of her toes touching the floor. The Indian bride, thought Hannie, as she headed for the pub where she had arranged to meet her sister. Cath had been at the clinic earlier on one of her regular trips from Brighton, and the two had secretly agreed to stagger their visits to their mother and meet afterwards for a chat.

Cath, wearing a purple sweater and skirt, was sitting by herself at a table at the back of the pub. Her white fur jacket was draped over the back of her chair. When she saw Hannie, she jumped up, hugged her and kissed her cheek. 'Want something to eat?' she asked. 'I'm famished.'

'So am I,' answered Hannie. 'Let's see what they've got at the bar.'

As they walked to the bar Hannie said, 'Oi! What have you done to your hair?'

'Like it?' Cath asked. 'I got tired of being mousey so I went blonde. Greg says people'll think he's a gangster, with me on his arm.'

'It's nice,' Hannie told her, considering. 'It makes you look more, er, zippy.' She added mockingly, 'Where would we women be without our disguises?'

'You mean, where would *you* be?' Cath retorted. 'I'll have to have the chicken.'

They ordered and went back to the table. 'Well,' Cath said, 'here's to Mrs Edwards' little girls. How do you think she was?'

'All right,' said Hannie. 'She's definitely not getting any worse.'

'If she's not careful she'll recover,' said Cath with a grin.

'Oh, come on,' Hannie said. 'Surely you've got more

faith in her than that.'

As they sipped their wine Cath leaned forward. 'You'll laugh when I tell you this,' she said, 'but I'm doing my O-levels.'

Cath had paid no attention to anything at school except the magazines she used to prop on her knees under the desk at the back of the class. She had left at the age of sixteen without passing any examinations and persuaded her reluctant father to get her an apprenticeship in a hairdressing salon. Since Hannie and Robert were both studying for degrees, her parents had not been pleased. Cath then made matters worse by marrying, at the age of eighteen, Greg, a young garage mechanic, and concluded her fall by having three children in five years. It was not until Greg had bought first one garage and then another, and started to make a good deal of money that Cath became a daughter her mother could be proud of. Now that they had a house in Brighton and a swimming pool in the garden, Cath was back in favour.

'It's not that I'm bored or anything,' explained Cath. 'As far as I'm concerned, there can't be enough coffee mornings and shopping trips to keep me happy – I'm not an intellectual or anything. But what I thought was that this is all very fine, but with one marriage in three ending in divorce these days I could look very silly if there was a bust-up. I couldn't keep up our standard of living on a third of Greg's income. So I decided I'd get some nursing qualifications. The south coast's full of nursing homes. I could pick my own work and my own hours and it wouldn't be too hard on the children.' She took another sip of her wine. 'Greg doesn't know all this, though. He just thinks I'm bored and want to go to evening classes. I've told him I'm doing pottery and batik – they're on the same night as the maths and biology classes.'

Hannie took a bite out of a chicken leg and said, 'Can't you tell him the truth?'

'Well,' said Cath. 'Why worry him? I'm the official nitwit in our family – no exams, doesn't know who the prime minister is, keeps on thinking about hairstyles. Greg works hard for all of us and he likes it that way, so why should I disturb him? He'll be quite proud when I get the certificates.'

Hannie nodded. 'You're a good steerer, Cath. I'm proud of you,' she said. 'You know how to get your way without pain.'

Cath smiled. Hannie was right about that. 'Anyway,' she said, 'how are you? Are the children and Adam well? How's your career in the SDP?'

Hannie grinned. 'All thriving,' she replied, 'family and career.'

Cath sniggered. 'We always knew, in the family,' she said, 'that your big interest in public affairs would lead to a career in politics.'

The truth was that Hannie, needing an explanation for her departures for two or three weeks at a time, sometimes five times a year, had hit on the idea of suggesting that she was engaged in political research for the Social Democratic Party, a job that might naturally take her away from her home in the country for conferences, research and meetings in London. She had a friend fairly high up in the party who was prepared to vouch for her if necessary. This friend would have been reluctant to provide cover for Hannie's real activities, so she had been led to believe that Hannie was having an illicit affair. But in fact no one ever asked about her career. Neighbours in the country found the notion of her job acceptable but dull and seldom asked for details. If they ever did, she could fall back on the adultery story – people usually believed a lie if it revealed something discreditable about the liar.

'Farm paying, then?' asked her sister. 'Job bringing in plenty of money?'

'Never quite enough,' Hannie said. 'There's always something. Cellars flood, tractors go over cliffs, children grow out of their wellingtons – the usual story.'

Cath regarded her carefully. 'It would save trouble,' she said, 'if you gave up that old country heap. That's what Greg says.'

'That old heap,' Hannie told her coldly, 'is Adam's family home, and my children's home. And when I want Greg's opinion I'll phone him.'

Cath spoke on bravely. 'Greg's a man,' she said, 'and men know more about these things. But I'm your sister, and I'm always worried about you. That's why Greg told me what he thought. I'm always worried about you, Han.' She dropped her voice and said, 'What you do is dangerous and illegal. I'm afraid for you. Supposing you get caught? What happens to Flo and Fran?'

Hannie said, 'Adam looks after them, of course. Anyway, as soon as I've got it all sorted out, I won't do it any more. In the meanwhile, what do you expect me to do? Lie on my bed painting my nails and watching the roof fall off and the rain flood into the house? You saw that place when we moved into it after Adam's father died. It cost £20,000 just to make it habitable. Every room was damp – it was rotten from attic to cellar.'

'It must make Adam very anxious,' Cath persisted, 'when he knows what might be happening.'

'Oh, don't let's talk about it, Cath,' Hannie said

impatiently. 'He knows I can take care of myself. And how else could we manage? The farm didn't make enough profit to keep the place going because it was in the same state as the house when we took over. But I am giving up when I can . . .'

'You love it,' insisted Cath. 'Go on, admit it. You do.'

Hannie laughed. 'Of course I do,' she said. 'Anyone would love it – travel, drama, surprises.'

'Then off home to the bosom of the family,' her sister told her. 'The perfect life.'

'For me,' Hannie said.

'You're a buccaneer,' Cath remarked. 'I'm glad I'm not.'

'Well, thank God I am,' Hannie told her. 'Sailing blue Caribbean seas with a knife between my teeth.'

'Have I missed anything?' Margaret Wilkinson asked, coming in at speed, stuffing a foolscap pad into her big handbag.

'We still seem to be in south London,' Elizabeth Lord said mildly. She stood up. 'Can I get anyone a drink while we're waiting for the action to start?'

'I'm getting there,' Hannie said. As Elizabeth poured them all a drink, she continued her story.

After lunch with Cath, Hannie went straight to her office above a furrier's in South Molton Street. When she went in there was a pile of mink stoles on her desk. She sat on them as she listened to the messages on her answering machine: one came from a woman who plainly thought Hannie was a hitwoman, and seemed to want someone, probably an absconding husband or lover, bumped off in Tenerife; the second came in the kind of voice she instantly recognized – a voice that meant drug-smuggling; the third caller had a strong East European accent, gave a number and asked her to call back. The last message was from a woman with a West Indian accent. She said, 'I need some help, but I can't afford to pay you very much. Jackie Fraser thought you might help me. If you're prepared to work for only a little money, to start off with, I hope you can phone me.' Then she gave a number and said, uncertainly, 'Thank you – goodbye.'

At that moment in came the proprietor of the shop, Gordon, with a pile of shaggy orange jackets over his arm. He looked embarrassed when he saw her, then said, 'Just popping these down in here while I make space in the cold store.' She sat on her desk with a heap of furs beside her, staring at him. Gaining confidence, he continued. 'Fancy one of these? Hundred and fifty – you can have it for a hundred.'

'What is it?' Hannie asked. 'Orang utang? Look, Gordon, this is meant to be an office. I come in – the door's open and there's dead animals all over the place. This door's supposed to be locked unless there's a fire –'

'Yes, yes, I'm sorry,' he told her, hastily putting the coats on a chair. 'I'll just clear a space, then I'll pick the coats up –' And he was gone, leaving Hannie thinking it was time to move on again. She could never stay anywhere for very long. Gordon's heavy doors and security locks had impressed her, but what was the point if he left her door open so that anyone could get in to play over her recorded messages?

She thought about the calls. She telephoned the number of the woman with the West Indian accent. There was music in the background as a young man's voice said, 'Who do you want?'

Guessing, she said, 'Your mother.'

24

'I'll get her,' he said. The receiver went down on a table, the music, a reggae beat, went on and she heard him calling. Then the music was turned down and the woman who had telephoned said, 'Hullo – Mrs Bennett? This is Sarah Fevrier.'

Hannie, to prevent her talking too much over the phone said, 'I'm interested. Can we meet?'

The woman hesitated. 'What are your fees?' she asked.

'It depends,' Hannie said. 'We can discuss that later. How did you come to know Jackie Fraser?'

The woman understood. She said promptly, 'She's on a course in child-care with my daughter – her best friend. My daughter –'

'Fine,' Hannie said. 'Well – shall we meet at your place?' She had found out long ago that it was better to visit the client at home, where indications of who someone is and what they want lie about, a clearly blazed trail any intelligent woman can read. After a pause Sarah Fevrier said, 'You can come if you want – but I'm watched.'

'Who by?' asked Hannie sharply.

'That's it – I don't know,' said the other woman. 'Maybe the police – but I don't think so. It doesn't matter to me if you know who I am and where I am. I can't post a letter without a car following me, but you –'

'They'll see me anyway, if they're following you,' Hannie said. 'I might just as well come to your house. I'll look like someone who might call anyway.'

'In disguise? Looking like the milkman?' Sarah said. She had a deep, husky voice and sounded amused.

Hannie was saying, 'Can you think – ?' when she heard what seemed to be the young man shouting across

the room. Sarah said to him approvingly, 'That's right.'
Then she said to Hannie, 'Simon says come pretending
to be a social worker. There's so many round here you
won't be noticed. Do you know what I mean?'

'I'm getting my bike out now,' Hannie reassured her.
'About four o'clock this afternoon?'

'All right,' said Sarah Fevrier. 'Not too much later.
I'm on shift at six.'

After she'd put the phone down, Hannie sat on the
fur coats and stared glumly at the address. Not exactly a
smart neighbourhood, she thought. Just off Portobello
Road, Notting Hill Gate, probably a council house.
And the woman had a job which took her out to work
at six in the evening, probably to a local hospital, or a
café. You couldn't say the situation smelt of big money
lying around in heaps. And she, Hannie, needed a good
£10,000 and preferably more by the New Year to cover
the overdraft and the cost of three new slate roofs on
the farm workers' cottages, not to mention next term's
school fees – and yet, she thought, the woman sounded
straight and her credentials were all right. That
mattered, in her business. The girl she'd mentioned,
Jackie Fraser, had been part of Hannie's scheme to get
the semen of a former Derby winner to an Arab oil
sheikh who couldn't be bothered to wait his mare's turn
in the queue for the popular stud. Jackie had been the
stable-girl Hannie had suborned to help. She'd told her
she only wanted the money to escape her low-paid job
at the stables and get to London to take a course in
nursery-school teaching. Which, evidently, she'd done.
A sensible girl, Hannie thought; too sensible to put
Sarah Fevrier on to her unless the prospective job had
some possibilities for both of them.

Gordon came in, picked up the orange coats from the

chair, looked at the pile of mink on which she was sitting and went to the door without saying anything. Taking pity on him, she stood up. He slipped back, picked up the mink stoles and, feeling bolder, asked, 'Sure you won't change your mind? If it's a question of principle this lot haven't been near an animal.'

Hannie was scandalized. 'With my hair?' she said. 'They'd call the fire brigade.'

'Have it your own way,' he said, and went out.

Hannie thought she'd better change offices in less than a week.

At that moment a tall, big, dark-skinned woman, wearing a mushroom-coloured raincoat and a light-patterned scarf tied tightly over her head, was coming out of her front door. She paused on the step and looked directly at the two white men in the large, dark blue car parked opposite her house. Neither looked back at her. The woman's expression hardened. She walked down her garden path, where two rose bushes and a clump of pampas grass struggled in a small flower bed against the diesel fumes from the traffic surging overhead on the motorway a hundred metres away. She opened the front gate and turned down the street. The car turned on the paved area under the motorway, travelled beside the railway line opposite the house for a few metres, then swung back on to the road. It followed the woman slowly as she walked, stiff-shouldered and angry, into Portobello Road. Later, buying yams, oranges and fish from the market stalls lining one side of the street she saw the car parked on the other side. Two men, dark-suited and wearing very white shirts, leaned against a shop front, watching her. She took her change, picked up her bag of fruit and looked across the street again.

She stopped dead as she saw a lean, tall boy of nineteen in jeans and anorak hurrying, almost bounding, along the pavement towards the men. Her son Simon. Behind him, travelling just as fast, was his friend, Selwyn, also in jeans, wearing a big, crocheted hat in green, red and gold. The woman was angry. She stuffed the fruit into her shopping bag and hurried across the street shouting, 'Simon! Simon!' If he heard her, it didn't prevent him from grasping one of the suited men by the upper arm and talking into his face. As a white van moved slowly past her, she stopped, then saw that the older man now had her son by the arm and was talking urgently back at him. Selwyn, standing close to both of them, was saying loudly, 'What you want, man? You tell us what you want.' As the woman came up the man dropped her son's arm, looked at his companion, who stood a little way off, and walked away. They both went to the big blue car and started to get in. Selwyn ran after them. 'Selwyn,' she cried, 'Selwyn – let them go.' He stopped in his tracks and all three stood on the pavement, watching the men as they drove away.

Sarah, turning to the two young men, said, 'You two have caused enough trouble in your short lives. What do you want to go and do all that for? Your mothers don't need any more trouble.'

'Why don't you go to the police?' demanded her son. 'How many times I ask you?'

'I don't need more trouble,' she repeated. 'Come home now, both of you. People are staring at us.'

In the end Hannie thought she might be overplaying her role if she took a bicycle. She settled for a pair of

28

round glasses, trousers, boots and a shoulder bag, out of which peeped a bag marked 'Portobello Health Stores' and a copy of the *Guardian* newspaper. The rest of her disguise consisted of a hurried walk, a concerned expression and a big brown beret to cover her too-noticeable hair. She walked up the cul-de-sac where Sarah Fevrier lived. A train raced past her on her right. Overhead the traffic on the motorway thrummed insistently. Pretending to ignore the big blue car parked opposite the house, she checked the address in her notebook, went up the path and rang the doorbell. The woman who opened the door was tall and strongly built. She had a prominent nose and her brown face was sombre.

'Mrs Fevrier?' enquired Hannie. 'I'm from the Social Services Department. We wrote to you.'

'I got the letter. You want to come in?' the woman asked, looking sternly at Hannie.

'May I?' said Hannie, stepping quickly inside.

In the hall Sarah Fevrier smiled, and Hannie smiled back.

'You looked really unwelcoming,' she said. 'You looked really – concerned,' Sarah said. 'Pleased to meet you, Mrs Bennett. Come in here.'

She led Hannie into the small front room, where there was a dark red three-piece suite, many photographs on the mantelpiece and a crucifix on the wall. One bar of the electric fire burned, driving off the chill of early autumn. A tall boy was sprawled in an armchair. He stood up when Hannie came in.

'No one can see in,' Sarah said, gesturing at the thick net curtains at the window. 'The problem is, when you're being watched you think they can.'

'Let's hope they're not fitted up to listen,' Hannie said.

'The car looks normal inside – no special equipment,' Simon said.

Hannie took his word for it. She sat down. Sarah sat opposite her. 'How long have they been there?' she asked.

'Three weeks,' Sarah told her. 'They're there all the time. Follow me to work – follow the bus home. Follow me shopping, going to church, even visiting the neighbours. I've tried talking to them – asking them what they want – they just look at me as if I wasn't there. One day I came out of work and I'm waiting at the bus stop in the rain. I went up to the driver and said to him, "We going the same way home – why don't you give me a lift." He just looked at me and drove away up the street. Next thing, I'm on the bus and there's the car again, still following.'

She seems a little too philosophical about it, thought Hannie. 'You didn't ring the police?' she asked.

The big West Indian woman shook her head. 'You think they're going to let the police catch them – clever men like that? And what else have they done – rob me? Attack me? They've done nothing.' She added, 'They may be the police. I don't know.'

But Hannie thought she did.

'You've got an idea what this is about, or I wouldn't be here,' she said bluntly.

'That's right,' the woman agreed.

'You never tell me that,' cried her son, who was standing in the doorway, on his way out.

'It's not you I'm afraid of,' Sarah told him. 'It's that Selwyn with his big, large mouth. What I tell you, you tell him, and then he tells everybody in the whole world, and then I've got trouble on my hands.'

'What kind of trouble?' demanded Simon.

'Interference – the kind we don't need. Now we've come to the important point. I want your solemn promise you say nothing to nobody till it's over.'

The boy was silent. 'You promise me,' she insisted. He nodded. 'In words,' she told him.

'In words, I promise,' he said.

Then the doorbell rang.

'That's Francine,' said Sarah. 'You open the door.'

'You tell her, though,' he called, going out.

'That's right,' his mother called back. 'Because your sister hasn't got any friend called Selwyn.' She said to Hannie, 'Excuse all this.' Hannie shrugged. 'Family life,' she said.

Simon came back into the room with a tall slender girl of about twenty. She had a smaller version of the family's big, straight nose. She smiled at Hannie.

'This is Mrs Bennett, come to see if she can help us,' Sarah said. To Hannie she said, 'Francine – my daughter. And you, Simon, don't stand there sulking at us, not till you know about everything. I told Francine because she's older and she was telling me about Mrs Bennett. And also,' she added, 'because, like I say, I don't want Selwyn and his back-to-Africa friends coming around making bad things worse. Sit down and listen to the story, which you are not going to like.'

The young man gave her a sideways look, but sat down. He shot a glance at Hannie too. She said nothing.

'I'll make us some tea,' Francine said, going out. Hannie asked Sarah Fevrier, 'You think the men watching you aren't just the police? And you don't want to involve the police in case they start asking awkward questions? Is that it? And, by the way, is there a Mr Fevrier?'

Simon cast a look at his mother who replied placidly, 'Mr Fevrier lives most of the time in Birmingham.'

'So those men haven't got anything to do with him?' Hannie asked. Simon's breath huffed out. He seemed about to speak. 'I've got to talk like this,' Hannie pointed out. 'That's what we're here for.' She knew she must look and sound like yet another white person demanding the answers to questions which were none of her business. Sarah, however, just said, 'Those men can't have anything to do with my husband. They came about a month ago. At first I thought they were DHSS snoopers, come to find if someone in the street was claiming benefit when they shouldn't. About that time I got the letter from home saying my mother was dying.'

Francine came in with the tea tray and began to pour the tea. 'You're not going to like all this, Simon,' she told him.

'That's what you keep on telling me,' he said. 'I'm getting tired of waiting to find out why.'

Sarah drew a deep breath and said to Hannie, 'We came to Britain in 1958, my husband and me. He was from the same island in the Caribbean, my grandfather's brother's son. Francine and Simon were born here, and we never went back – never could spare the money. But my sister, Angelina, and my mother and father are still on Beauregard, where we all come from. My two brothers are on St Colombe, the big island.' She gestured towards the photograph hanging on the wall. Hannie had already seen it; there was a couple in their thirties and two big girls and two younger boys. They were all in their best clothes, boys in suits, girls in starched dresses. The girls were tan-skinned, the boys blacker.

Sarah went on, 'Beauregard, our island, is just a small

island, coral, very beautiful. The big island, St Colombe, is only five miles away across the sea. There's a few other islands there, but nobody lives on them – they're too small. The whole of Beauregard belongs to one family – the Corringtons. They've owned that island for hundreds of years. The family used to be French, like most of the families round there, but in my granny's time the owner's daughter married a Corrington; that made the island English, in a way. Then it went independent, along with St Colombe, just after we came here to Britain.'

Sarah Fevrier paused, looked at both her children, then said, 'And here's the real story. This goes back to the nineteen thirties, when Edmund Corrington married a Miss Hugon, from Martinique, and they had a boy, Victor . . . No need to go looking at me in that way, Simon,' she said suddenly to her son. 'If you think this is one of those old island stories, then you're wrong. This matters to you and the whole family.'

She went on, 'So Miss Hugon, Mrs Corrington, died having the second child, and the child died, too. And Mr Edmund Corrington, he shut himself up with the boy in the big house on Beauregard and never saw any other white people, just took my mother, Sarah, into the house to look after it, and the boy. She was only fifteen.'

Hannie, suspecting what was coming, saw Francine sigh. So did her mother.

'That was how it was in those days,' her mother told Francine. 'So,' she said, 'two years after that Angelina was born and a year after that, I was born. Edmund Corrington was our father.' She paused. 'I think he loved her,' she said. 'I don't know – Mother never told me about it. Then he married again, and after that I don't think he was happy. The boy, Victor, turned out weak, and maybe he wasn't content with Mrs Julie Corrington, his new wife, although she was a rich heiress with property all over the place – St Colombe and Barbados and other places. Mr Corrington never came back to the island after the honeymoon. The old house fell to pieces – he sent a lawyer over from St Colombe to collect the rents from the islanders. He never took any more interest in the island, but he never sold off one inch of it either. Before he got married, he gave my mother a little bit of land, about an acre, for herself. The rest of the land he rents to her and her husband, just to make it look like he didn't give her anything. After that, of course, she married another man from the island, my father –' She looked at her son. 'Don't blame your granny. Things were like that in those days, in that place. What was she to do? – a poor girl only fifteen years old who'd never been farther than the next island in her life. And she wasn't ashamed – not my mother. She was proud of Angelina and me, like she was proud of the boys, your uncles.'

Simon just looked at his mother. Hannie was glad to interrupt. 'But what's the connection between the letter about your mother being ill and the arrival of these men in a car outside your door here?'

Sarah told them, 'That was when they took my mother to St Colombe, to the doctor there. First, she wasn't well. Then she got really sick, so they went to the doctor. There's no doctor on Beauregard, no doctor, no school, no electricity either, no water, except from the wells – it's like a hundred years ago. And Angelina wrote to me that my mother was very ill, might die. But even before the letter came, the men in the car were here.' After a long pause she sighed and said, 'She's got this letter, you see, from Edmund Corrington. He wrote it two years before he died and in it he gives her the whole island when he dies. Now my mother is dying, they think she, or Angelina or me, will show the letter and claim the island. I think that's why those men are here – to watch and make sure I don't do anything. I'm worried now. I'm afraid for my family. I want to go there, but Angelina tells me not to go. She thinks if I go things could get worse.'

'Is the letter witnessed?' asked Hannie.

'By old Mr Squires, the lawyer, but he's dead now, and by another man, a respectable white man from Barbados.'

'What did Edmund Corrington's will say?' Hannie pressed. 'If he left a will when he died –'

Sarah shrugged. 'I don't know about that. All I know is no Corrington's been to Beauregard since he died nearly four years ago. They've been watching and waiting to see what my mother would do. Now she's dying they want it finished.

'The Corringtons are going down. They need that land, for money. Men've been coming round to see the family, too. Not often, and they don't say much, but they come. That's why I'm afraid. There's no one there to help my mother and my father and Angelina. Everyone's poor and afraid. That's why my mother never claimed her rights when she could have, after Mr Corrington died. On that island it's still like slavery days. The white man says what's got to happen and nobody argues with him.' Looking at her children she said, 'Your granny was happy with her little bit of land, a few animals, her garden. Now something's got to happen – the peace has gone.'

'So why doesn't she take the letter to a lawyer?' demanded Simon.

'She doesn't trust the lawyer,' Sarah said. 'She thinks he's in with the Corringtons – gets a lot of business from them. That's why she doesn't send it here. She thinks the mail's interfered with. It's a small island, everybody's everybody's cousin. The black people are afraid of the white people.'

Simon, looking at Hannie, said, 'So why's she here?'

'I want that letter to be brought here to England,' Sarah said. 'Here, where the Corringtons can't reach out. None of us can go out there. Everybody knows us, or they know all about us. I thought about it, believe me, even chartering a boat from somewhere far away and landing on Beauregard at night. But we're still black people, arriving somewhere, chartering a boat. It's too unusual. One phone call, and we're found out. They could catch us. A white woman pretending to be a tourist can get to Beauregard and take the letter and bring it back here, all without anybody knowing, that's my idea.' She said to her children, 'We make one mistake, and those men might kill the family on Beauregard – or us. If they take all that trouble to watch us here, where will they stop? It's not like it is here, not around those islands. You talk discrimination – you're probably right, but on those tiny islands things go bad fast, faster than here –'

'All right, all right,' Simon said angrily. 'I hear you. Don't say any more. How we going to get the letter, that's the point now.'

'Don't talk to your mama like that,' Francine warned.

'If it's five miles from St Colombe to Beauregard I can go on a package tour,' Hannie said. 'Then, with a boat, I can be on Beauregard, collecting the letter, before anybody knows it. Can you send a message so they expect me?' she asked Sarah.

'Have to be clever,' she said. 'That postmaster on Colombe could be opening the letters.'

'How do we know she won't sell the letter to the Corringtons once she got it?' Simon asked, looking at Hannie who said promptly, 'You don't. You're all going to have to study me now and phone me later if you trust me.'

'The problem is, I can't pay you much,' Sarah said. 'Only the cost of your trip and a thousand pounds.'

Francine was horrified, 'All you got.'

Sarah said firmly, 'If that island's ours, willed to us by my real grandfather, then it's ours. He meant us to have it. It's Simon's future, and yours. And the future of all the others there. I'm investing.'

Hannie, choking a bit, for the idea was against all her principles, suggested, 'Supposing I do it just for the expenses? I invest, too. If it works, you can pay me properly later – say £20,000? It seems a lot, but that island is worth tens of millions. And that'll reduce your worries about me turning dishonest – if I've got a stake in the business.'

The Fevriers looked at little shocked. 'I could be risking my life,' Hannie pointed out. 'You've said yourself these people are dangerous.' She stood up, adding, 'You don't have to agree now – talk it over. Can you see me out, Mrs Fevrier, looking a bit upset, as if I'd brought you bad news?'

On the step she was seen to reassure Sarah, as Francine looked towards her brother as if reproving him for causing trouble to the family. And Hannie walked down the street still looking busy and caring, conscious of watchers' eyes on her back. She took a bus to the Town Hall, went up in the lift and only left when she was sure she had not been followed.

She felt rather cheerful. She guessed the Fevriers would decide to hire her. And this was exactly the kind of job she really enjoyed – and the £20,000, if she pulled it off, would come in very handy too.

Later that evening at the White City dogtrack, she asked Jean-Pierre Hoffmann, 'Why is it that I can't stand the boring jobs?'

There was the sound of a bell, a brief roar from the bystanders as the dogs ran, then silence. Jean-Pierre looked disgusted. '*Merde!*' he said, and threw his ticket down on the unswept concrete.

They were standing by the barrier and it was drizzling. Hannie looked at her card and then at her companion. He wore a sweater and a tweed jacket, casual trousers and suede boots. His camera was round his neck, as usual. As she watched him, he scribbled on the card, raised his camera, pointed it at a crowd of men and women farther along the rail, took a picture and asked, 'Have you picked a dog for the next race?'

He raised the camera again, focused it and took a picture of something on the other side of the track. Hannie looked at the card and picked a name at random.

'Sam's Return,' she muttered. 'What about you?'

'I think I'll have Turn of Fate and Belle Hélène,' he said. He was getting dull and dour, she recognized, the way gamblers do when the luck is neither good nor bad. They walked to the tote and placed their bets. Hannie listened to the hare rattle and the murmur of the crowd as the dogs ran while she wondered vaguely if Sarah Fevrier had told her everything. Sam's Return won at 50-1, and Hannie collected a hundred pounds, saying, 'Dinner's on me.' Jean-Pierre won fifty on the next race and a hundred on the last, but he was still not happy. He was a news cameraman. He had been everywhere in the last twenty years, from Stanleyville to San Salvador, and he did not go to the White City dogtrack just to break even.

Hannie, relieved to get away from the drizzle and the too-brief thrills of the track said, 'Let's eat.'

Over the meal she asked him again. 'Jean-Pierre, why can't I stand the boring jobs?'

The eyes of a man who had seen massacres and scurried out of Saigon at the last moment in a plane crammed with frightened Vietnamese and desperate Americans looked at her steadily.

'Hannie,' he said, 'you're like a kid.' He hesitated and then said, 'My God, I hope one day you don't find out what a kid you are.'

'Jean-Pierre,' she said, 'I don't go where you've been. I don't have to see death and political corruption.'

'You will one day, Hannie,' he told her in a firm voice.

'Phooey,' Hannie said, disturbing an elderly lover and a young girl at the next table. 'You're just tired and gloomy, Jean-Pierre. Saying dismal things to bring me down.'

'Sometimes you're a pig, Hannie,' he said. 'Let me tell you this: there's no such thing as a free lunch. No easy job. I know that because I got one ten days ago. I turned up at a smart restaurant to eat and photograph Elizabeth Taylor, if she came. I was standing in for another photographer. So I was sitting there, eating my lamb, when the Arabs suddenly blew up the restaurant. I got the worst war wound I ever got – there are twenty-three sutures under my pullover and right down to my balls. I saw the blood and thought, My God –

it's gone. Now you come to me and accuse me of being in a bad humour.'

'Phew,' Hannie said. 'I'm sorry, Jean-Pierre.' Then she enquired, 'Is it gone?'

Jean-Pierre winked at her. 'Find out for yourself.'

The next morning, Hannie rolled over in the bed at the Hilton and yawned. After a night spent making love, and a visit from the hotel doctor when he panicked about his stitches, Jean-Pierre was fast asleep. Hannie got up and collected her tumbled clothes. She took them quietly into the next room. She had the knack of waking at any time she wanted. Her plane left in an hour and a half for Paris, where she had to collect some money.

She was drinking coffee when Jean-Pierre came in, naked, his stitches livid in the dawn light. He took the cup from her hand, drank the contents. 'Ah, Hannie,' he said sadly, 'Paris now, and then straight back to the *bon ménage* on the coast of England. When shall we manage to spend some time together like human beings. Always hotels, hotels, hotels.'

'You've forgotten the back of that truck leaving Beirut,' Hannie pointed out. She had been badly caught out there. After finishing a long hop from Australia to Jerusalem with the formula for a fuelless car, and a short hop from Jerusalem to the American University with the scrolls of the newly-discovered fifth gospel, she had just been paid off in gold when the first Israeli bomb hit a building six hundred metres down the street. In the end she and Jean-Pierre had made a dash for it in a truck full of antique furniture. They had made love on a pile of Turkish rugs. And half an hour later he had banged on the back of the driver's cab, made the truck pull up by the roadside, got out and gone back to Beirut.

Jean-Pierre again removed her coffee and drank it. 'Nevertheless,' he said, 'one day, we shall spend a week in the country together. We shall walk, eat, make love . . .'

'For two days, until you get out and go back to Beirut,' Hannie interrupted him, perhaps a little shiftily, for although she was fairly certain that Jean-Pierre was happy to be like a ship that passed in the night, could you ever really be sure about people whose lives were so affected by the times they lived in and the countries they went to? They presented to the outside world a personality like a pebble which had been rolled and grated by the tide for aeons – smooth, featureless, almost without colour. Yet for all she knew she was Jean-Pierre's last chance to get off the beach and find a cleft in the rock where he could safely lodge.

She pushed the thought away and stood up. Jean-Pierre stepped forward and embraced her closely, murmuring, 'Back to bed now. Get a later plane.'

And later, as they lay talking, he said, 'You leave the good husband and the delightful children and – what? – take a plane to some hotspot to smuggle something in or out of the country. You get dirty, tired and frightened, no doubt, like we all do. You don't need to do this. If you don't like the husband, well, you can find another.'

Hannie, who had been dozing, said blurrily, 'My husband could not be bettered.'

'If you say so,' remarked Jean-Pierre.

'I expect you believe women only do anything as a kind of comment on their relationships with men,' Hannie said. 'And sometimes that's true, just like it is with men. But I'm remembering.' She paused, still feeling rather tired. 'You see, it was about eight years ago. We had the old house in Devon, where we live

41

now. It's a lovely place, very green, with the sea not far from the house. And the gentry called on us, and we called on them. I was pregnant and very happy. It seemed like a life I could easily lead for ever and then –'

'You found out,' said Jean-Pierre, 'that your husband was sleeping with another woman.'

Hannie sat up and stared at the picture on the opposite wall. It was a bad print of a Renaissance woman in heavy brocade and pearls. 'No,' she said. 'No, it wasn't that. On this particular day Adam went off fishing, as he often did, but the sea suddenly got up, and he was late. I struggled up the cliff path to the headland in the wind so I could look out for his boat. I wasn't that worried, I don't think. Just a little bit. But there I was, looking over the stormy sea. I couldn't see the boat, and I began to think that I was expecting twins and I might be a widow, and the wind was whipping round me – and do you know what I saw?'

Jean-Pierre was laughing. 'I see the heroine of some Gothic novel – the kind they sell in paperbacks at airport bookstalls all round the world. They always have a woman standing on a cliff on the cover. She has a long cloak and a big skirt.'

'That's right,' Hannie said angrily. 'That's exactly what I saw, too. Me, waiting. I was fed up. It suddenly seemed to me that while everything had looked so wonderful I'd booked myself for a twenty-year wait. Waiting for Adam, while he went out in the boat, waiting for the children to come home from school, or the man to fix the roof or the groceries to arrive. I went down that hill in a bad temper, all wet, and I was thinking that I wouldn't be able to stand it. All this waiting. Anyway, it was like an omen because before I got to the bottom I realized I was in labour, nearly a month too soon. So I got in the car and drove myself to hospital and had the twins.'

'What had happened to your husband?' asked Jean-Pierre.

'Oh, he'd had to put into a small port down the coast. The phone lines were down. By the time he'd dried out, driven home and then driven to the hospital I'd had the babies. It was very quick. The doctor was more frightened than I was.'

Jean-Pierre looked at her intently. 'You made up your mind that next time he could stand on the cliff in labour with his long red hair streaming in the breeze, and you would be in the boat?'

'Don't give me that one, Jean-Pierre,' Hannie said impatiently. 'I get enough of that sort of thing from the clients. I've confided in you. Don't start rubbishing me. The smuggling started by accident because I live on a smuggler's coast. Always has been. And it's something I can do without spending three-quarters of my life away from my husband and children, like I would if I worked for the Post Office. And I make a lot of money, which we need. So you don't have to start telling me I have some strange psychological reason for trying to keep my husband at home. He's a farmer, after all.'

'That wasn't what I meant,' he said but she thought that he had meant it. She realized that he was probably paying her back because she had taken his near-romantic declarations too lightly. Even Jean-Pierre was not incapable of doling out a little male spite when the need arose.

After a silence he said, 'Oh – all right. That is what I meant.'

'You've been around a long time,' she told him. 'You see me as a silly amateur. Someone playing grown-up games she doesn't understand.'

'A beautiful woman who won't look any better after ten years in a Bolivian gaol. And,' he said, earnestly, 'to tell the whole truth, I am not in love with the tradition you belong to. I am very fond of you. I have another friend who is the same, and I love him too. But it is your horrible, English, bourgeois ideal. It is the rose garden with its ancient walls, and the rooks in the old elms – your countrymen have spent nearly two hundred years now moving all over the globe, cursing the heat or the cold, dreaming of the gentle rain over fields, exploiting, looting and enslaving. And all for your rose gardens and your tennis courts and your scones and jam under the oak tree. The world is still trying to deal with the results of all that, and so is your country, but you cannot see it. And you and your kind are still doing it and you'll go on doing it until the last green eye of the little yellow god has been taken away to restore your beams or to send some poor helpless child away from home at seven years old so that he can go to a school where they'll teach him the same lesson. The little, puny English dream – you want to pretend to be lords of the manor. And those manors can only be kept up by plundering the world and not mentioning that the money comes from "heathen" countries.'

Hannie lifted the phone and asked for breakfast. Putting it down, she said, 'Look, Jean-Pierre, I'm not a big political thinker. I'm just doing the best I can to get by.'

'I have an obsession,' he told her. 'And also, I should like you to be safer.'

'Then we should never meet,' Hannie pointed out.

'I would go to live in a thatched cottage near your house,' Jean-Pierre said gallantly.

44

Not long after that she left for Paris. And, a week later, for St Colombe.

Hannie moored her boat to a tree standing near the water at the edge of a crescent beach of glittering white sand. She stepped ashore. Birds wheeled overhead as she walked, under a brilliant blue sky, towards the fringe of trees behind the beach. It's Eden, she thought. Edmund Corrington had protected Beauregard, twenty miles square, with a population of one hundred people, so that, as she had approached in her boat, she had felt like the buccaneer her sister had accused her of being – about to set foot on an island in the Caribbean, all coral and white sand under a piercingly blue sky, and as the guidebook told her, in the interior of the island, pleasant woodlands, fresh streams and groves of wild banana trees.

Hannie wore a floral dress, wide straw hat and sunglasses. Over her shoulder hung a white canvas bag. The only item distinguishing her from a normal tourist was a pair of strong but flexible purple suede boots, lacing well above the ankle, into which she had changed in the boat. If caught, she hoped the colour of the boots and the fancy style would make it look less as if she had planned an expedition where she might have to do tough walking in the vicinity of creatures which could bite and sting.

She had carefully established, among the others on her tour, the character of a nervous, divorced woman whose husband had recently gone off with his personal assistant. She wore dark glasses a lot and carried several jars of capsules in her bag. These she took piously, with the air of someone receiving the sacrament, not a difficult bit of acting for the daughter of Mrs Edwards. She hoped that hiring a boat and disappearing at dawn for Beauregard would be considered a stupid impulse she'd followed because she was so disturbed. Not that the boatman could believe that; she'd had to show her competence round the harbour before he'd let her have his boat.

She sat down under a tree, in the sand, and stared quietly out to sea. Theoretically, craftily composed letters should have ensured that one of the Fevriers arrived at the beach every morning to see if she'd landed. If the messages had gone wrong she'd have to go and find them. In the meanwhile, half an hour in this lovely spot, studying the pink of the clumps of coral studding the sand, hearing the cries of the birds wheeling through the blue sky and the faint sounds of the breeze in the palm trees, would not come amiss.

She had been three days on St Colombe now. It was hot, depressing and built on black, volcanic soil. The evil-hued beaches made children cry and their parents vow to expose the travel agents who had put misleading pictures in their brochures. The town, also named St Colombe, was, underneath its top-dressing of hotels, bars and ornamental gardens, a tired French colonial city, gone to seed. The streets were dusty, the verandaed buildings unpainted, the back end of town was too close to the centre, so the shacks, the chickens scratching, the thin, Black barefoot children, the heavy women with buckets and bundles, the discouraged men, were painfully obvious to tourists venturing only a short distance from their hotels. And over everything loomed the heavily wooded mountain, *la Veuve Colombe*, the Widow of Colombe. There's something sinister about a volcano, however extinct, thought Hannie, so no wonder it was cheaper to get a package tour to St Colombe than some of the other Caribbean islands. No wonder she was pleased to be sitting here on the beach at Beauregard.

Now there were voices speaking gently behind her, not far away. Then, at the edge of a clump of trees nearby, two figures appeared. Hannie stood up, left the beach and went to where they stood on a narrow path leading through the trees.

She recognized Angelina Fevrier by her height and build. She had the same candid eyes as her sister, although she looked older. The man beside her was a little shorter, his face heavily lined by years, Hannie guessed, of very hard work.

He said, 'Good morning,' but spoke with an accent, a little like French, which she could hardly understand at first.

Angelina said, 'Better go now, before the sun gets strong. We live only about a mile from here.' Hannie walked behind her, with Angelina's father at the back, up the track between sparse trees and scrub.

'I'm Regius,' said Angelina's father. 'Hannie,' she told him, her eyes on Angelina's strong bare feet hitting the track. She wondered if life on Beauregard was not so paradisal. Maybe people would prefer an owner who violated their peace by building a hotel, putting in a generator and piped water, and running in supplies of Coca-cola and steak. She said as much to Angelina as they went. Angelina replied, 'I don't know. We thought about that. On St Colombe they got jobs at the hotels and taking the tourists out in the boats. They got electricity but they have to live off the visitors. Here we got poverty and our land. Which is best?'

'Pity that has to be the choice,' Hannie replied.

'But those men came back – four of them,' Angelina said.

Hannie, having difficulty in keeping up with her in the mounting heat, said, 'What! When? What did they do?'

'Yesterday,' she said. 'Late on in the day. They landed in a boat. I was putting water on the plants. It's dry; the rain's late this year. Father was in the house looking after Mother. They came up to me and said they had to see her. I went inside, and Father told me to tell them she was too sick. The biggest one said I had to tell her Mrs Julie Corrington heard she had a letter which was useless but Mrs Corrington wanted to have it to protect the good name of the family. They said to say Mrs Corrington would give five hundred dollars for the letter. Then they hung around for a bit and went away – said they'd be back for an answer soon.'

'Then what?' asked Hannie.

'Then they said wooden houses burn well, then they left,' Angelina reported impassively.

Hannie stopped. 'Look,' she said urgently. 'You'd better come back to St Colombe in the boat. It's dangerous here.'

From behind Regius said, 'My wife is near death. I don't want to move her and I'm not going to leave her. I've told Angelina to go –'

'I can hold them off,' Angelina said. 'I'm staying here. And are you telling me for sure it would be safer on St Colombe? I don't know.'

Whatever holiday mood Hannie had conjured up on the boat on the sparkling sea had evaporated quickly. Now they reached a big half-acre clearing. Crops grew in rows. Near the one-storey wooden house with its corrugated roof stood a stone-walled sty from which Hannie heard the sound of a sow and her screeching piglets. A stream ran beside the house and behind the rows of plants, where the trees began, were two tethered goats. Big flowers grew up the sides of the house.

Inside were three rooms. The one they entered first had an old-fashioned kitchen range, a highly polished mahogany table and matching chairs, a heavy sideboard and a neat dresser with a big blue and white dinner service – plates, cups, saucers and tureens – arranged on it. There was a battery radio, and on the walls and sideboard, pictures and photographs. Hannie saw the picture Sarah Fevrier had in London showing the couple, old Sarah and Regius Fevrier, and their four children.

'Best if you see Mrs Fevrier now,' Regius said as they stood there. 'She has to have her medicine soon – that makes her tired.'

The old woman, who was, Hannie realized, not very old, (sixty-four, she later learnt), lay in a big wooden bed under a white coverlet. Hannie and Regius walked quietly up to it and looked down. She was very thin and grey in the face. She seemed to be asleep. Then she opened her eyes, saying in a weak voice, 'I'm glad you came. Regius must give you the letter, and you must take it to England quickly. I want my Sarah's children to have this island. If Mrs Corrington gets it she will take it all, even this –' She paused, exhausted, then whispered, 'This is our land – we have looked after it.'

Hannie said, 'Yes – don't worry. I'll take the letter to England.' And Regius said, 'Come away, now. Come away.'

'Give it to her, Regius,' said the woman. But he had already opened the drawer in the small polished table beside the big bed. Holding the letter in his hand he walked from the room, saying, 'I'll give it to her, Sarah. Sleep now. I'll bring the medicine in just a little while.'

In the doorway Hannie turned to look back at Sarah. Her eyes were open. Hannie said, 'I'll do my best, Mrs Fevrier.' Sarah's mouth moved, but Hannie heard nothing. She went out and shut the door.

In the other room Angelina poured dark fragrant coffee while Hannie read the letter. It was dark in the room, but she could read easily. Edmund Corrington's writing was clear and the ink he had used was black. The envelope had a stamp on it and the postmark read St Colombe, June 2nd 1981. So far, so good, Hannie thought, checking the signatures at the bottom of the second page of the letter. Percy Squires and Hugh Metcalfe had both signed their names and added the date. Then she began to read:

My dear Sarah,
It's a long, long time since I have been able to communicate with you or the children. You can't know how much I regret this, but I'm afraid it has been necessary because my wife has always been very upset by the thought of you and what happened between us, although I, God knows, have never regretted any of it for an instant. I sincerely hope that you feel the same although I know you have the right to resent me, after what I did and, alas, what I didn't do. I should probably have married you, dear Sarah, and to hell with what the others would have said. But what's done is done, worse luck, and all I can say is if I've hurt you I'm sorry. At least Regius is a good man and if I've hurt you, I think I've hurt myself more. The last forty years have been agony to me. All I've been able to do is preserve your home from intrusion, and even that hasn't been easy, believe me. And now, Sarah, I'm ill. I think I might

be dying. All the Corringtons die young. So I believe that however much I've missed you, and the dear little girls, I must now do something sensible for you because once I've gone the family will own the island and do what they like with it. I've decided to make a will leaving the whole place to you. This will be properly witnessed by the two gentlemen who are in the house with me at this moment, and then one of them will take it for me to Mr Corneille. Pay attention to all this, Sarah – don't go off into one of your dreams – because it's vitally important you understand everything. I may never get the chance to write to you again, or see you. All I can do is look after you. What you have to do, if you ever hear of my death, is this; go to Mr Corneille on St Colombe, *with this letter*, and ask him to execute the will. Then the island will be yours. Don't listen to anything anyone says to you about this, whoever they are, just take the letter to Mr Corneille. This, dear Sarah, is all I can do for you after all these years so please do as I ask. Remember, the island is yours. And now, they are waiting for the letter so goodbye, my dear Sarah, and remember me well, as I do you.

Hannie put the letter down on the table, studying the superscription, 'With all my love, Edmund,' and the two signatures beneath. After a while she said, 'Yes – yes, I see. But I'm afraid we need the will. Apart from anything else there could be a later one. Or maybe the Corringtons could produce something fraudulent – we need that will.' She looked at the two silent Fevriers, father and daughter, and said, half-apologetically, 'There it is – we must have it. Where is it?'

Angelina said, into the silence, 'I told Sarah we

51

should have it. The problem is old Corneille, the lawyer, died. It's his son now. Not an honest man. I asked, but he said he'd never seen it. Never found it when his father died.'

'He could have destroyed it then,' suggested Hannie.

Angelina shook her head. 'People like that don't dare take that last step,' she said. 'And when I talked to him I could tell there was something wrong – he had that will in that room while I talked to him, I know it. He won't have it there now, though, that piece of paper will be hidden away. That was the worst day's work we ever done,' she added, 'when we told him we still had that letter. Then those men began to haunt us and Sarah. Now we can't move in case we make it all worse for us.'

Already Hannie, in the dusky room, surrounded by old, heavy pieces of furniture, was sensing the strength of the forces ranged against the Fevriers. She stood up, putting the letter in the envelope, saying, 'I'd better leave quickly. I'll try to get into Corneille's office and find that will.'

'It's dangerous,' Regius told her.

'I don't like to leave the job half done,' she said. 'That way I get no satisfaction and no profit. How can I get a message to you here without anyone knowing?'

'My brother, young Regius, knows you're in St Colombe. He may have seen you by now, but he can't go near you in case he gets spotted. He'll find a way,' Angelina said with some certainty.

Regius was putting some medicine in a glass for his wife as Hannie and Angelina set off down the track, back to the boat. Hannie told her what she was planning to do with the letter and said, 'I wish you'd all get in the boat and come with me.'

Angelina told her, 'We can hold those men off for a

52

little longer, pretending we're going to sell them that letter.'

Hannie, speeding the boat over sparkling sea, looked back at the fringe of white shore and trees of the beautiful little island and reflected how vulnerable the Fevriers were and how fast she must act now.

In the late afternoon she returned the boat, deliberately bungling her approach across the harbour and telling a story of having landed on an island she thought might have been Beauregard, or a smaller island farther on, where she had fallen asleep, then got lost on the way back. The owner of the boat seemed to accept her story, but she was not sure he really believed her.

She walked back to her hotel and took careful note of Corneille's office, a wooden building with peeling white paint and a good collection of loungers in T-shirts hanging about on the veranda outside. The sight of them with their hand-rolled cigarettes and beer cans was not encouraging. A respectable lawyer, the kind who would be trustworthy about wills, would have cleared them off the premises. Hannie hoped Corneille did not employ any of them as guards – they looked nasty. But as she walked back to her hotel, which was in the next bay, about a mile from the town, she wondered who else was involved in the plot to do the Fevriers out of their island. The Corringtons sounded like people who had once been rich Caribbean landowners but were now going downhill. Their lawyer's office had a small-town, disreputable air. Yet someone had quickly organized watchers in London as soon as they found out Sarah Fevrier was about to die and had been asking about Corrington's will. And the watchers were white men, in a big car – it began to look like more than a local job, as if somebody efficient, with money to spend, had joined in with the Corringtons. As it was, it didn't seem likely the will was still in Corneille's office – unless he was hanging on to it in order to stay in the game. She'd have to be quick, she realized, not just because the Fevriers were in danger but because on a small island people soon find out who you are and what you're up to. Her surprise value would soon wear off.

'Enjoy your trip?' enquired the receptionist as she collected her key, which confirmed her fears, since she had told no one about her trip.

Hannie shook her head. 'My husband used to take me out in a motor boat, but on my own I was confused. I wish I hadn't gone.'

As she got in the lift, she could feel his eyes on her back. She wasn't even sure the character she had invented was convincing. Whatever marks slavery and oppression left behind, one of them was alertness to body language and facial expression. Even if her dejected air and inoffensive ways were deceiving her white companions, she might be betraying herself to the black people on St Colombe.

Nevertheless, she went into the bar, sat down with a couple from Essex, awarding herself a vodka, a couple of her tablets and five minutes' talk of the kind which goes, 'Sometimes the people you trust the most are the ones who let you down the most in the end.' Then she declared she had a headache and told them she would miss dinner, deciding to rest rather than spend any more time on her persona.

At midnight she put on a dark shirt and trousers and, carrying a black shoulder bag, climbed from her veranda on the first floor out to the vine which grew up from the ground below. She dropped down. To her right she could see lights and people sitting out at tables with their drinks. Inside the hotel the disco was going full blast. As she moved quietly towards the corner of the building she found three men under a tree, smoking. They must have heard the rustle of the vine and the soft thump as she dropped to the ground, but they only said 'Evenin' as she walked past. She returned the greeting, hoping that vine-clambering was a regular occurrence among the guests at the hotel.

The road was dark and silent. There were trees on one side and the sea lay below on the other. She walked for perhaps ten minutes until the road began to move upwards in the direction of a big, white building which overlooked the harbour of St Colombe. Approaching, she heard the sound of reggae, not the crude rhythms the hotel calypso band served up to the guests, but more complex and sophisticated. As she heard a phrase repeated, she realized she was hearing live music. Then the sound stopped and two big doors opened at the top of the hill. In the light thrown outside she saw two long lean figures, arms round each other, stagger out, laughing. She watched them reel about and fall down in the grass of the hillside, out of sight. The face of one gleamed in the darkness, the other didn't.

A big figure appeared in the doorway shouting, 'Come back here – we going to be here all night.' Other voices started calling, 'Come back, man. We got to get on –' and then one of the fallen men got up and wandered back inside. Hannie, meanwhile, started walking again. She had gone past the white house when she looked back. On the hillside a figure stood watching her, presumably that of the second man for she saw a white face. She was alarmed. White people here usually meant authority; authority was what she didn't need. But as she turned away, she thought she saw him give her a thumbs-up sign. Reaching the hot, deserted main street she reflected that here was yet another person who knew about her midnight walk into town.

Turning off the main street, she walked down the passageway between the wooden walls of Corneille's office and the shabby shop next door. She found herself in a dried-up yard, about a hundred metres long. Tired creepers hung on a fence. She walked round an old bucket and the inside of a TV to get to the back door. Somewhere a dog started barking furiously. She was relieved to hear a chain rattling as the animal evidently hurled itself to and fro, unable to get free. The door was bolted top and bottom from the inside, but a small window next to the door had a simple catch, which she lifted, as a second dog joined in with the first. As she stepped through the window, she heard more dogs, then the enraged shout of an owner. She stood inside for a little while, until the noise died down. The beam of her torch, which she shone down towards the floor, showed scurrying cockroaches, the bottom of a fridge, a cooker, a bag of vegetable peelings spilling on the tiles.

She eased open the kitchen door and walked down the passageway to the front of the house. The narrow beam of her torch revealed an old desk, a telephone, a typewriter on another desk, a filing cabinet. Business didn't look good, she thought, which was just as well, because the filing cabinet was so old she could open it easily. Even as she did, she guessed that the will, if it still existed, was at Corneille's house – Angelina had told her it was at the foot of the mountain. Well, one step at a time, she told herself, as she went through the filing cabinet, finding plenty of information about cows and goats which had died in suspicious circumstances, a wealth of paternity suits, and arguments about land. There were even wills, but none of them the one she wanted.' The desk contained stationery, unanswered letters, a bag of what smelt like herbs on a leather string, plenty of green tags and three copies of *Playboy*.

She crept up the uncarpeted wooden stairs. There were two rooms upstairs, one with only a table and a pack of cards on it, chairs all round. The other was completely empty. As she went down again, she decided she'd have to go to Corneille's house. The manoeuvre went against her better judgement but she knew time was running out. Better a last bid than no bid at all.

She climbed out of the back window, pushing it to, and at the same time the dogs started barking again. She groped in her big bag for her can of hairspray. As she did so, a large Alsatian outlined itself against the wooden fence at the bottom of the yard, scrabbled over it, claws scratching wildly, and bounded towards her. Hannie crouched, holding the hairspray. The dog stopped, baring its teeth and preparing to spring. Just as her finger hit the button a hand fell on her shoulder and a voice said, 'Mrs Bennett – we better talk.' Now the dog was blundering round the yard, whining.

'OK,' she said. 'But let's go fast.' Voices were beginning to call out as they ran out of the yard and back into the main street. There they slowed to a walk. 'That stuff blind the dog?' asked her companion as they strolled.

'Too far away,' Hannie told him, still holding the can. 'Where are we going?'

'Recording studio,' he told her.

'That white building by the sea?'

'That's right.'

'Who are you and what's it about?' Hannie asked.

They were on the road out of the town now.

'Don't worry. I'm on your side. I'm Regius Fevrier.'

Hannie looked at him carefully. He was tall, thin and younger than the sisters, only about thirty, but he had the same big nose. She capped the can of hairspray and put it back in her bag.

'We're going in the wrong direction. I want to have a look round Corneille's house. You could help me.'

'That will's not there,' he told her. 'No way that family would let Corneille keep it. He's too careless and too lazy.'

She was tired now. She said, 'Look, I can't stay here much longer. Too many people know about me – and I think you should go to your family.'

He nodded. 'I got a message from a man bringing over fruit and vegetables for the market. Angelina says to tell you they came back after you left. One of them showed her his gun. My brother Martin's coming from the other side of the mountain, where he works, tomorrow. Soon as he arrives, we're leaving for Beauregard. That way we'll all be there.'

They walked up the path to the white building. Regius Fevrier opened the doors and they went in. It was one large room with a sound booth at the back. Against the long wall were ten or twelve steel drums. Six men sat near the drums, drinking beer from cans. Two were playing cards.

'You're a musician?' she said to Regius.

'I got a job in one of the hotel kitchens,' he said. 'But I write some songs and play.' He indicated a guitar propped up against the wall of the sound booth. 'They let us have this place when the regular bands aren't using it, the big ones, from England and the States. We're just a local band – a few records on a local label.'

They sat down opposite the group of six men. Regius went to a fridge in the corner and got Hannie a can of beer. She drank it gratefully. 'I'm glad you're going to Beauregard,' she said. 'I tried to get them to come here – thought it'd be safer.'

'Old Sarah wants to die there,' he said. 'Plus – who says it's safer here? Could be worse. Funny people about.'

'Yes?' Hannie said.

'Yes,' he told her.

'Thought it was getting hotter,' Hannie murmured.

'The Corringtons arrived from Barbados this afternoon,' Regius informed her. 'Mrs Julie and the son, Victor. By charter plane. They're not that rich, to spend that money unless there was something happening. One of the men at their house says they're going to Beauregard tomorrow.'

'What for?' asked Hannie.

He shrugged. 'Get the letter?' he suggested.

'Where do you think that will is?' demanded Hannie.

'My guess is old Mrs Corrington's got it. If she asked Corneille for it, he wouldn't dare say no. He's got all the Corrington business and God knows what else he knows and owes them – plenty of skeletons in that cupboard.'

A big man with a lot of grey hair strolled up. 'So, Regius?' he enquired. He had big, intelligent brown eyes.

Regius nodded easily. 'This is Jacks,' he told Hannie. 'Mrs Bennett,' he explained to the big man.

'Mrs Bennett,' Jacks said agreeably.

'Just talking about who got the Corrington will,' Regius explained. The big man evidently knew the whole story. 'Old Julie Corrington, that's my guess,' he said.

'She won't still have it, though,' Hannie said. 'She'll have destroyed it – wouldn't you?'

'I would,' Jacks said. 'But we're not rich. She is, and that's why. People like that don't get rid of anything useful. They might change their mind; they might want to use it for blackmail. She's got that will. But she'll have it well protected.'

Hannie looked at Regius. Regius shook his head. 'No, not me,' he told her. 'They got everything at that house – big wall, shotguns, big dogs roaming round the gardens, burglar alarms. I wouldn't try it, not without a parachute regiment too.'

Hannie drank her beer and said, 'There's got to be a way.'

He nodded. 'All I want to see is that will in a lawyer's hands before my mother dies.'

He turned to another man who had drifted up. He wore steel-rimmed glasses and a black T-shirt with Che Guevara on it. Regius said, 'All I don't want to hear at this moment, Arthur, is that property is theft.'

Hannie asked them, 'Who's behind the Corringtons? From what I hear it's one elderly woman and her stepson, feeble Victor. But they've got expert threateners, enough funds to hire men to watch Sarah Fevrier in London. You can feel there's extra power coming from somewhere –' She broke off and stood up, saying, 'I'm tired. I'd better go back to the hotel and get some sleep. Maybe I'll think better in the morning.'

The three men walked her down the hill. Arthur stopped. 'There it is – I'm sure of that, I just felt it.'

The three men looked up at the mountain, *Veuve Colombe*. Hannie stared up, too. Jacks said, 'Know, Arthur, I didn't believe you and your old daddy's strange thoughts.' He paused. 'Now I'm not so sure.'

'Not an eruption!' exclaimed Hannie in alarm.

'*Veuve Colomb*', *elle brûle, elle brûle,*' sang Arthur, evidently remembering some old nursery rhyme.

As Hannie watched, she was sure she saw a spark fly

up into the air above the mountain.

'My father's been trying to tell them for months,' Arthur confided, 'they keep on saying he's mad – don't want to drive away tourists – say *'Veuve Colomb'* just grumbling up there, as usual. This is a poor island. We can't afford an active volcano.'

By now the hotel was in sight. Hannie said, 'Maybe you'd better go back. We don't want to be spotted together, especially me and Regius. Thanks for the walk.'

Arthur said, 'Good luck.'

As she walked in quietly, the receptionist appeared to be dozing and Hannie, who had taken her key with her when she climbed out of the hotel, tiptoed across the lobby and up the stairs. On the way up she began to feel uneasy. She crept along the corridor to her room, thrust the door open with her right hand and, still holding the handle, felt quickly for the light switch with her left, snapped on the light, jumped back and banged the door shut. Outside, she flattened herself against the wall. She had seen three men in the wreckage of her room, although there might have been a fourth in the bathroom. Now she was too afraid to run, in case they shot her in the back. So she would have to fight. She caught the first one across the neck as he hurled out of the room, looking for her. He fell in the doorway. Two others holding guns came out too fast. As the nearest man tried not to trip over the body Hannie grabbed his gun and hit him over the side of the head. But she knew that, unless he was very slow, the third man would now have located her and levelled his gun. He was, indeed, standing in the doorway of her room, the gun pointing at her. She flung up her arms, still looking for a chance to attack him but realized he was standing too far away and not planning to let her come any closer. 'In here,' he said. And Hannie walked into her room as he backed away from her. There had been a fourth man in the room. He now stood behind the man with the gun, who said, 'Get them inside and shut the door.' To Hannie he said, 'Sit down in that chair.' Which she did, as the other man hauled the two out of the corridor and back into her room.

Glancing round, she saw that the contents of the drawers had been turned out on to the floor, her shoes lay scattered about and her suitcase had been ripped to pieces. It lay, lining out, on the bed. Quicker and less painful, she thought, to tell them immediately where the letter was. On the other hand, once they knew, they might kill her. She'd have to hold out as long as she could. Perhaps the noise of the struggle had disturbed the guests, perhaps someone would ring the desk to complain.

So she sat there saying, 'What's going on?' The man with the gun said, 'Where's the letter?'

'What letter?' said Hannie. The man she had chopped across the side of the neck groaned and began to come round. And the man with the gun smacked Hannie round the face and made her teeth rattle. She screamed. Then she screamed again. 'Leave me alone,' she cried. 'What do you –?' The other man clapped his hand over her mouth, which was open. Hannie bit him hard. She screamed, 'Help! Help!' as he snatched away his hand. The second man smacked her hard and another hand went over her mouth. Hannie, with her face aching and a cruel hand wrenching it to one side, shot a vindictive glance through streaming eyes at the man whose hand she had mauled. There is something outrageous about being bitten by another human being. He was staring at

62

his dripping hand, in shock. Hannie was pleased. Underneath that, she was frightened.

Then, what she hoped for happened. A key grated in the lock of the door. The hand suddenly left her face, the gun disappeared, and as the door cautiously opened, Hannie was left sagging in her chair, holding her face in a littered room where one man lay unconscious on the floor, two had just got up groggily and one was trying clumsily to staunch the blood from his hand with tissues from the dressing table. The receptionist, with Regius, Jacks and Arthur crowding behind him, stared into the room. Hannie stared back. 'Sorry,' she said. 'Things got a bit out of hand.'

'Keep these men here,' the receptionist told her. 'I'm going to phone the police.'

'Just get them out of here,' groaned Hannie, still holding her face. 'I don't want any of this to come out. It was a mistake — it went too far.'

The receptionist looked round the room, beginning to be relieved that there would be no scandal. He couldn't really believe, Hannie thought, that there'd been an orgy involving an unconscious man, a bitten man, a turned-over room and a ripped-up suitcase. But he seemed ready to try as Hannie groaned again, 'Just get them out of here. Get them out of my sight. I'll pay for the damage.'

So the three men, supporting the fourth, followed by the receptionist, left the room. Regius closed the door.

'Phew!' Hannie said, slumping.

'You all right?' asked Regius.

'Thanks for coming,' Hannie said. 'It wasn't a moment too soon.'

'Lucky you screamed,' Jacks said. 'Arthur suddenly told us he thought this might happen, so we came back.

That receptionist tried hard to stop us from coming up.'

'He wouldn't have been so fast if you hadn't been there,' said Hannie.

'They paid him,' Arthur said with certainty.

Hannie went into the bathroom and washed her face. As she brushed her hair, she heard Arthur asking Regius if he thought the bar was still open. They went downstairs and walked into the bar which was empty except for two drunken tourists who scarcely looked at them. Hannie, sipping her drink, said, 'Well – we know something. That letter is dangerous to the Corringtons.'

'And something else, those men were Americans,' Regius said.

'Right,' said Hannie, nodding.

'Means I'm right,' said Arthur. 'Organized crime – they got the Mafia in on this one. That's where the money's coming from for all these thugs and hoodlums.'

'I'm afraid they've hurt my family,' Regius said. 'Else how did they know you had the letter?'

'The boatman knew I took the boat out,' Hannie said. 'Three men under a tree saw me climb out of the hotel tonight when I went to Corneille's – this place is like a whispering gallery – everybody knows everything.' She hoped she was right.

'I'll come over to Beauregard tomorrow,' Arthur said to Regius. 'Apart from all that, I don't like this volcano. You better get out of here too,' he said to Hannie. 'They won't leave you alone till they get that letter.' Suddenly alarmed, he said, 'Hey – they didn't, did they? You still got it?'

'Not exactly,' she said and told them where it was. Then they had another drink. But Hannie said, 'I'd really like to get my hands on that will. There's something about getting slapped round the face that makes you angry.'

Jacks said to Regius, 'Some nasty people going to get their hands on that island if you don't prove it's yours.'

Regius said, 'I don't like the idea that anything's happened to the family over there.' After a pause he said to Hannie, 'All right, let's try to get that will from Julie Corrington – but I have to leave first light for Beauregard.'

'Plenty of people tried to get in that house,' Jacks said. 'All they got is shot or dog bites and gaol sentences. The only way you can get in there is if they invite you, and that's a fact.'

Hannie thought a bit and decided, 'They can invite me. Why not? They want the letter; they'll be pleased to see me, day or night, any time, if I look as if I'll co-operate.'

'True,' Jacks said. 'But if you go and if you get the will, then you've got to get out. That's the hardest part.'

'I'll work it out as I go along,' declared Hannie.

'You're mad,' Arthur told her. 'Look who you got against you. Could be the Mafia – could be there's a heavy political angle. These islands are strategic. Whoever they are, they're powerful. They could kill you.'

'I doubt it,' said Hannie, and got up to phone Julie Corrington.

'I wish she wouldn't do this,' Arthur said. 'It could be the CIA, the Cubans –'

'Could be the Primitive Methodists,' Jacks said. 'I just hope the Corringtons won't let her come. But,' he said, brightening up, 'remember who's in that house, an honoured guest?'

Regius and Arthur looked at him and began to smile.

'Forgotten about that,' murmured Regius. 'Now that's a nice idea. How're we going to let him know about this?'

Arthur shrugged. 'If she goes at all, she can go in my taxi. I can get a message to old Rob, the servant up there.'

'This is getting interesting,' declared Jacks as Hannie, looking satisfied, came back and said, 'All fixed up and taxi coming.'

'Cancel it,' Regius said promptly. 'Arthur here, he drives a taxi. It's parked up at the recording studio.'

'All right,' Hannie agreed. 'Keep it in the family.' She yawned. 'Another little walk. I'll go upstairs and get out of my burglar kit.'

Out in the hall, while they waited for her, Regius told the receptionist, 'You let those men in.'

'They climbed in,' the man said.

'They paid you so they could search the room,' Regius said.

'Get out of here, trash,' the receptionist said contemptuously. 'Musicians, criminals, dopedealers, just get out.'

'We'll be seeing you,' Jacks said agreeably as the four of them left the hotel. The receptionist stared after them, looking worried.

The taxi wound up the road in complete darkness. There were thick trees and bushes on either side. From this angle Hannie could not see the top of the mountain, *la Veuve Colombe*, and as they twisted up the wooded hillside over which a sickle moon rolled, casting fitful light, she found it hard to believe the stories about an imminent eruption.

The Corringtons' house was surrounded by a high wall.

66

Arthur had to shout their names into a grille next to the gates before the doors swung open. They went up a long drive bordered by flowering bushes and plants, tangled and overgrown, until they reached a big white plantation house, two centuries old. Hannie, whose career had been helped by the invisible compass she carried in her head guessed the house overlooked St Colombe harbour.

The front door was open and a figure stood on the steps. As soon as the car stopped, Arthur jumped out, ran round, flung open the door of the car and then dashed straight up to the man on the steps as if they were both expected to welcome her to the house. Hannie got out of the car, bewildered, and walked up to join them. Seeming to ignore Arthur, who had just whispered something in his ear, the elderly man took her courteously into the house. In the silence Hannie heard Arthur start the car and drive away. As she walked over the marble floor of the hall, under huge ceilings, she felt a peculiar tingle in the soles of her purple leather boots. She followed the servant stolidly into the empty drawing room, where he left her. The wooden floor was well polished. A great spotted gilt mirror hung over an ornate marble fireplace and lamps stood on low tables. At the end of the room two huge bow windows looked out on the bay. Hannie stood staring into the darkness, just able to make out the glitter of the water as the moon wove in and out of the clouds. Once upon a time, she thought, some old Corrington, or the like, had been able to stand here in the early morning watching his slaves loading his sugar or his cotton aboard schooners bound for Liverpool. What did the owners see today? Holiday craft, tourists with dark glasses and cameras, flowered shirts, big hats, buying souvenirs from the shops around the harbour. Or did they, she wondered, look out through binoculars to the left, towards the white shores of the tempting little island of Beauregard?

Ten minutes, a quarter of an hour passed. Hannie, guessing that the old trick of making the subject wait was being played, sat down and relaxed, making her mind a blank and letting her muscles go as limp as possible. The man or woman who makes the other wait, whether in a drawing room or a prison cell, gains control. The counter-move was to relax and make the time work for you. When the manservant came back into the room, he thought she was asleep and coughed politely. 'What's your name?' she said immediately.

'Robert, madam,' he replied. 'Mrs Corrington apologizes for the delay and says she will be with you shortly.'

'Thank you,' said Hannie and waited another five minutes.

Finally, a party of three people came into the room. 'So sorry,' said Julie Corrington, in her high, soft voice. 'Sorry to have left you by yourself for so long.' Two men were helping her into the room. The one with his arm round her waist was surely her stepson, Victor. He was tall, overweight, and pale. The man on the other side, holding her upper arm, was shorter, a calm-faced, square-jawed man, with gold spectacles. He had brown hair and his eyes, when he glanced at Hannie, were cold, intelligent, and, she decided, far from sentimental.

But it was Julie Corrington, small, dark and heavily made-up, especially round her very blue eyes, who riveted Hannie's attention. She wore a long, dark red dress and as the two men assisted her to a brocade sofa, Hannie saw she was shod in very small, high-heeled soft cream shoes. Now she leaned against the corner of the sofa, one white arm ending in a white hand covered in rings extended along the edge. 'I'm pleased you decided to visit me, Mrs Bennett. Not before time. But luckily you're here now. Let me introduce my son, Victor –' and she indicated the big man standing by the sofa. 'And this is my business adviser, Mr Brown.' The calm man in gold glasses was sitting between herself and Hannie. She turned to her son. 'Do sit down, Victor, dear. There's no need to hover. Mr Brown will pour us all a drink, I'm sure. What would you like?' she asked Hannie.

'Some whisky,' Hannie said vaguely. 'Just a small one.'

'With ginger – soda?' Mr Brown said, from the drinks table near the wall.

'Er – ginger,' Hannie said. She decided to be as confused as possible since her only way of robbing the house was to be in it overnight. She needed to be disarming enough to be invited to stay. In the meanwhile she understood why Julie Corrington, small and soft-voiced, had arrested her attention – she was the same age, and had the same style as her mother, even down to the little, useless feet. Julie Corrington was her mother, manipulating, disguising power by the appearance of weakness. But here it was more frightening – the victims weren't just her own family. Hannie suddenly imagined the soft beringed hands torching the Fevriers' wooden house on the island, burning them up as their pigs squealed from the stone pen; saw Regius and the others arriving the next day to a pile of smoking ruins, and heard Julie Corrington ask softly, 'Well, my dear, what have you come to tell me?' Hannie, glancing at her and for a moment into the cold eyes of Mr Brown thought, 'Better get this one right or you could wind up in the bay with heavy weights tied to your feet.'

As though hardly knowing where to begin, she pointed to her face, where a bruise had developed. 'See this? I can hardly believe it myself, but when I came in, there were four men in my room. They'd emptied all the drawers and ripped my case to pieces – I got in a panic. I started hitting them – I can't remember what happened except that eventually I was in the chair with one of them hitting me and asking me for a letter. At the time I couldn't even understand what he was talking about. Then some men I'd met casually that evening' – and here she tried to give the impression that she had let herself be picked up by them – 'suddenly turned up and got rid of them. I don't know what would have happened if they hadn't.'

Mr Brown came over and took her empty glass. He refilled it. Hannie took it and drank deeply. Julie Corrington said, 'How appalling. Did the police give you any idea who they were?'

'Police?' Hannie said. 'I didn't want the police involved. You hear such things about the foreign police and getting into trouble abroad. Besides, have you seen them? That's to say – I don't want to be rude – but they're not exactly the sort of police I'm used to –' She trailed off, as if embarrassed.

'I do see what you mean,' Julie said soothingly.

'Gang of louts,' said Victor Corrington, getting up and helping himself to another brandy. 'No better than the men they're supposed to be catching. Sorry, does anyone want topping up?'

'I don't think so, Victor,' his mother told him silkily.

'Terrible experience for you,' he said to Hannie.

70

'I just told the man from the hotel to get rid of them,' Hannie said to Julie Corrington. 'I'll buy a new suitcase and claim it on the insurance when I get back. Forget all about it – that's all I want to do.'

The attentive Mr Brown again took her empty glass and refilled it while Julie Corrington pretended not to notice. Hannie was worried about Mr Brown. The men he had hired to rob her room could have reported back to him already. If so, they would have told him her reactions had not been those of a normal woman tourist. And her performance here would be pointless. Nevertheless, she took a drink from her glass and said self-consciously, 'I hope I'm not getting drunk.'

'You've had a shock,' Julie Corrington told her. 'Really, this island's gone to pieces, with all the tourism. It causes the most frightful problems.' She looked at Hannie from a little ivory face, through big, forget-me-not eyes and asked, 'But how did you come by the letter? What made you think it was mine?'

Hannie launched gladly into her tale. 'I took a boat out, you see. I had the idea I wanted to do something a little bit daring – I hadn't slept well that night – I expect I wasn't thinking straight. Now I wish I hadn't gone because I went astray somehow and landed on this island, and there was a man there fishing who sort of latched on to me – I could hardly understand what he was saying – but he told me to wait on the beach, so I did, mostly because I'd been trying to ask him if he'd take me back in the boat to St Colombe. But he hadn't seemed to understand what I was saying, so I thought I'd wait for him to come back and try to make him see what I wanted. And the next thing was he appeared on the beach with this tall, black woman, who he said was his daughter, and she asked me to take a letter back to

71

England and deliver it to the Queen. Of all people! When I said why didn't they post it to her, it'd get there quicker, they said all the mail in and out of St Colombe was tampered with by the postmaster. Well, quite honestly, I didn't believe it. In fact I thought they were just simple people who lived on this island and had gone a bit cuckoo. I felt quite sorry for them really. They looked quite poor, and the woman didn't have any shoes on – and anyway I wanted to get away because there I was stuck on this island with a couple of people who might not be in their right minds – so I said yes.' Hannie paused, took another drink and said, 'Anyway, much as I wanted to get away, I didn't like to agree to anything which might get me into trouble, so I just said all right, as long as there isn't anything in this letter which the customs might not like when I go through – I mean, the tour people were pretty quick to warn us about agreeing to deliver packages for people on the island to other people they said were their relations in England.'

She looked at Julie Corrington who assured her, 'You were very sensible.'

'So they opened the envelope for me,' Hannie explained. 'And I read the letter inside, and they told me it was their claim to the island.' She looked again at Julie Corrington. 'I've got to apologize if I've seen anything I shouldn't. I was just in this predicament, you see. No choice, really.'

Again, Julie Corrington reassured her. 'It was all a very long time ago. Such things used to happen here, years ago.'

'Human nature, I suppose,' Hannie said wisely. She sat for a moment staring into her glass, then rallied herself. 'That's it, really. I took the letter and said I'd make sure the Queen got it. The old man showed me where I had to point the boat and I pointed it, and got out. To tell the truth I'd more or less forgotten I'd got the letter until this business with these men. Then I got frightened and remembered your name. I thought the sooner I got it all sorted out the better, so I rang you up from the hotel. I'm sorry it's so late but, you see, I thought they might come back.'

Brown spoke for the first time, in a well-modulated New England voice. 'Very frightening, all of it. You were quite right to come here and I, personally, don't care about the time.' He said to Julie Corrington, 'It's just as well all this has come to a head. You've been too tolerant in the past. I believe I've mentioned to you several times that this affair should be resolved straight away, before it came to some kind of crisis. Now see what's happened – this lady has been inconvenienced, frightened by thugs – and it has to be settled, once and for all. Will you explain to Mrs Bennett, or would you prefer it if I did?'

'I think you can make it clearer,' Julie Corrington said. 'But, please, could you pour me a tiny brandy first?' It was Victor Corrington who poured his mother a tiny brandy and himself a large one. He topped up Hannie's glass, too. Mr Brown rattled some ice into a glass and poured Coke on it saying, 'This is all I'm allowed, regrettably.' He sat down and said to Hannie, 'The position is simply this. Mrs Corrington's husband, Mr Edmund Corrington, died four years ago. He owned certain property on this island and on Barbados and, of course, the island of Beauregard. He left a simple will, which he had in fact drawn up before his marriage to Mrs Corrington, and this states that in the event of his death half his entire property, and money of course, should go to his son by his previous marriage, Mr Victor Corrington, and the other half to his future wife, Mrs Corrington. There were slightly altered provisions covering the disposal of the property in the event of there being children of the marriage, but since there are no children, that has nothing to do with us here. The main point is that there is a perfectly valid will, drawn up by Mr Corrington, when in his right mind. I stress his mental state because later, unhappily, it altered.'

Aha, thought Hannie, relieved to hear there was no will, fraudulent or not, of a later date than the one she had come to steal. So that's the problem, then – Corrington was out of his mind when he wrote the letter.

'Now, here,' Mr Brown said, 'we come to the unfortunate part. It's a pity it has to be said all over again, but you have a right to hear. Not too long before his death, Mr Corrington became mentally disturbed. At some point during the course of his mental illness he conceived some idea of making restitution for what he saw as a terrible wrong he had done to the woman Sarah Fevrier and her two daughters. As you'll know,' he said to Hannie, 'it's not uncommon for patients suffering from depression to develop ideas of exaggerated guilt and responsibility for all the terrible things that happen in the world –'

'But they were his children, weren't they?' Hannie asked. 'I mean – forgive me, Mrs Corrington – he did have two children by this woman, didn't he?'

'So far as we know they were his children,' Mr Brown said smoothly, but Angelina had shown Hannie her birth certificate and Hannie knew there could be no doubt about the parentage of the two Fevrier daughters. 'So,' she said, 'perhaps he did owe them something.'

74

'Not an island worth thirty million dollars, over half the value of his estate,' Mr Brown said. He looked at Hannie, challenging her to dispute the point. Hannie merely said, 'Oh – I see what you mean.'

'Indeed,' Brown said, 'Mrs Corrington won't mind my telling you, I'm sure, that thinking some moral debt perhaps lay undischarged, she recently made an offer of money to the family.'

'I felt I should show some generosity,' Julie Corrington murmured.

'And I disagreed with you,' Brown said. Turning to Hannie, he said, 'But then, I'm a man of business, not a woman of sentiment.' Hannie nodded. She was not nearly as drunk as she was pretending to be, but the whisky was going to her head a little – and this scene was nauseating. But that, too, might work in her favour. She said, 'I feel quite upset.'

'I'm so sorry,' Julie Corrington said, 'that you have to suffer all our family secrets at one go. Please, Mr Brown, do let's get this over with as quickly as possible. Perhaps you'd like to stay the night here, Mrs Bennett – I'd feel dreadful turning you out of the house at this hour, after that terrible experience at your hotel and this not very pleasant story.'

So if I don't give you the letter you can take it, Hannie thought, delightedly. We'll soon see about that. She said, 'Well, that's very nice of you – very nice. I'd love to.'

'Just find Robert and get him to prepare a room,' Julie Corrington said to Victor. 'The blue room.'

Hannie, who had noticed the not-so-new suit worn by the manservant, wondered how he felt about getting rooms ready for guests at three in the morning. As Victor left, Mr Brown said, 'I'll finish the story quickly.

You must be very tired.'

They were working well together, he and Julie Corrington, Hannie thought. They've decided I might be too sentimental to hand the letter over without taking it to the Queen, so they're planning to rob me tonight. Tomorrow the house will have been turned over, and the same gang who tried to get the letter before will be blamed. There'll be a lot of talk about the crime rate on the island and no one will care anyway, because by then, they think, they'll have what they want.

Brown continued smoothly, 'It's a sad story from now on. Poor Mr Corrington, his mind unfortunately full of guilt and self-reproach, wrote the letter promising the woman the island, persuaded his friends to sign it – presumably they thought he was rational at the time – and then posted it off to Beauregard. Obviously, Mrs Corrington knew nothing of all this. Of course, he never made the will he speaks of in the letter. In this disturbed frame of mind he probably forgot. Unfortunately,' he added, 'it's been impossible to persuade the Fevrier family that he never did it. As you'll have seen for yourself, the Fevriers are very simple, uneducated people, and they simply don't believe this. For years now they've suffered from the *idée fixe* that the letter means the island belongs to them. However many times this is explained to them, they never change their views. But, equally, they never proceed with a claim.' He made a slight gesture with his hands, his open palms towards Hannie. 'I guess it's just one of those things simple people use to maintain themselves in rather constricting circumstances. They pretend to be the rightful heirs to something, imagine that their lives would change if only they had their rights –'

His voice tailed off. He looked confidingly at Hannie who responded, 'Oh, yes – I do see it now. But,' she asked helplessly, 'what am I supposed to do about the letter? I promised them I'd help.'

Julie Corrington said easily, 'Well, my dear, I'm sure Mr Brown would say hand it over to him immediately, and he'll see it properly disposed of. But if you feel you ought to keep your promise to these people, then I say you should do exactly what you said you'd do – take it to Buckingham Palace.' Her glance at Mr Brown was almost flirtatious.

Mr Brown said to Hannie, 'I don't suppose you know that Sarah Fevrier has already been given land by Edmund Corrington – this was at the time of the births of her children – several acres of land, free and clear, on an island ripe for tourist development. She or her heirs are hardly going to suffer in the future.'

'My goodness,' said Hannie, impressed. 'Is that true? They're going to do quite well out of it, then, in the end? But,' she added after a pause, 'I think I ought to do what I promised. After all, if they got a letter from the Queen, or whoever she passed it on to, all signed, sealed and official-looking, they'd feel they'd been properly dealt with, wouldn't they? They wouldn't go to the end of their days feeling they'd been defrauded.'

'You are *so* right,' Julie Corrington agreed. She said to Mr Brown, 'You must be able to see that Mrs Bennett's plan is the best idea. After all, don't they say justice just be seen to be done, or something –' She trailed off and Mr Brown supplied, 'Justice must not only be done, but must be seen to be done, is the phrase, I think. By all means,' he said to Hannie, 'get the letter to Buckingham Palace if you'd prefer it. And now,' he said, stretching his shoulders, 'I think I'll go to bed. It's been a long day.'

'Perhaps you'd tell Victor to bring Robert to help me up,' Julie Corrington said. 'In a moment, after Mrs Bennett and I have had a little nightcap.'

'I will certainly do that,' said Mr Brown. 'Goodnight, Mrs Bennett, a pleasure to have met a lady who's dealt with a confusing situation so well. I hope you enjoy the rest of your holiday.' And, saying goodnight to Mrs Corrington, he left.

'What a nice man,' Hannie said. 'It must be very reassuring to have someone like that to depend on.'

'Oh – he's wonderful,' said Julie Corrington. 'Perhaps,' she added, holding out her glass to Hannie, 'you could just pour me another small brandy, just a tiny one. And,' she added, as if it were an afterthought, 'do fill up your glass.' Which Hannie did, with her back turned, making sure she put little whisky in her glass. Sitting down, she said, 'I really shouldn't – not with the pills I'm taking.'

'Nothing seriously wrong, I hope,' said Julie Corrington.

'Just to see me through a bad patch,' Hannie replied, slurring her words a little. She added, 'It's not much fun when your husband leaves you for a woman ten years younger.'

'Oh, my dear,' said Julie. 'What a tragedy. Why do they do it?'

'What baffles me is how any woman who does that can look at herself in the glass in the morning without being sick,' Hannie said vehemently.

'She'll be punished in the end, I'm sure of that,' said Julie Corrington firmly. 'And you'll meet someone else and be very happy.'

'I'll drink to that,' said Hannie, raising her glass.

The door opened. Victor and the manservant came

in. Julie Corrington raised her arms slightly and said, 'What a nuisance I am to you.' 'Mother,' said Victor in humorous reproach. Hannie felt sorry for him as he devotedly, as if it were a privilege, bent down. The white arm encircled his waist and he gently lifted her from the sofa. The woman, supported by her son and her servant, left the room. Hannie stayed downstairs, listening to the faint sounds which told her roughly where the two men were taking her. A few minutes later, Robert came back and told her where her room was. Not long after that she went to bed.

The room was huge, painted pale blue and had one light, hanging from the middle of the ceiling. Hannie put on the cotton nightdress lying across the big bed with its hard bolster, went into the huge bathroom which led from the room, bathed in tepid water, cleaned her teeth and collapsed into bed. There she lay dozing, waiting for someone to come and search her handbag, hoping they would come soon so that she could conduct her counter-search of Julie Corrington's room before dawn.

Less than an hour later the door to her room eased open and, after a pause, someone came in. Hannie lay quite still, breathing heavily. As the figure approached the bed she had a quick look, distinguishing the heavy but compact figure of the capable Mr Brown. He reached out and took her bag, which she had put conveniently on the table beside the bed, retreated a step or two and dropped quietly to the floor. She heard the sounds of familiar items moving gently against one another in the bag and guessed he was shining a small torch into it. Then he seemed to be taking everything out and laying the contents on the carpet. Then he put everything back, straightened up and returned the bag to the table. Now came the moment when he would feel under the bolster, thought Hannie, and relaxed so that the feeling hand would sense her head heavy against it. He did the same on the other side of the bed and then went to the chair where she had left her clothes. He seemed to stand by the chair after he had investigated her pockets, wondering where else the letter could be, then left the room.

Hannie lay still for another three-quarters of an hour. Hearing no noise, she got up and put her clothes on. It didn't sound as if Brown had gone to tell Julie Corrington he had found nothing in her room. All she could think was that he had still not heard from the men who had searched her hotel room. Perhaps they had seen her go out and had gone back for another try. Which meant, thought Hannie, picking up her bag and putting it over her shoulder, that Brown might still be awake, listening for the telephone and that she would have to be quick, and even more careful about making any noise. She left her room silently and crept along the wide landing to where she thought Julie Corrington's bedroom might be. The landing was lit and she could see down the wide, curving staircase to the hall, where lights also burned.

As she opened the door of the bedroom she froze, half in and half out of the room. Someone inside the room was talking. The voice said, 'You're no good, Edmund. No good at all.' Hannie saw a huge room with large windows in which net curtains floated, catching the breeze from the sea. There was a big four-poster bed with soft white draperies, and beside the bed, on a table, a brass lamp, surely an old oil lamp, for the light it gave out was mild and a little smoke came up from the glass chimney at the top. The rest of the room was dim and seemed to be full of heavy furniture.

Hannie, stuck in the full light of the landing, was terrified. 'What a failure you are,' commented the voice, mildly contemptuous, and Hannie, in a flash, realized that the speaker was Julie Corrington and remembered the name of the late Mr Corrington, former owner of properties in Barbados, St Colombe and the disputed little island of Beauregard. Julie Corrington was talking to her dead husband.

Hannie's position was too dangerous for her to feel any horror. She was concerned only about whether Julie was asleep or awake. 'You've sold our land, Edmund, and you've spent our money, and what we have now is because I've done everything to conserve what we have. Everything,' repeated the voice. Hannie decided to risk it and slipped into the room, pulling the door to behind her. 'You just sit and drink,' the voice went on remorselessly, 'dreaming your drunken dreams about the black beauty on Beauregard. "The only time you've ever been happy." Happy! Happy – while I manage everything, take care of you and there's no one to take care of me. Take care of me,' came the voice, like its own echo, as it trailed away, and there was silence.

Hannie stood there, breathing as softly as possible, while a moth circled the lamp, hit the funnel with what seemed a loud thump, circled again, hit the lamp again and fell on the surface of the table. Then came a deep breath from the curtained bed, then another, then something like a snore.

Hannie in the softly lit room with the softly blowing curtains knew that somewhere in the room there must be a safe. Julie Corrington, like a peasant, might never destroy the valuable paper and, like an autocrat, might never give it to anyone else. But Hannie guessed she wouldn't leave it in her handbag overnight – she would observe certain standards, and not dumping down a handbag swollen with the day's detritus would be one of them. So where was the safe, wondered Hannie. Pound to a penny, behind the portrait of the thin-faced, tired man in a white suit, the portrait of her late husband hanging above the beautiful inlaid cabinet on her left. If it wasn't there, or if Julie Corrington religiously handed over the keys of the safe to the manservant at night, then Hannie was in trouble. As she would be, too, if the safe had a combination lock. She crept over the carpet to the cabinet and gently lifted down the portrait. There was the safe, and there was the keyhole. Crouching, now, behind the cabinet, she started thinking about the key. It would be near Julie unless she gave it to Robert every night. She began to move stealthily across the room to the bed but stopped in her tracks as the sleeping woman began, in her soft, monotonous voice, to speak again. 'I could be a better wife to you, Edmund,' she said, 'if only you'd face up to your responsibilities and if only you'd finish the business on Beauregard. The only thing you prevent me from doing, the only thing, while I take responsibility for everything.' And once again she repeated the word, 'Everything' and was silent.

Hannie risked a few more steps over the carpet to the bed, then a few more. The keys to the safe were not on the table. Perhaps they were inside the drawer. Now she could see Julie Corrington through the thin curtains. She lay with her face turned to the ceiling, her eyes shut, her hands folded over the lace breast of her nightdress. She didn't look asleep – but then she didn't really look awake either. Hannie opened the drawer and touched metal with the tips of her fingers. With great care she lifted the large bundle of keys. If they rattled even once, Julie would wake. She looked like the sort who might keep a dainty revolver under the pillow. Then at last Hannie had the keys safely in her hand. She turned and began her stealthy walk back to the safe in the wall.

She was there when Julie began to speak again. 'I'll have it when you're gone, Edmund, you know that. I'll have Beauregard. If you won't get rid of her now, I'll get rid of her when you're dead. Why should that coarse, savage woman sit there on Beauregard, on our land, while I toil here day by day, trying to hold things together, trying to preserve something, our land, our money, our way of life?' After a pause she said, 'We'll see, Edmund. We'll see what happens when you're dead.'

Hannie, despite her preoccupation with robbing the safe, was appalled by the vindictive whisper. She began to see why Julie Corrington was prepared to go along, on any terms, with people ready to help her fight the Fevriers' claim to the island. In fact, if the Fevriers weren't dead already, it was probably more because the Mr Browns of this world would prefer to get their way without unnecessary violence and the resulting complications than because Mrs Corrington was holding them back. For her, Sarah Fevrier wasn't just an inconvenient legatee, she was a deadly rival, the woman who had ruined a white lady's life.

Hannie very quietly put the keys on the carpet and, still hiding behind the cabinet, went through them. Two keys on the bunch seemed likely to fit and, when she stood up and tried them, the second one worked – the safe door came open, with a slight creak. Hannie paused, waited, then examined the contents. There were three shelves; the top two contained letters and documents. On the bottom shelf was an unlocked cashbox full of bundles of US dollars and Swiss francs. She took all the documents, put them quietly in her shoulder bag, closed the safe, put the picture back, put the keys on the top of the cabinet and crept to the door. As she opened it, she heard Julie begin to speak again. 'Edmund. Edmund, come here. I want to speak to you.' Hannie hoped for poor Edmund's sake there was no afterlife.

She made her way back along the landing and had nearly reached her room when suddenly the lights shivered, the floor trembled and the whole place went black. In the darkness she felt the floor tremble again. In one long, swift thought she saw Julie Corrington waking, and reaching for her lamp, going straight to the safe to grab her documents in case they had to evacuate the building, then, finding them gone, start to scream. At the same moment she heard a door bang open and Victor Corrington shouting, 'Mother! Mother! I'm coming!' Hannie decided to risk the dogs in the garden and Robert's gun. She grabbed the banister and felt her way to the top of the stairs. Someone banged against her heavily. Victor shouted, 'Mother!'

'I'm not your mother,' snarled Hannie Richards and found the top of the stairs. Suddenly there was a light at the bottom. She saw Robert standing there, holding up a candelabra in which five candles burned. She ran down.

As she passed he said, 'The door's open.'

'Thanks,' she called, tugging it. 'Aren't you coming?' she shouted from the moving steps.

'In a minute,' he cried. Hannie saw two Dobermans streaking past her, running, she guessed, downhill, but she decided to take the route she knew, down the drive and, she hoped, back on to the road to St Colombe.

On her right, as she stumbled along the drive, she could see sparks shooting up into the darkness like fireworks. Birds were squawking now, flying up. Suddenly the path shook so much that she staggered and nearly lost her footing. There was the crash of a tree higher up the hill. Then she heard running feet close to her, and a hand fell hard on her shoulder. The hand found hers and began to drag her backwards.

As she tried to wrestle free, crying, 'Let go! What are you doing?' a man's voice said, 'Wrong way. I'll get you down the cliff path – there's a couple of boats there – take one over to Beauregard. It's safe there.' As he spoke, above the growling of the mountain and the crashing of shifting trees, he was tugging so fiercely at her captured hand that she had to move with him to keep her balance.

'Who are you?' Hannie yelled, made aggressive by fear. Why would anyone on the Corrington estate be helping her?

The man said, 'Come on – I'm a friend. Trust me,' and as Hannie decided to go willingly, he gasped, 'That way you could have been killed.'

The path heaved again, like a ship at sea. A small animal, running, brushed Hannie's leg. She thought of snakes as they struggled through the darkness, past the big white house, where candlelight shifted from window to window and she caught the sounds of shouting voices above the rumbling of the mountain.

She found herself at the top of what looked like a path to the sea. At the bottom there was a gleam of water. The moon came out and went behind the clouds as they slid down the path, caught at by thorns and stones.

Hannie's companion, in front, shouted, 'What did

you do with the letter?'

Hannie gasped as a small stone hit her smartly on the cheek, 'I collected it from Beauregard, took it to Barbados in the boat the same afternoon, posted it to my lawyer.'

'That's right,' he said.

They were nearly at the bottom now. The sky was filled with sparks. He groaned, 'Oh, Christ.'

'What?' she asked.

'Stone hit me in the back,' he told her. 'They're really going to start coming down now.'

A shower of small rocks just missed them. The mountain roared.

'I'm down,' he declared, and Hannie was soon on the shore beside him. It was darker there, and she glanced at him. She had the idea he might be the man who had come out of the recording studio with Regius and fallen down in the grass, laughing; the man who had given her a thumbs-up sign as she took the road into St Colombe. And perhaps she'd seen him, even before that, somewhere. But with the beach now quivering beneath her feet, she decided this was no time to ask who he was or why he was helping her. 'Boat's over there, fully fuelled,' he shouted.

He seemed to be turning back to the cliff. 'What about you?' she said.

'Got to go back up and see if anyone wants a hand.' She couldn't make out his face properly in the darkness.

'Good luck – thanks,' she shouted at his back as he started to climb. Then she ran for the boat.

Under the silver moon, from the safety of the sea half a mile out of St Colombe, she saw one white wall of the Corrington house slowly crumble and collapse sideways. She watched a great piece of wall stagger its way

86

downhill, then plummet off the cliff to the sea. Slowly, as if she were dreaming the sight, the roof fell in on the house and the wall nearest her pushed out and began to fall. Then the moon went behind clouds.

Hannie turned back to the wheel and concentrated on the difficult business of navigating in intermittent darkness in strange waters. She wondered if the strange man who had helped her had escaped. She wondered about the Corringtons, Robert and Mr Brown. She checked the compass, turned the wheel and went towards Beauregard.

It was raining again as Hannie parked her car opposite the small house in London, near Portobello Road. This time there was no big, blue car in the street. The door opened before she could ring the bell. The hall was full of boxes. 'Come in – excuse the mess,' said Sarah Fevrier. 'It's not very comfortable, but I wanted to thank you – and pay you, of course.'

She led her into the sitting room, now stripped of the photographs. 'I'm leaving the furniture for the people who are moving in,' Sarah said. Her son Simon was opening a bottle of champagne. Francine told Hannie, 'I'm staying on to finish my course. The lawyer says it's OK for Mum and Simon to go to Beauregard and start acting like owners.'

Hannie took the glass Simon offered her and said, lifting it, 'To you. All the luck in the world.'

'We had the luck,' Sarah Fevrier replied. 'Now it's down to the hard work.'

Francine laughed. 'Typical – typical, isn't it? Comes into a fortune – and she can still turn it into work.'

Hannie was very curious. She asked them, 'What are you going to do with the island now you've got it?'

'We're going to build some nice little tourist cabins, you know,' Francine answered. 'Very rural, very posh, very Beauregard, that sort of thing.'

'Nothing low-class,' added Simon. 'Charge a lot for them, scuba diving, sea gliding, all that. We can rent them or sell them – we got no objection to the money, then we build up the place, the farms, small industries, like that, try to keep the place self-supporting and independent.'

'Sounds good,' said Hannie. 'You get to sit at the UN as President of the Republic of Beauregard. I hope it works out.'

'It'll work out,' Simon assured her.

'Tell me,' Hannie asked Sarah, 'your mother –'

'She died,' Sarah said. 'She died five days after you saw her last, when you landed on Beauregard the night of the volcano. The Corringtons lived,' she added. 'Even Mrs Julie Corrington, that frail, tender lady. She's tough and strong – and she never had to work like my mother did, that's for sure.'

Hannie said, 'I'm sorry.'

'Grandmother lived long enough to see that will, though,' Francine said, 'with her very own eyes, in that bundle of papers you brought over. Auntie Angelina said that helped her. At least she died happy knowing that Mother and Auntie and all the rest of us would be all right.'

'And that Edmund Corrington kept his word,' added Hannie. 'In any case, people like Mrs Corrington are dead already.' She told them about the terrible voice, talking into an empty bedroom to a dead man. 'What difference does it make if people like that are breathing in and out?' she said. 'They're not really living.' And she lifted her glass yet again. 'Anyway, here's to the

Queen of the Islands,' she said.

'Ah, yes, thank God,' replied Sarah, and meant it.

At the Hope Club the women now sat smiling in the darkness. While Hannie had recounted her story, evening had come, but no one had got up to put on the lights.

Elizabeth Lord said cheerfully, 'A happy ending.'

'And here's the Hope Club's share of it,' Hannie added in a practical voice, taking out her chequebook.

3. The Adventure of the Small African Child

Three months later a seedy Christmas filtered through the narrow streets of Soho. Silver Christmas trees twinkled in sex-shop windows; restaurants bulged with office parties; weary, footsore women who had lost their way in Regent Street or Oxford Street trailed past strip clubs looking for somewhere to get a refreshing cup of tea.

Recently the Hope Club had begun to change. The members had decided to expand the premises, and Elizabeth had been put in charge and quickly got the plans under way. With money from the club's account, she bought the house next door from some departing Maltese businessmen who were glad of a fast sale with no questions asked. Then she got planning permission and knocked through some of the rooms. The renaissance of the Hope Club had begun. Forgetting a five-year-long breakdown, Elizabeth bullied, nagged, cajoled, checked plans and accounts, greased palms and buried the sums involved deep in the accounts.

By December there was a new façade to the club over the second house. A large lobby had been set into the front of the building. Inside was a small porter's lodge to be run by Mr or Mrs Knott. Beyond that lay a vast restaurant with acres of white tablecloth and subdued lighting. In the basement there was to be a sauna and a gym. There was already a writing room, a library and a small computer Elizabeth was using at present for the accounts. More bedrooms were added. Elizabeth had even bought up, lock stock and especially barrel, a gentleman's wine cellar.

Above the portico, in gilt letters, hung the sign 'The New Hope Club'.

At lunchtime one day Elizabeth, Margaret and Julie all met in the restaurant and then moved to the chairs by the fire in the long, cream sitting room. At the end of the room, double doors led into the writing room, which was not yet in use.

Elizabeth, holding out her hands to the fire, said, 'I'm glad no one suggested Christmas decorations. It's a relief to find one place which doesn't remind you of turkey and bath cubes.'

'We should think about the opening of this place,' Margaret said. She was due back in court later and wore a black suit with a white stock at her neck. 'Is it members only or do we want some prominent women as well?'

Elizabeth looked startled. 'Do we want publicity at all?' she asked. 'We've got enough members to fill up the Club and quite a lot who'd like to join. Anyway, I've got a vested interest in keeping quiet. My husband knows what I've been doing but not quite on what scale. He's pleased that my little job has cheered me up, but still can't understand why it takes so long for me to get carpets cleaned. Frankly, you can think what you like, but I'd rather he didn't find out from the papers that I've been in charge of buying, gutting and planning a whole building.'

'You can't tell him the truth?' Julie asked.

Elizabeth said bluntly, 'It's hard enough telling myself the truth. I know he wants a well woman, but only in his way, and his way makes me ill. I'm working on a solution which means I can have the man I love and the father of my children and still manage to get out of bed in the morning. But I'd just like to keep the opening quiet. Apart from that, I can't see the point. The women who come here like the privacy. This is where we come to talk, relax and sometimes just hide out, or if we want a good laugh, time to be alone and think, or support and advice from our friends. If the club gets too much publicity, it could become the kind of place everybody rings when a woman goes missing – "Try the police. Try the hospitals. Try the women's refuge. And now, try the Hope Club."'

'But my instinct tells me that we ought to face that out,' Julie said. 'That maybe we're not private, but hiding. That maybe we're acting like women always have done, talking in secret like slaves and hush-up when massa comes around.'

Margaret nodded. 'Men's clubs have always worked because men could go there when they wanted to relax among friends or their wife was threatening a row. And they've worked as places where you could swap professional information and get tips on the Stock Exchange or the 2.30 at Kempton Park. If them – why not us?'

'Why not us?' said Elizabeth. 'Why not us?' She looked at the others. 'I don't think you live in the same world as I do. I live in the one where men think that a conspiracy is three women and a baby being together for three-quarters of an hour and *not* talking about nappies and knitting. And it's not getting any better; as women start doing more and men's jobs start being more threatened, it gets worse. A lot of men are very frightened now. They daren't admit it but they are, and men are trained to hit out when they're frightened. Put this place on the map with a public opening, Margaret, and we'll have to cope with everything from domestic spite to getting our windows smashed in by men who think that it's a lesbian club. Or we'll leave our houses with a barrage of jokes in our ears – "Out for a night with the girls, then, are you? Don't lose all the housekeeping money playing poker. Let me hear all the dirty jokes when you get back!" And if we put this place on the map, it'll start looking desirable and friendly and nice, and men don't like the feeling they're excluded from nice places by women. And what about reprisals? Not just sarcastic remarks and nasty atmosphere. You're a barrister, Margaret. You know the statistics about violence against women.'

Margaret looked at her soberly. 'I don't like the idea of being intimidated,' she said.

'All right then,' Elizabeth said. 'Try this one and see if you like it. Men are a problem. What about women?'

'What about them?' Margaret asked impatiently. 'I'm due back in court in three-quarters of an hour . . . '

'She's right,' Julie told her. 'Women have got a lot of problems. This place could look like the spot where they find solutions.'

'We look privileged,' Elizabeth said. 'No wonder – many of us are. Some of us earn a lot of money. Admittedly, some of us have nothing, but I'm the person with the pocket calculator here and I'm telling you that most of us are better off than the average and some of us are very well off indeed. If that weren't so, we couldn't keep the place open at all. So we have a lot of women with large incomes and many more with skills and abilities. And outside the walls of the club there are women in trouble crying out for support. Their children have been taken away by the local authority and they can't get them back. Their husbands beat them up and they don't know where to go . . .'

'We can refer women to the people who can help them,' Margaret said stiffly.

'That's where they've already been,' Julie told her. 'And what about the new problems, where there isn't anybody to go to? Would you have believed ten years ago – fifteen years ago – that one day you might have to start thinking about Asian girls who were being pressured into marriage? Or maybe some girl who's had a baby for money and now she doesn't want to give it up?'

'There are laws to cover these things,' Margaret said doggedly. Julie looked sceptical. 'Anyway if we're so rich and clever,' she continued, 'why should we have to hide from men, in case they punish us? Or from women because they think we could help them? It's a bad idea to hide – things usually catch up with you in the end and when they do, it's worse.' She glanced at her watch. As she stood up, the telephone rang. Margaret answered it. 'It's for you, Julie,' she said.

Julie raced over and took the phone. She spoke for a minute and banged down the receiver. She turned back to the others.

'They double-booked the recording studio,' she said in rage. 'This album will be released the day my first grandchild is born.'

'I must go now,' said Margaret, picking up her briefcase. But just as she made for the door the telephone rang again.

'It's for you, Margaret,' Julie told her.

Now Margaret spoke for several minutes and replaced the receiver. She looked furious. 'That was my clerk. Five members of the jury have gone down with gastro-enteritis. They think it must have been something in their lunch. The judge says he'll call off the trial for this afternoon and try again tomorrow. Otherwise he'll have to swear in a new jury and start the trial afresh. Oh, well, I might as well sit down again for a while. We can go back to this question of the opening. It isn't just a matter of the opening. It's a whole set of principles we're talking about.'

Julie yawned. 'Why don't we all get together after Christmas. Everyone should have a chance to speak.' She thought about it for a minute and said, 'I expect I'll be able to speak. In a kind of strangled voice.' Dropping into broad dialect she said mockingly, 'Me moder – me auntie – and me auntie girl, her wid the baby which never sleep, not one second of the day or night he close he eye – they all comin' to London to see they Julie. Oh my. Oh my, oh my.'

The others laughed.

Margaret said snobbishly, '*This* Christmas I'm entertaining my husband and his mother, my father and my lover, and my lover's two young sons. That's the nucleus. There may be more. *This* year I'm making my husband and my lover pay contributions towards the cost of extra help. *This* year I shall maintain the normal, rational, pleasant nature of my life for the full fifty-two weeks, not just fifty-one and a week spent presiding over the court of misrule. *This* year plans will

95

be made, contingencies covered, and I shall lie on the sofa, doing no more than keep the peace.'

'Between Edward and Robert?' asked Elizabeth incredulously.

'No, between Robert and his mother and between Edward's sons and my father's dog. But *this* year,' she emphasized, 'I shall have all that under control.' She leaned back in her chair.

'Congratulations,' Elizabeth said.

The door opened and a tall, elegant figure came into the room.

'Oh you're here,' cried Hannie as she swept across the carpet. 'How wonderful!' She was in evident good spirits, wearing a flashy purple cape and thick leather boots and carrying several bags.

'Hannie,' shouted Elizabeth and Margaret with one voice, 'where have you been? You've been gone for weeks!'

Slumping into a comfortable armchair, Hannie lit a thin cheroot and said, 'I'm surprised to find you all here. Why aren't you out at work? Or chopping down the turkey or stuffing the Christmas tree? How can you sit there idly at this time of year and call yourselves decent women?'

Margaret smiled. 'We don't want to think about all that now. Tell us where you've been and what you've been doing.'

'I will,' Hannie said promptly. 'And, in a way, it's a seasonal tale . . .'

And so, as the Salvation Army band struck up in the street, and a rendition of 'Oh Come All Ye Faithful' wafted up to the windows of the Hope Club, Hannie Richards began her story.

96

Hannie thought of water – mineral water, tap water, iced water, fountains, waterfalls, water in abundance. The hot sweat flowed down her back as she bumped in her Land Rover along a track, once part of the old Mediterranean trade route, in the Republic of Chad in central Africa. Far, far away she could see through the haze the faint line of the mountains of the Tibesti region, where she was headed. Otherwise the long plain, dried-up and sparsely covered with small, scrubby trees and bushes, seemed endless, stretching ahead, behind and all around, parched and featureless. She had been travelling like this for three days. The village should, if her calculations were right, be thirty miles ahead. If they were wrong, she was in trouble.

Meanwhile, she was desperately thirsty. She dreamed of that neglected bottle of mineral water which had lain so casually on the marble surface of the table where she had been sitting, under a plane tree, just a week ago in warm Roman sunshine.

The man opposite her had been plump and middle-aged. He wore a smart, pale suit such as successful businessmen wear. He had gold cuff links and a slim gold watch. He had mild, clever brown eyes and spoke impeccable English, better than her own, in a low, calm voice. He puzzled her.

'The matter,' he said, 'is obviously made complicated by the civil war which has gone on there for many years. I should never have thought of sending a woman, but when I looked at the male candidates, I had to reconsider the question. They were drug-runners, mercenaries, men of the worst character. They were, if it does not seem too exaggerated to say so, stamped with vice. To employ them was unthinkable. Fortu-

97

nately at that moment someone suggested your name. You were recommended to me as a woman not dead to all feeling and, above all, honest. Since the matter involves a child –' he shrugged, 'I can think of no one better.' He looked closely at Hannie and said, 'You seem doubtful. We are offering a good price. What are your objections? Is it the danger?'

'I should like to know more,' she told him.

'The civil war in Chad has gone on more or less since the French gave up responsibility for the area twenty years ago. Should we agree that you are to go, I shall provide you with a complete briefing. For the moment, imagine an enormous area, five times the size of Great Britain in fact, half desert, containing 192 peoples speaking 110 different languages. The war is basically between the Islamic groups, living mainly in the north, and the Christians of the south. The French left control in the hands of the southerners. Ever since then the battle for leadership has gone on. There are factions, factions of factions, loyalties of faith, family and tribe. Violence, corruption and treachery are never far away. The Libyans have backed the Islamic side, the Christians have called in the French. They sent the Foreign Legion. The neighbouring states have tried for agreements to end the war, but no solution has remained in force for long. The area to which you would go is in the uplands, among the foothills of the mountains. It is a very arid area, quiet at present so far as we know, but our intelligence is poor. At any rate it is 600 miles from the border with Nigeria and frighteningly close to the real Muslim strongholds in the mountains – and a people called the Toubou, so well known for their ferocity that some have called them the Sicilians of Chad. As you can see, there is danger.'

A white-coated waiter flicked two pigeons from a table on the other side of the tree.

Hannie felt inclined to confide in this soft spoken and very calm man. She said, 'I often find that the most doubtful part of the jobs I do is not the job itself but the people who hire me. I usually prefer to know who they are and why they need me. You've already said that you won't tell me. You need an African child exported from the Republic of Chad with no questions asked. You've satisfied yourself that I'm not from the back end of my business, where the personnel are scum. You've failed to find your Bogart, or Mitchum, tough, a little frayed around the edges, perhaps, but still capable of chivalry to the ladies and fidelity to friends. That's because they don't exist. Ninety per cent of the people in my trade know that women and friends are for using, not helping. I'm not exactly like that – which is why I'm the person who asks the questions. There's a child, as you point out, involved here. I have to examine the risks, which include you, before I take on the job. Otherwise I may lose my life, and the child may lose his. If he does, I'm the one who has to watch him die, not you.'

She looked into his peaceful face and realized what was unusual about him. He was not challenging her as men almost always did at this stage in the proceedings. This man – Signor Sebastiano he had called himself – was not even thinking of her as a woman. He was measuring her as if he wanted a servant for a position of trust. More than that, he was measuring her in many different ways, so many that she could not be sure what he was looking for. He said nothing and she went on, 'Let me put it this way. Matters of this kind usually involve politics, money, sex or the family. Perhaps you could give me some indications.'

He was reading her, she thought resentfully, a great deal better than she was reading him. She still could not fit him into any context. He was not a politician, not a businessman, certainly not a crook.

He said unhesitatingly, 'The closest definition is – family.'

Hannie felt furious. She should never have offered him categories into which he could fit himself. He had taken advantage of this to mislead her. But the truth was that she and Adam were short of money. That simple house in the country, that wholesome country life, even with their earnings from the farm, cost a fortune to maintain. She needed this job. She asked, 'Can you tell me more than that? The word family doesn't really seem to explain a lot, here.'

He said, 'I'm afraid I can tell you no more. Each of us must trust the other. I have been as honest as I can about the dangers. I am very eager to get the boy out of that dangerous country, where famine and illness are probably a greater peril than bullets.'

Hannie said, 'All right. But I want 40,000 dollars, over and above expenses. And I want it in gold.'

His smooth, rather pasty face did not move. 'Of course,' he told her. 'I'll give you half now, if you'll tell me what arrangements you would like to make. The other half, naturally, will come to you when you return.'

Hannie thought – half stays here; from now on only half of anything goes back to England. She surprised herself by this thought. What was she – a squirrel burying nuts for the winter? She stared up into the leaves of the plane tree, autumn leaves. Well, she thought, if it's autumn that's what I'll be – a squirrel.

'Is something troubling you?' Sebastiano asked. Hannie looked at him. He was fast, very fast. She said, 'No, nothing.'

100

'The rainy season's ended,' he told her. 'So you can travel any time now.'

'As soon as possible,' said Hannie. A leaf floated down on to the marble top of the table. It lay beside the half-empty bottle of mineral water.

She mopped her brow as she drove along. She had water in the back, plenty of it. But Arnold had told her, 'Never drink, and when you do, drink half as much as you want.' He had also reminded her that if anything went wrong she should stay by the Land Rover and not forget the radiator was full of water. People had been found dead of thirst beside cars, he told her, with their car radiators full. All this had suitably frightened her. The landscape completed the message – flat, pale-brown, cracked earth, a few scrubby trees, rocks and glaring sun. Beside the tracks, wheelmarked where other vehicles had gone during rain, months, or perhaps years before, there was sometimes a heap of cattle bones, a skull, a pair of long, curved horns.

She checked the compass on the dashboard, and every two hours, when she stopped, she checked it against a navigating device, a Cruiserfix, she carried in her jacket pocket. She drove on steadily over the bumpy, cracked earth. She should arrive at the village an hour before nightfall and, with luck, would be able to turn straight round and begin the journey back that day. The harsh hills came closer as the sun grew lower in the sky. She had seen some villages as she drove, tall thin herdsmen driving gaunt cattle with wide horns, a woman, followed by two big girls and a little one, walking along the horizon with pots of what she thought must be water on their heads. She hoped she had navigated correctly. She hoped that Sebastiano's information about the village was right. She hoped the right child would be there when she arrived. She hoped, if there was a village and there was a child, that the villagers would let her have him.

'They are animists,' Sebastiano had told her.

'They're savages,' Arnold had told her. 'You know — pots full of chickens' blood, rags tied over bushes, all that sort of thing. They think there are spirits in everything — rocks, trees and all that. They reckon people can get possessed by an evil spirit. Then along comes the witch doctor and the town band to drive it out.'

'Are they dangerous?' Hannie asked in alarm.

'Funnily enough,' Arnold told her, 'they're not. As religions go, they're fairly peaceful. You'll see more trouble in the Falls Road or a Celtic Rangers match in five minutes than what you'll see around these ju-ju merchants in a month of Sundays. The thing is not to get put off by anything. It can look at bit disgusting if you're not used to it.'

She had met Arnold in Lagos at a bar to which she had drifted as if by accident, but really from instinct. There was always a pub, a bar, a hotel, even a hut where the counter was a couple of planks raised up on two crates. It was often near water — sea, river or canal — and it always contained the same kind of transients, the seamen, the soldiers, the young drifters, the real travellers, those who could not stop travelling, the petty criminals, the veterans of wars, civil and national, the mercenaries and, usually, the girls. Hannie knew these places, sometimes smart spots, sometimes dumps, by the clientele. Those tanned bone-tired faces, those stale, empty eyes, were the same anywhere you went, from Boston to Hong Kong. She walked into Sam's in Lagos, looked round and sat down. As she did so she wondered vaguely how long it would take her to become marked like this with the stamp of her trade. Perhaps the signs were etched there already, but she could not see them herself.

A boy in a white coat hurried over from behind a long, polished bar. She asked him if there was anyone around who knew Chad. Two minutes later Arnold was sitting opposite her. He was between forty and fifty, short and strong-looking. He had no little fingers, only the stumps of where they had been, on his gnarled, brown hands. Arnold had found her a Land Rover which was up to making the trip. He had driven with her to Kano to check that the vehicle was in good order and point her in the right direction. They slid out of Kano one day to reconnoitre.

He said, 'Here's where you slip off to get over the border into Niger by night. After that you can get back onto a tar road until Zinder, if you want. Then go north-east using the old trade route, if the rains haven't washed it out. Then you've got 300 miles of desert to the Chad border, avoiding people. You should be able to trickle over the border at night. If you make it, you've got another 300 to do till you're there. You'll be lucky to do twenty miles an hour. If you try to do more, you're mad. You stop every hour to let the radiator cool and check the vehicle. Don't drive more than six or seven hours a day if you can help it. You've got a first-aid kit, flares, steel planking, shovels – the lot. You still need God's help, and if you meet anybody nasty even He can't help you. Your worst enemies in that terrain will always be heat, thirst, mechanical breakdown.'

They were driving, in intense heat, back to Kano,

where she would leave him. He said, 'The best advice I can give you is not to go. I can put you in the way of some cargo to take back to the UK if you want. Make the journey worthwhile.'

What would it have been, Hannie wondered, as she drove – a consignment of cannabis resin, leaking into her luggage, or a letter from a Nigerian politician or businessman too sensitive to be trusted to the ordinary mails? When she refused he said, 'OK. But I hope you're lucky.'

'I am,' she'd replied.

'Then I hope you know when it begins to run out and stop trusting it,' said Arnold.

She stopped the Land Rover, picked up her water flask from the floor by her feet, drank and rubbed a little of the water over her face. She was wearing a khaki bush hat and shirt and a bright yellow skirt she had bought in the market at Kano. Her long red hair was tucked up in the bush hat. The important thing, she knew, was not to obstruct the sweat in any way. Let it trickle coolingly from the crown of your head to the soles of your feet. Then she heard, in the distance, the sound of drums and behind it the even fainter sound of the flute. She got out, checked oil and water, got in and checked the instrument panel. She drove on.

The conical huts were thatched in groupings of three to six. There were about twenty of them. She pulled the Land Rover up about thirty metres away from the nearest hut, by a thorn bush. As she walked into the village she passed a forked tree trunk with a big pot lodged in the fork. Outside the first hut sat a woman nursing a baby. The noise of the instruments, drum, fiddle and African flutes, grew louder, coming from behind the village where big rocks lay tumbled at the foot of high, bare hills. The woman looked at her incuriously. Hannie stood there as the music got louder still. From behind the huts came a procession. In front, a woman with a length of red cloth wound round her half-staggered on the arm of an elderly man. Behind were thirty or forty men, women and big children and, among them, a man with a drum, which he played, another with a round, stringed instrument across which he drew a bow and some others playing pipes. The people, some naked, some of the men in shorts, some of the women in dresses, stopped when they saw Hannie. The music stopped too. They were all very tall and thin. Their faces bore no expression. Hannie, conscious of the sinking of the sun which would, in less than an hour, disappear, plunging the place in sudden darkness, started back.

She said in English, 'I have come for the child,' and repeated the same thing in French. Before she had finished speaking, a woman of about thirty, with a baby at her breast, a much older woman and three men had come out of the crowd and were standing in front of her. They examined her. She bore their scrutiny as calmly as possible. They were not, she thought, hostile. She knew they had not understood a word she said. They might be expecting her to be someone she was not. They might expect her to do something. The sun seemed to be going down too fast. The crowd stared at her in silence. The next few seconds would determine what they were going to do – drive her out, strike her down, turn away and ignore her completely.

None of those things happened. The two women and the three men began to talk. The younger woman nodded. The old woman started to make some remarks. Her voice, speaking the incomprehensible language, went on and on. At one point she raised her voice and called something out. She went on speaking. The older man in the group interrupted her and began to talk. The sun went on sinking. Then a skinny boy in a red robe which came to just below his knees pushed through the front ranks of the crowd. He put himself just in front of the family group and stood and looked up at Hannie. He was, she thought, about eleven or twelve but tall and spindly for his age. His skin, like that of the others, was so black that it had a bluish sheen, like a dark plum. His brown eyes were big and, she thought, intelligent. He looked long and peacefully at Hannie, who breathed out in relief. She had been sent to collect a child. Here was a child. It looked as if she had found the right place. Sebastiano, when she had asked about credentials, had simply said, 'They will know when you come.' Hannie had doubted if it would be that easy.

The group was now silent. Then the boy disappeared. 'Oy!' said Hannie, staring at the crowd into which he had gone. Meanwhile, one of the men was trying to make her understand something. She thought she caught the words, 'Frolinat – Tebescu – ' She shook her head. He spoke again in his own language, then paused and said, remembering the word, 'Soldats'. Hannie nodded. Whatever he was trying to tell her was not good news. He pointed behind her at the hills. She nodded again. He must be telling her that Frolinat troops were in the hills. But where was the boy? Was he, in any case, the right boy?

He was at her side holding a small bundle, wrapped in the same red cloth as his robe was made of. She looked at his alert face and back at the group facing her. The younger woman, with the baby, stepped forward and embraced the child. The others did the same. There was a chorus of voices – Hannie took the child's hand and led him to the Land Rover. He squatted on the back seat, his bundle beside him. Then, seeing her sitting in front of the wheel, he sat down himself. Hannie turned to look at the now silent group of tall Africans, standing in front of their thatched huts, at the sun folding down over the hills on her right. She started the engine and drove away.

Later she looked at the boy. He sat on the back seat, gazing gravely ahead. He had not shown any sign of distress at leaving them. The villagers, even his own family, had not wept or seemed very sad. Only the woman with the baby, who she decided must be the boy's mother, had been grave. She felt puzzled.

She drove for another half hour, getting out occasionally to check the track. Then, suddenly, it was dark. Even so she drove on, very slowly, following the track with the headlights. It grew cooler as she bumped through the bleak landscape. Each time she looked at the boy he looked back at her seriously, seeming calm and in no need of reassurance or consolation. He had no fear of her or of the future.

Three-quarters of an hour after darkness had fallen, she decided to make camp. It was reckless to drive on alone over the rough road, and the headlights might attract attention if there were troops about. She pulled up just off the trail, by a big rock, cooked millet and some chicken from a tin over a portable gas burner, gave it and water to the boy, who ate and drank. Then she unrolled the sleeping bags and showed him how to get into his. She also found out his name by pointing at herself and saying her own.

'Bambarake,' was what she thought he said.

'I'll call you Bob,' she told him. She had an idea it

might be important to give the boy a short name she could call out in an emergency. He agreed to the name.

Now she was tired. Three days of driving in boiling heat and enduring the contrasting cold at night had left her exhausted. She had travelled faster than she should have done, and her physical reserves were gone. She propped herself up against the rock in her sleeping bag, smoking. She looked at the boy from time to time. He was not asleep but lay, his big eyes gleaming, staring at the stars, which were huge in the clear sky overhead. Once he turned his head and smiled at her. Hannie began to calm down. She sat up all night, dozing now and then, keeping rough watch. Towards dawn she heard a camel roar. In the distance she heard the sound of engines and even, she thought, a shout. She sat farther upright, waiting, with the rock digging into her back. Nothing came near. The boy slept.

A pink light appeared, as if painted, along the horizon. She stretched, welcoming the chance to get moving but not looking forward to the heat, the dust, the monotony. She made tea. They breakfasted off the remains of last night's supper. As they packed up the Land Rover quickly, she discovered that the boy followed what she was doing intelligently and copied her. And then they were on their way again. As they went, Hannie looked around her and indicated to the child, Bob, that he should do the same. She was afraid troops of some kind were still in the region. The sooner they reached the border with Niger the happier she would be.

When they stopped to rest, she tried to strike up a conversation with the boy, naming various objects around them and asking them what they were in his dialect. He had a quick and merry attitude to all this.

He learned so much faster than she did that she began to wonder how far she had been impaired by the journey. At one point he began to point at an imaginary child beside him, of about the same size as himself and then, pointing at her, said, 'You – boys –' and nodded, holding up two fingers. He smiled at her, as she stared at him, and said, 'You,' again, then made the gesture of suckling two children at the same time. Was he really telling her that she was the mother of twins, or just that he was a twin himself? It was mystifying, but she nodded obligingly and agreed. In any case, as a travelling companion the skinny black boy was better than most. He was not fearful or depressed. He was helpful, uncomplaining and cheerful. If anything, he made her feel better, not worse. The animists of a poor village in Chad, she thought, had a lot to teach Europeans about child rearing.

That night she slept peacefully and next day made good speed. The following day was equally good. They crossed the Niger unobserved, and it was only late on the third day, when they were barely seventy miles from the border with Nigeria, that the boy suddenly stopped singing – they were passing time teaching each other songs although, again, he proved much more able at it than Hannie. He said, 'Look.' She turned slightly and saw him pointing upwards. She saw nothing but two birds circling overhead. Then the birds were gone. She shook her head. Five seconds later she heard the sounds of an engine. A little after that she realized it was a helicopter. Ahead of them, about half a mile away across the scrubby plain lay a range of low hills, about five hundred metres in height. Instinctively she accelerated, bumping and jolting down the track. She looked up sharply. Behind her, the boy, unalarmed, pointed back and to the right. Now there were two helicopters, still tiny, but heading in their direction. She came off the track, into the dusty, cracked earth and drove slowly for the hills. She would try to hide the vehicle until the 'copters had gone. She suspected they were border patrol. Neither she nor the boy had respectable credentials, and here, miles from anywhere, in the hands of uncertain border guards, anything could happen to them. Ahead she saw a narrow, rocky gully running into the hills. She drove in, over the rocky surface, hoping the helicopters had been too far away to identify them.

As she jolted on in the lurching Land Rover, between steeply banked rock, she looked for some overhang which might conceal them. She found it and pulled over as the two helicopters whirred over and disappeared. She waited. Less than a minute later they were back. She could see the men inside peering down. They were not dressed in the khaki camouflage uniforms she had expected. They were not in uniform at all. They were wearing, as far as she could see, civilian black shirts and black trousers. And she realized they had spotted her, or guessed from searches farther on where she must be. They now buzzed incessantly overhead, circling round and round. She had driven past these hills on the way in and remembered they were only about a mile in length. After that the plain went on and on. So even if the gully was a way through and not a dead end she would, if she drove on, still be out of cover in a matter of minutes. Once she was in the open they could swoop down on her and land near by. And they could not stay here for ever. The helicopters could land elsewhere, and the men rush in and take them. There were four or five men in each, and all but the pilots had rifles slung over their shoulders. She looked up again, able to pick out the features on each face. It was only then that she recognized the fact she must have noted before – the men were not Africans. The majority were dark-skinned and might have been from somewhere around the Mediterranean. One of the pilots was blond. If this was a border patrol, she thought, they should be Africans, from Chad or Niger.

She sat and thought for a moment but, in the end, whoever they were, they had her boxed up and the only answer seemed to be surrender. If she resisted, they might use their rifles on her and on the boy. The only hope was to hang on, hoping that their fuel was low and that they would have to retreat. Then she could try a dash for the border and hope to get over before they returned. Once in Nigeria her position as a British citizen on her own, authentic passport would be secure. It was a slender chance, but anything was better than facing eight heavily armed men in a wilderness. She looked up at the helicopters, as if surprised that they were still there, then turned to the boy and indicated that they were going to eat. She made a small camp on a flat stone under the overhanging rocks and got out the portable gas rings and blankets to lay on the boiling rock. They had tea, tinned beef and rice and peaches.

Hannie ate dry-mouthed, chewing resolutely, as the noise of the helicopters spinning overhead filled her ears and the buzzing and burring drove holes in her head. The boy sat back, leaning against the rocks, eating calmly. Hannie could not tell what he was thinking. Flies clustered round them. A string of large black ants headed for a section of peach, lying on the stone.

Then both helicopters made a noisy, low-flying sweep

across the gorge – and were gone. The sound of their clattering wings grew less. Hannie, thinking that perhaps they had been forced to go off and refuel, started packing up the camp slowly, listening all the time. A scream began. It was so startling that at first she could not work out what it was. The boy looked up as the noise grew louder. A small fighter plane, probably a Mirage, swooped over the gorge, flying dangerously low. It too disappeared.

Hannie went on putting the gear into the Land Rover, thinking furiously. All this air activity over one spot did not make sense. It could be airforce manœuvres. It could be an extension of the war in Chad, straying over its boundaries. She could hardly believe that so much technology was being directed at her, her Land Rover and one little black boy.

They were sitting on the vehicle when they heard the helicopters returning. Behind that noise was the high scream of the jet. Suddenly, from behind the hills, there was a bang, and a flash. One helicopter gone, thought Hannie. A little later one helicopter came flying over the rocks. Another deafening bang rang round and round the gorge as it exploded, rolled over and over in flames and fell. It lay, suspended by a wing of the machine on a rock, burning, some 200 metres away from the Land Rover. Inside it Hannie saw two faces, distorted in agony. She turned to the boy, sitting beside her, intending to cover his eyes so that he could not see, but he sat there solidly, looking sad and muttering something, an incantation perhaps. Inside the fuselage another figure moved in the flames. There was nothing she could do. As she put the car into reverse and started to back down the gully the machine exploded again. Some metal clattered off down the rocks, but it still hung there, burning.

She set off for the Nigerian border in a sober mood still wondering what had been going on. There was nothing to be seen of the Mirage but a faint white trail in the sky. It had done its job and zoomed off to the south. Unexplained event, thought Hannie, who was fairly used to unexplained events. She drove on through the blistering heat, deciding to risk crossing the border in daylight so as to get the boy to the rendezvous point and off her hands.

By nightfall they were driving, legitimately, on a tar road, through a few trees, to the Anglican Mission, near Kano. The journey and its dangers over, Hannie realized she did not quite fancy handing the child over to just anybody. She hoped the people who were to receive him would be all right. She had grown fond of him.

A big truck, full of people and goats, sped past her on the narrow road. She drove by a crew of men doing construction work near the road under arc lamps. They gave her a cheer. She waved. A few miles on she entered a small town and, slowing down, looked for the Mission. It was there, on the left, a low, white building set slightly back from the road. In the gap between that building and the next she noticed a parked Mercedes. She stopped the Land Rover outside the building and said to Bob, 'Here we are.' He picked up his little red cloth bundle and got out.

Taking his hand, she walked in through the open archway. In a big, cool reception area a plump white man in khaki trousers and a white shirt sat under a fan. He got out of his basket chair and came towards them. Conscious of her stained bush jacket and crumpled skirt, Hannie looked at him carefully and said, 'I'm Mrs Richards. I think someone's expecting me.'

'They're in there,' the man replied glumly, waving at an archway behind him. All she could see in the darkness of the room behind was part of a long table, with benches. Then, through the archway came a tall, middle-aged woman in a grey dress. She walked up to them and looked at the boy. He said, composedly, 'Hullo, lady.'

Her rigid face moved. She smiled and said, 'Hullo – do you know any more English?' She spoke in the clear, authoritative tones of the upper-class headmistress of an expensive girls' school. Hannie felt baffled and, having been for some time an unsatisfactory pupil at such an establishment, uncomfortable and threatened. This was possibly the last person in the world to whom she would have wished to entrust the amiable Bob. On the other hand, such women were not brutal or likely to neglect the physical welfare of a child in their care. Nevertheless, she gazed in some horror at Bob's new protector. The boy, in the meanwhile, had picked up what she meant by her question and replied, 'Bed. Camp. Hannie.' He gave her his brilliant smile and added, 'Soldiers.'

The woman shot Hannie a glance which made her feel scruffier than she was and suggesting that she should be ashamed she had not passed the journey teaching Bob Wordsworth's 'Daffodils'. A second later, however, she rallied, and said, 'My name is Angelica Simms. I expect you could both do with a bath and something to drink before we have dinner. The others are in there waiting, but we did not want to overwhelm the child. This way.'

As she led the way to the bathroom, Hannie asked her, 'Have I got the right boy?'

'I think so,' said Angelica Simms in a crisp voice. 'I expect we'll soon find out.'

Hannie thought that she was not going to get much

information out of Angelica. Now that the mission was over, she was increasingly curious about why anyone had paid her so much to snatch a twelve-year-old African child. She walked past Angelica, who had opened the bathroom door and turned on the taps to the bath.

'I'll go first and show him,' Hannie said, sitting on a stool and pulling off her boots and then her socks. 'I'm pretty stained,' she said to the woman, who seemed shocked and glanced at the boy as Hannie took off the bush jacket and the crumpled skirt.

'What is his name?' she said, as Hannie got into the bath with a sigh of relief.

'I've been calling him Bob,' Hannie said, squeezing a sponge of water over her grimy head. She washed her hair with the soap, smiling encouragingly at Bob, who stood in the doorway staring. She ducked under the water and came up, saying, 'It's lovely. Nice – have a splash.' She turned the taps on and off so that he could feel the water.

'We had an incident, by the way,' she told Angelica, 'not far away from the Nigerian border.'

'What incident?' asked Angelica.

Hannie got out of the bath and wrapped herself in the towel Angelica, eyes averted slightly, handed her. She pulled out the plug. The boy watched the water swirling away down the plug hole. Angelica's eyes watched him.

Hannie said, 'We got chased by two helicopters. The personnel were Arabs, or something, armed with machine guns. Then someone came along in a fighter and shot down the helicopters. I don't know why any of it happened.'

Angelica went on watching the boy as he put the plug back in the hole and turned on the taps. She said, 'Nasty for you.'

Hannie said, 'Could you get someone to fetch my bag? From the Land Rover?'

Angelica called 'Matthew!' but her eyes stayed on the boy. He now turned off the taps and began to wave them out of the bathroom. 'Out,' he said.

Hannie turned round and went out. In the passageway she said, 'Could I borrow your comb?'

A black boy brought her bag and a pile of fresh clothes for Bob. Angelica lent her the comb from her handbag in no friendly way. Hannie stood in the passage and put on fresh clothes from her bag, a European cotton dress in yellow, combed the tangles from her matted hair and said to Angelica, 'Who are the other people we're to meet?'

'Mr Omovo is a Methodist minister,' she told her. 'Mr Martin is a Roman Catholic clergyman, Sister Anna is a nun and Mr Dugdale-Smith is an expert on African dialects from the child's region.' Her tone was cold. She added, 'When will you be leaving?'

Hannie knew the acceptable answer to give was, 'Five minutes ago,' but instead replied, 'Tomorrow morning. I'd prefer not to do any more driving today. If there's no room here I'll find somewhere else to sleep.'

Bob came out of the bathroom in the now stained red robe.

'Put these on,' said Hannie, holding up the shorts and shirt. He looked at them and said, suspiciously, 'Boy clothes?'

'Yes.' Holding up her dress and pointing at Angelica's skirt she said, 'Girls' clothes. These are boys' clothes.' He nodded, and took the clothes back into the bathroom.

As they walked down the passageway Angelica said, 'I believe there could be a bed for you here.' They went

116

past the plump man in the reception area, still in a basket chair under his fan, and went into the room beyond. The rest of the party were sitting at a long table to the right of the room. The two clergymen, one older and one younger, were both Nigerians, as was Sister Anna, the nun. Dugdale-Smith, who rose with no alacrity when they all came in, was white. The three Nigerians all looked at the boy, who advanced to the table. There was a complete silence which was broken by Dugdale-Smith, who said, 'I'm Robert Dugdale-Smith. I suppose you're Hannie Richards.' He introduced the others.

Father Martin, the older of the two Nigerian men, said, 'Let us all sit down. You must both be tired and hungry.' Hannie looked at the younger clergyman. He was large and strong, she thought, and wondered why it mattered. As a Nigerian boy brought in platters of rice, chicken and lamb, she realized she was apprehensive about something. She picked at her food, wondering how this respectable middle-class British lady, a nun, two clergymen from different denominations and a language expert were all connected with the clever Italian in the café in Rome and why the centre of the whole thing was the Chadian boy who now sat at the table, talking to the clergymen politely in fractured English and eating his food neatly with his fingers. Six hundred miles across the desert to fetch him, the destruction of two helicopters and their crews which, because the whole affair was so odd, she was now prepared to consider as part of the scenario, a handover to a religious group at a mission – nothing made any sense at all. Perhaps, she told herself, she felt uneasy because her working life was normally conducted among people whose lives ranged from, at one end of the spectrum, seediness, to, at the other, downright evil. There was no one sitting here to whom you would not entrust your life savings in complete confidence – that, she thought, might be why she felt so rattled. At the bottom end of the table the black-suited clerics, the black-habited nun and Angelica spoke quietly. She and Dugdale-Smith had somehow got stuck up at the lay end of the refectory table.

'You speak Bob's language?' she asked him.

'I'm not expert,' he said, 'from what I hear from that end. I know a related dialect, though. The only two people really up to this one are both in France. The others will be in Chad.'

'Move down the table a bit,' she said, 'so that you can join in. I'll sit here and eat quietly. I'm tired anyway.'

So Dugdale-Smith joined the group at the other end of the table in the big, quiet room and Hannie sat and ate silently, in a daze almost, listening and not listening to what passed. She found herself checking the catches on the French windows in the wall opposite. They looked flimsy. She wondered why she cared.

At the other end of the table Dugdale-Smith and the boy began a halting conversation. It soon became plain that Bob was learning faster than the professor. Hannie, tired, refused ice cream and went outside the building and leaned against the wall. It was cool and very dark. The stars were huge. Little knots of people stood in the street, gossiping and laughing. She sat down and rolled herself a cigarette.

'Can I join you?' asked Dugdale-Smith, appearing beside her. He squatted down and rolled himself a cigarette from her tin, using only one hand. 'This is a funny business,' he said. 'What's it all about? Who's the boy?'

'I don't know,' said Hannie. 'I thought you must know. I was just hired by an anonymous Italian to go and collect him. They're very exclusive in there. They'd like me to leave this minute – in fact, I got the impression they would have been pleased if I'd dumped the boy and gone away immediately. I thought you were one of them.'

'Not at all,' said Dugdale-Smith. 'I teach at the School of Oriental and African Studies. I was contacted a few weeks ago by a friend of a friend of mine at the club I belong to. This chap just said he wanted someone to teach a boy from Chad English as he was arriving in Nigeria shortly and his relations wanted to get him off to an educational start. The pay was good, and I love Africa, so I said I'd do it for a couple of weeks. I went to a man I know at the FO to check on the fellow who'd approached me just in case it was politics. Africa's so full of politics even innocent academics like me have to be careful. But the man was what he said he was – the relative of a local bishop – there's the ecclesiastical connection coming in again, you see. I came out and what do I find? Not the jolly Nigerian family I'd expected, hundreds of aunties and uncles and first, second and third wives and lashings of arguments about everything under the sun, just this slightly melancholy collection of clerics, the admirable Miss Simms, who frightens me only fractionally less than the headmistress of my first school, and – the amazing boy. The boy's amazing, you see. He's obviously straight out of the bush. He eats with his fingers. He knows nothing. He learns like wildfire. He experiences no culture shock. I'm not exaggerating – when he sat down at that table he'd not only never seen a watch but he can't have had any notion of what time is in the western sense. When I left, he could tell the hours on this.' Dugdale-Smith pulled a large pocket watch out of his shirt. 'In English – he learnt words and numbers together. A child like that could learn fourteen languages in two years. I've an idea that's not all he can do, either.'

'Meaning what?' asked Hannie.

'They've trained him up as a sorcerer back at his village. You can tell by the way he raises his head, like smelling something.'

'I don't know about that,' said Hannie, who got bored when she had to listen to superstitious tales from fellow travellers. 'I found him to be a very nice boy, that's all. Cool as a cucumber, too. We got attacked *en route*. Two helicopters which might or might not have been after us got taken out completely by a Mirage. Can you think of any kind of fighting which might be going on around the Niger–Nigeria border?'

'Not a thing,' said Dugdale-Smith promptly. 'Do you think there's going to be any trouble?'

'I hope not,' said Hannie. 'But I'm sleeping in the boy's room tonight.'

'Oh, Christ,' said Dugdale-Smith. 'I'm going back inside to ask what's going on – I didn't come here to risk my skin.'

'I don't think they'll tell you the story,' said Hannie. 'And I'm certain they don't expect anything. Only I do, and I'm not sure I'm not just tired and desert-struck.'

'In that case,' said Dugdale-Smith, 'I'll make use of my deep knowledge of, and sympathy for, Africa to go over there and see if I can get anything to drink. I didn't realize I was in for clerical gents and total abstinence when I signed on for this trip. You'll join me, I hope?'

'I will,' said Hannie. After Dugdale-Smith had

strolled off into the darkness, she walked round the building and checked the windows. At the back there was a small garden, surrounded by a wire fence. The dining room had arched windows and french windows, and on either side there were other windows, for other rooms. It would take ten men inside to stop intruders from coming in, and two or three would have to guard the front door leading into the building. The only thing to do was to hope she was having paranoid fears – there was no way of protecting the Mission with the few people they had available. As a last try, she went indoors to talk to the others. The two clergymen, the nun and Angelica Simms were still sitting at the table. Bob, they told her, was in bed.

Hannie sat down unasked and said, 'I don't want to alarm you, but I wonder if you've considered the possibility of an attack on the Mission tonight. I think it could happen – I think those two helicopters may have been after us. I think it might be as well to put some guards on duty.'

Father Martin said, 'I cannot see why we should be attacked. It seems a most peculiar idea. Have you any reasons for thinking we are threatened?'

Hannie sighed, 'I'm afraid not. I just feel it might be wise to find some guards. I'm sure the police would take anything you said seriously.'

Father Martin looked at her and said sympathetically, 'The rigours of the journey have been great, Mrs Richards. I think you may be over-reacting.'

Hannie stood up. She said dryly, 'I've noticed that the moment when people start telling you you're over-reacting is the moment, usually, to be most on your guard. But I hope you're right and I'm wrong. Goodnight.'

After she left the room she heard them talking among themselves. She checked where her room was with the Nigerian boy and looked in on Bob, who was in the room next door, near the end of the corridor. He was fast asleep in an iron bed, under a white coverlet. Above the bed was a huge iron crucifix. She went out and rejoined Dugdale-Smith outside the Mission. As she sat down he handed her a paper cup and told her, 'It says Johnnie Walker on the label, but I don't believe it.'

Taking a sip she said, 'Neither do I.'

He was tipping something from a screw of newspaper into a cigarette paper on the ground. He completed his expert roll-up, lit the cigarette and handed it to her. 'You've been doing some effective foraging,' she remarked. 'Did you pick up any gossip? Anyone new and strange in town? Any unexpected vehicles?'

'Nothing,' he told her. 'But a couple of the women said they felt something was going to happen. Sometimes they're right.'

'Yes,' said Hannie, 'and just as often they're not.'

'What's new indoors?' Dugdale-Smith asked, nodding at the Mission. 'Same old iron curtain,' Hannie said. 'I asked what they'd think of getting a few guards for the inside of the building or maybe a policeman or two. They told me not to over-react.'

'Such a bad sign,' Dugdale-Smith said.

'I wish I knew that Bob would be all right,' Hannie said.

'He'll always be all right,' Dugdale-Smith told her. 'He commands respect, affection, even loyalty, even at that age, even from men like me. We're supposed to go up to a hotel at Jos tomorrow, all five of us. Do you think I'd spend a weekend up there with that cheery crew if it weren't for the boy? I'd be on the next plane in a flash.

122

I'll stay for the boy – I even want to. I can't understand it.'

'Funny,' she said.

'Very funny,' he told her. Hannie saw a man with a secret, a bad one, in Dugdale-Smith. She didn't want to know what it was.

They sat peacefully on for half an hour, saying little, until she stood up and said, 'I think I'll turn in now.'

The boy, Matthew, helped her to carry her mattress into Bob's room. When he had gone she jammed it against the door and lay down in her clothes to sleep. She hoped nothing would go wrong.

But it did. At two in the morning she awoke, listening. Two seconds later she heard the sound of a door being closed, very quietly, down the corridor. They were looking for her and the boy. She got up and, in a single movement, wrenched up the mattress so that it lay, widthwise, across the door. She turned and at that moment came the sound of breaking glass and a black figure launched itself through the window into the room. He fell in a crouch and Hannie, at the same time, pulled the crucifix from the wall behind Bob's bed and hit him over the head with it. He fell down immediately, blood streaming into his eyes. He wore a black balaclava, black shirt, black trousers. Bob sat up, looking frightened.

'Under the bed! Under the bed!' Hannie yelled, pointing. She saw him get out of bed – he was back in the red robe again, she noticed – and then spun round, the crucifix still in her hand, and struck a black shoulder which was trying to push the door open. There was a cry and the shoulder went back. Hannie slammed the door and kicked the mattress further back against it. She had heard another man come through the window.

She charged him with her crucifix but he was on his feet and ready for her. He seized her arm. She kneed him in the balls. He groaned and doubled up. There was no sign of Bob. He must have got under the bed. Behind her, the door strained. The man she had hit over the head was on his feet, looking groggy. The other man was doubled up on the floor. Standing above her on the window ledge was a third balaclava-ed figure, also all in black. The mattress gave way, finally, and a man half-fell into the room. Hannie hit him with the crucifix but she was tired and the blow had no force behind it. He came on. There was another man behind him and another behind that one. She gave up and stood there gasping. The third man, now in the doorway, had a machine gun.

'All right,' she said. 'What do you want?'

'Just the boy. He's ours,' said the man in front, his hand to his head. He had an American accent.

'What for?' she said, still breathless. 'He's only a boy. Leave him alone. Who says he's yours, anyway?' She knew she sounded like a child in a school playground. She knew that people in such situations almost always did.

'He's not yours,' said the man with the American voice.

'I didn't kidnap him,' said Hannie.

'You took him for money,' said the other. 'Where is he?'

'He's under the bed,' said the man Hannie had kicked in the groin. He was standing up now, his face twisted with pain. At that moment Bob came out from under the bed. He looked at the men, at Hannie, at the machine gun.

Hannie said, 'Don't fight. Do what they say.'

124

'All right,' he said, standing beside her. 'All right. I am happy.' He turned round and collected his red bundle from the foot of his bed. 'I go with you,' he told the one of the men. 'You fight nobody.'

'Whatever you say,' agreed the man.

'I'm responsible for him,' Hannie declared. 'You tell me who you are and where you're taking him.'

The man said, 'You don't know what you're in. Just shut up and keep back.' But she walked behind them down the corridor, calling out, 'You tell me where you're taking him.' Just ahead of her the two injured men leaned on each other. Ahead there was a knot of the others, with Bob invisible in the middle.

As they approached the reception area the limping man in front of her turned round and said, in a guttural accent, 'Go away. You can do nothing. We do not want to hurt you.'

In the hall Father Martin, the nun, Mr Omovo, the plump white man and Angelica Simms stood guarded by two men with revolvers. As the party from the corridor moved towards the front door these two backed away from the captives, following them.

Angelica Simms said, 'You will bring about a tragedy by this. May God forgive you.' Hannie thought she saw one of the men with revolvers smile. At that point Angelica walked straight towards him and his companion and out into the street where the other men were with Bob. She watched the tall woman go up to the party, push through and say, in a clear voice, 'You'll have to kill me before you take this child.'

Hannie had to admire her. If one of the men on their side had moved he would have been shot instantly. Only Angelica had the power of her age, her sex and her assurance to throw them off balance in this way.

She challenged them now to shoot their mother. It would not work, but you had to respect the attempt. And yet it did work, in a way.

From inside there came a shot, a cry from Father Martin of 'Omovo!' The young Nigerian minister appeared in the doorway, holding a revolver he had snatched from one of the attackers. One of the men in the street raised a machine gun and riddled him with bullets. After that there was complete silence. Hannie stood looking at the splashed body in the doorway and at the group outside in the street. Behind her a woman, the nun, wept. Then, by the buildings opposite the Mission, she thought she saw a shadow move. She took a few steps towards the door, as if to go to the minister's body, and as the party in the street were attacked by what seemed like ten, twelve, black-clad bodies, as shots were fired and a voice cried, 'Dolce Chris –' she, who had placed the exact position of Bob seconds earlier, was into the throng and pulling him out by one hand. She found Angelica had his other hand and together, in a chain, they ran past the Mission and round the side of the building. They crouched in the garden, under a tree, hearing shots and cries from the front of the building.

'Oh, my God,' gasped Hannie, 'what the fuck's going on.'

Angelica said, 'They're inside the Mission.' Hannie turned. A black figure showed in a window. There was shooting. The figure leaped, twisted, fell. There was an explosion. Another window shattered out. Fire sprang up inside the room, throwing a patch of light on to a bed of flowers.

Hannie whispered, 'Where are the keys to the car?'

Angelica whispered, 'In the Mission. We'll have to

get to the open country back there – find shelter.'

Hannie thought if they took to the countryside behind the Mission garden they would be easily found at dawn. There was no alternative, though. Here, they would be spotted by someone soon. Then she heard, beneath the cries, the shots and the crackle of fire, the sound of an engine starting up.

'That's the Mercedes,' Angelica hissed.

Hannie, bent double, crept as fast as she could through the garden to the side of the building. She tripped on a heap of stones and, as she recovered herself, saw a dim figure sitting in the driving seat of the car. As she scuffled up to it a hail of machine-gun bullets hit the wall opposite the vehicle. Plaster and brick showered down. She wrenched open the door of the car. 'You!' she whispered fiercely. 'Listen! We're in the garden. Keep the engine running and wait.'

He was trying to shut the car door. 'Fuck off,' he said. 'I'm leaving.'

Hannie kept on pulling at the door. 'You wait,' she said, 'or I'll kill you now. I mean it.' It was true that as she half-crouched, hauling on the door he was trying to shut, she could have killed Dugdale-Smith with her bare hands in order to get the car. Pure conviction carries weight. 'Hurry up, then,' he said. She did not trust him so, in order to keep hanging on to the car door, she had to stand up and call out, 'Angelica! Run over here!' There was a rustling and Angelica and Bob appeared suddenly. As they scrambled in and got down on the car floor at the back Hannie said, 'Are you any good as a driver?'

'Get in,' he ordered. As he put the car in gear he muttered, 'I used to drive in rallies – shut up, get down. I'm risking my skin sitting here.' He backed, horribly

127

fast, down the entrance. Two men with guns who had just appeared round the corner fell back against the wall. As he pulled the car back into the street he hit another. In front of them, an attacker with a machine gun raised it, then lowered it again. Dugdale-Smith put his foot down, and they screeched off. A moment later the back window was shattered by machine-gun bullets. Dugdale-Smith said, 'Ugh,' and the car swerved as he took the impact of a slug. Hannie, crouched in the front seat, thought that he might be dead. At any moment his feet would slip from the pedals and they would career off the road. She grabbed for the handbrake and found Dugdale-Smith had a firm grasp on it. She straightened up. The jacket of his white suit was red.

'You're hit in the shoulder,' she said. 'Pull over, I'll drive.' He glanced at his coat and said, 'Christ!'

'Pull over,' she said urgently. 'When you feel it, you'll lose control. Hurry, they're going to be chasing us.'

He pulled up. She got out and raced round the car as he half-fell into the passenger seat. She got in and started the engine.

Dugdale-Smith groaned and said, between his teeth, 'Get me to a hospital. I'll bleed to death. Get me to Kano.'

'I'm going,' said Hannie, wondering how fast she dared travel on a road she'd only driven once. The mirror had shattered. She said to Angelica, 'You and the boy can get up now. Keep an eye on the road behind – look for their lights.'

Glass tinkled as they rose from the floor.

'I've got to make a phone call,' said Angelica.

Hannie drove faster. They should be able to outrun nearly anything in the Mercedes, given luck.

'I must make a call,' said Angelica.

'When we get to the hospital,' said Hannie.

'There must be somewhere nearer –' said Angelica.

'Shut up,' said Dugdale-Smith. 'Are you mad?' He was now in great pain. Hannie flinched when she thought of the smashed bones in his shoulder. From the corner of her eye she saw Bob's black hand travelling over the back of the seat towards the spreading red patch on Dugdale-Smith's jacket. 'No!' she cried out. 'No! Bob!'

She braced herself in anticipation of Dugdale-Smith's sudden leap when the hand touched his wound. He might even faint on to her as she drove.

'All right, Hannie,' came Bob's voice as the hand landed softly on the bloodstained coat. Hannie bit her lip. Dugdale-Smith breathed out, as if relieved. The hand stayed on his shoulder. He said, 'Ah – better.'

Meanwhile Hannie drove on grimly. On this long, flat stretch of road it would be easy to see if there was a vehicle in pursuit of them.

'Angelica – anything behind?' she said.

'Oh –' said Angelica. Then she said, 'There are some headlights.'

'How far?' asked Hannie and, getting no reply, repeated, 'Angelica – how far?'

'Sorry,' said Angelica. 'About half a mile.'

'Keep your eyes off the boy and on the road,' Hannie said grimly. Bob's hand was still on Dugdale-Smith's shoulder. The man's head had dropped back against the seat. His eyes were closed.

'Sleeping now,' Bob said reassuringly.

Angelica said, 'Thank you, Bob. That's wonderful.'

Hannie, sensing mysteries, which she hated, thought: Passed out cold, that's what he's done. She drove on furiously and said, 'Keep your bloody eyes on the road, Angelica. How far away are they now?'

'I think they've gained a bit,' said Angelica.

'They must have rockets,' said Hannie.

The other car, a low black vehicle containing four men, was on their back wheel as they entered the suburbs of Kano. As they screamed up to the hospital Hannie prayed they would be left to get Dugdale-Smith out of the Mercedes in peace. She noticed a police car outside the hospital and thought, thankfully, that the men in the car would not dare to give them any trouble. They swept past looking straight ahead. Dugdale-Smith was pulled out by attendants and taken to the operating theatre. Angelica Simms took over. First she drew a sister to one side for a whispered conversation. She disappeared for two minutes, returned, took the police inspector aside for another consultation, disappeared again, came back, talked to the Matron and then led the whole contingent, by now ten strong, into a small sitting room, where something like a party began.

Hannie sat on a vinyl-covered bench at the back of the room, with Bob sleeping beside her under a blanket. He lay on his back, sweet-faced, like a boy carved on a tomb. Even so, everyone in the room came over to see him from time to time. They stared down at him with curiosity, respect and affection. They ignored Hannie. She thought it must be something Angelica had said. A small nurse brought her a cup of tea. She sat and sipped it, wanting now nothing more than a hot bath, a good sleep and a one-way ticket home. And, she supposed, to see the boy on his way to somewhere good. In the meanwhile, how did Angelica have all this influence over nurses and policemen and local bigwigs? Why did

130

they all inspect Bob regularly? Above all, why the constant attacks on them?

She thought she should not sleep in case of another arrival by terrorists. But she did sleep, dreaming that she was back at the head of a long column of men, women and children walking the rocky, dry trade route through Chad. Vultures swooped overhead. Flocks of goats and sheep marched among them, or to the sides. Donkeys carried bundles and packs. The sun beat down on their heads. Hannie felt thirst, heat and weariness. She was holding the hand of a little girl, who stumbled and fell. She bent over her, tried to get her to rise, but knew she was too ill. Round her the people still moved. Then at her side was a tall man, dressed in a robe, with a beard and a staff, which had something carved on it. She knew the man could help the child. She pleaded with him, but he could not understand her. Then to her great relief and joy he touched the child with his staff. The child stirred, got up. Hannie, knowing the man was Moses, awoke and found Angelica in front of her, calling her name. She looked into the severe face and felt depressed.

'They want a statement from you, Hannie,' said Angelica. 'Then we can go.'

'Where to?' asked Hannie.

'Rome,' said Angelica.

'Why Rome?' asked Hannie.

'I can't tell you. But you can get a flight back to England from there.'

'All right,' said Hannie. 'Is Bob coming with us?'

'Yes,' said Angelica.

'What happens to him then?' asked Hannie.

'I don't think that's any of your business,' Angelica told her. 'Of course, we're all grateful for your help.

131

You've been very brave. And I acknowledge that if we'd put guards at the Mission as you suggested, a great deal of danger would have been avoided. Nevertheless, that doesn't entitle you to ask questions. This matter is highly confidential. Now, will you come over here.'

She had commandeered a desk. On one side of it stood a police inspector, on the other a consular official, looking tired and holding a cup of tea.

'Mrs Richards,' he said. 'The Nigerian authorities have decided that there is no need for the innocent victims of an attack, which is now under investigation, to remain in the country. What they would like is a statement about what took place from your own point of view. Just as regards the attack, of course. Then you and Miss Simms may go.'

Hannie, reluctantly, began to write as short an account as possible of the event. She much disliked the idea of giving written evidence, under her own name, to the authorities. In a world full of computers, every time her name appeared her professional life grew more dangerous. A traffic offence in Bogota could now link her to a strange attack in Nigeria and, as it happened, to a false arrest in Prague, which had been reported to the consular authorities, on a charge of smuggling out state secrets. The charge, a result of an informer's passing on of a rumour, had been dropped, and Hannie had got out with what she was actually carrying, in micro-fiche, in the false bottom of a bottle of vodka which had been made by a sympathetic worker in one of the Czech glass factories. It was just a few poems, a testimony from a labour camp, a writer's last letter to his son, photographs' scraps of paper left over from the Inquisition. Hannie was surprised to get the bottle of vodka back after they had torn her luggage apart. This drifted through her mind as she wrote, slowly, using her left hand, on the grounds that there was a good chance she could dispute the handwriting at a later stage if she had to. The consular official looked at her pityingly as she struggled slowly through her story. She put in a few spelling mistakes to add to the impression.

'Did you catch them?' she asked the police inspector as she signed her name badly. She was fairly sure they had not, or the questions would have been harder to answer, but it seemed an obvious thing to say.

'Three dead men were left behind,' he told her, 'but there was no evidence about who they were. They must have taken the wounded with them.'

'Hope you catch them,' she said and went to ask the Matron how Dugdale-Smith was faring. They were, she heard, surprised and pleased by how little damage had been done. The bones had pieced together nicely. He had lost less blood than they would have expected. As she spoke, the Matron glanced, involuntarily, at Bob, who was still asleep. Hannie, crossly, went over to Angelica, who was in animated conversation with two clergymen, one a bishop, and waited for a pause in their chat. She had seen Angelica's signature on the statement she had made. It showed her to be an Anglican nun, Sister Angelica Simms, from an organization called the St Anne's Orphanages, in Lagos. This was obviously a good way to explain Bob away and provide him with papers claiming him to be a Nigerian orphan. It also answered Hannie's questions about why Angelica was playing a dominant part in the affair.

'When are we leaving?' she asked Angelica.

'In half an hour,' said Angelica. 'The Inspector's kindly arranged an escort to the airfield.'

They howled through Kano and not long after were

airborne in a small private plane containing only Hannie, Angelica, an Irish Jesuit priest, Bob and three burly stewards. Since the priest and Bob had craftily fixed it so that they could sit with the pilots, Hannie and Angelica were forced to make the best of each other's company. It was five in the morning so they had coffee and toast side by side.

'You were very brave, back there, when you invited them to shoot you before they took the boy,' Hannie said, by way of making agreeable conversation.

'It was my duty,' said Angelica.

'Well, not everybody does their duty,' Hannie told her.

Angelica said implacably, 'I try, but I do not always succeed.' She added, 'Yours is a strange way of life. Are you happy in it?'

'I never think about it,' said Hannie. 'I do it for the money.'

'Is that all?' asked Angelica. 'Is there no other reason?'

'What other reason is there?' asked Hannie. 'Don't start telling me to examine my motives – that's just a way of saying they bloody well need examining, if not scrubbing out with disinfectant. I mean, you're sitting next to me with a kind of Salvation Army look on your face – "And how did you come to be in this position, you poor girl." Well, I'm not poor and I'm not a girl. I'm a successful smuggler. That means I break the law, but what laws? I might break a law preventing me from taking whisky into Saudi Arabia and come back and break a law preventing me from taking marijuana into Scotland. If I got the consignments mixed up and took the marijuana into Saudi Arabia and the whisky into Scotland, I'd be in the clear. I can walk into the Soviet

Union with a suitcase full of Communist literature but I can't bring anti-Soviet material by their own writers out. I can take the anti-Soviet literature to South Africa in truckloads. What happens if they catch me trying to come in with Communist propaganda? You'd be surprised what's considered contraband from place to place – contraceptives, instant coffee, marigold seeds, frozen panda semen without a licence, brandy for the parson, baccy for the clerk – the laws I break aren't the ten commandments. They're just what suits a particular government at a particular time. Don't forget they used to have to smuggle in the English version of the Bible. I dare say when they did they hired some depraved character like me and then sat in the back of an ox-cart with him asking him why he led the life he did. These governments make the rules their way, and I break them my way. And, come to that, Bob's contraband and you're a receiver.'

And with that Hannie drank some more coffee and sat back in her seat. What had he said, Bob, when she woke him up and gave him some tea and cakes and told him he was going in an aeroplane? He had nodded, hadn't he, and said, 'I must.'

Not sure that he understood what he was saying she had asked him, 'Must?'

He had waved round him at the room, still full of people and said, 'I –' and then, lost for words, had circled his arms, wide, as if embracing an invisible person. And Hannie, feeling the great impulse to love, protect and nurture in the gesture, had smiled and shrugged, saying, 'I don't know about all this. I hope it's all right.'

'All right,' he had assured her. 'Very all right.'

In retrospect, the generosity of the gesture, the hope

and love on the face of the child filled her with fear for him. What would the world do to his trust and bravery? She had told him, instinctively, 'Be careful.' And, 'Not careful,' he had said and had widened his arms, as if to include everything and everybody in the room.

As she thought about this, Angelica said, 'I'm sorry if you think I was trying to lecture you. All I really thought was – well, drugs, guns, you seem like too nice a person to be mixed up – I'm not putting this very well. It's just that in some respects you're very unlike the usual kind of person –'

'I just do it for money, that's all,' said Hannie. 'I lead a very expensive life.'

Bob came laughing out of the pilot's cabin. He said, 'I took it up to 25,000 feet. The pilot said it was good.'

The priest said, 'I think that's enough now. You must have some breakfast.'

'Yes,' agreed the boy.

'Angelica,' Hannie asked, 'what is he? Why are we taking him to Rome?

Angelica said, 'Honestly, Hannie, I don't know. Initially, my bishop asked me to meet you, with the others you met, and take the boy to Jos and settle him a bit and get him to learn a little English. After you arrived, the orders changed. Father Martin got a phone call from the bishop saying the boy must be brought to Lagos. At the hospital I used the bishop's name – plans changed again. This time we were to fly to Rome in a special plane. That, I imagine, was because of the attacks. But those orders didn't come from the bishop. He had to make another call before he rang back with the plan.'

The priest, who had been having his breakfast with Bob, came down the plane to them. 'Does he often do that?' he said to the women.

Hannie turned round. Bob was sitting still, in the back seat. He looked straight ahead. She had often seen him do it while they were travelling in the Land Rover, even while they sat on the rock with helicopters racketing overhead. It was what he had been doing on that first night as he lay staring up at the stars in his sleeping bag. It was true that in these abstracted moods he rarely blinked, which was strange, but she had thought his habit of drifting into periods of stillness and consideration must be tribal and, in fact, a vast improvement on table-leg kicking, asking for the *TV Times*, checking the fridge for Cokes and all the other ways of passing the time adopted by twelve-year-olds in her own culture. She had also wondered if it might be a symptom of *petit mal*. She mentioned this to the priest.

'That could be,' he said sombrely. He went back to the pilot's cabin.

'So you really don't know what it's all about?' Hannie said to Angelica.

'My bishop said that I was not to ask myself any questions, even if I wished to,' Angelica told her. 'I have to obey.'

'Pretty hard not to try to put two and two together,' Hannie said. 'I'd think you could hardly help yourself, sometimes.' She looked back at Bob's small figure, still as a statue. She added, 'I began to wonder if his breathing didn't slow down when he went like that. Now I come to think of it – it resembles a trance condition. I wonder if that's it.'

'I'm forbidden speculation,' Angelica said.

'I couldn't manage that myself,' said Hannie.

The priest, coming back from the pilot's cabin, bent over and said, 'Mrs Richards. I'm to ask you if you could spend a few days in Rome after we arrive. There are some questions we should like to ask you.'

'Who's we?' said Hannie, who had a built-in dislike of answering questions.

'Your employers, I should have said.'

'Who are –?' said Hannie.

'I'll have to check if I'm at liberty to tell you,' he said, moving back down the aisle of the plane.

'Remember – no names, no information,' Hannie called after him. Then, rather to her own surprise, she went to sleep. She seemed to be back in the column of people she had been travelling with before. At any rate, she had the same young child by the hand, and, walking beside her on the other side, two fat lambs. In this strange company she walked the dried-up trail, but this time without any pain. She was at peace. Then the others were no longer there. They climbed a grassy hill, and Hannie knew that when they got to the top they would see something wonderful which would make them very happy. As they took the final slope she was very excited and so was the child. She skipped beside her. The lambs ran a little before them. At the top of the hill the lambs stopped. Hannie and the child arrived and they all stood, awe-struck, gazing at – and then she woke up. Angelica was shaking her.

'Oh, Angelica,' she complained. 'I was having such a wonderful dream. It isn't every day I have a wonderful dream. Most of the time I have lurid anxiety dreams. I could kill you, Angelica.'

Angelica's stiff face smiled. 'You sound like one of my children,' she said. 'The children at my orphanage. I'm sorry – we're putting down to refuel. I only wanted to tell you so that you can go and stretch your legs. What was your dream?'

'It was –' said Hannie and of course, she had it. She'd

got it. 'Oh, my God,' she groaned. 'I know what it is. I know why we're here. I know what this is all about.'

'What?' asked Angelica.

'Do you really want the purity of your ignorance sullied?' said Hannie. 'Are you sure it isn't against instructions? They could take your badge away.' She felt very depressed.

The priest came hurrying up and said, 'I can tell you who you will be seeing in Rome. They wish you to know.'

'I already do,' said Hannie. 'Tell me – was it done by computer?'

'I believe it was,' he said. 'On the other side, at least. But I have a problem here, now. I told them I thought that you, who have been involved with the whole situation all the time, might suspect the truth, or part of it. It seems you have. And you can imagine we want none of this made public.'

'You can trust me,' Hannie said promptly. 'I'd never breathe a word of all this. I hope that it's all a lie, an error, a terrible mistake. I believe none of it and the sooner you find out you're wrong, that there isn't a particle of sense in the whole business, the better for all of us.'

He looked at her sorrowfully. 'I cannot believe you mean that, Mrs Richards,' he said.

'Then you haven't looked at the history of the last two thousand years,' she declared. She went up the plane and sat down by herself.

Twelve men were dead already, she thought, watching the Irish priest and Angelica talking with their heads close together. The eight in the helicopters, three in the attack on the Mission, and Mr Omovo, the Methodist priest. If the second wave of attackers on the

139

Mission had been Italian, as she supposed, then they were defending the party inside, especially Bob. That made the men who had come through the windows to kidnap him the opposition. So who was the opposition?

Somehow both sides had, presumably with the help of a computer, worked out that the new Messiah, son of God, had been born and was living in a desolate corner of an ignored and desperate African state. One side had decided to rescue him from the obvious dangers of famine and war. The other had either found out and decided to get him for themselves, or had started off on the quest at the same time. Anyway, Hannie's team had been quicker. In the excitement, twelve men had died. Who would want to lay hands on the son of God? Islam could make use of a new prophet. Judaism could make use of a Messiah. She was extremely lucky, thought Hannie, that she had not had to face Jews and Arabs simultaneously. Unless, she thought suddenly, she had. It could have been a three-cornered contest. How would she know? And with that idea came terror. They were not safe anywhere with that boy aboard. Three faiths, two of them over a thousand years old and one far more ancient than that, were separately in political conflict all over the globe. A real religious leader, to inspire and transfigure his followers, would be invaluable – to, say, the Catholic Church in Poland and Eastern Europe, to Islam in the battle with Israel, to Israel itself – a religious leader backing one sect of a faith, Christian, Islamic or Jewish, would be invaluable to the sect. And twelve men had already died. How many more would there be? They themselves were in danger on the plane. They would be in danger on the ground. If the boy was accepted as prophet or saviour by anybody, the whole world would be in danger of crusade, jehad and holy war by the power which had him, against whoever had not, whether they were Christians or Muslims, Jews or Communists, Protestants or Catholics, Reformed, Orthodox, Sufis or Holy Rollers. Standing in front of all this would be skinny, black Bob, his embrace for the world turned into a stranglehold. He was an H-bomb. Already twelve men had died. Poor Bob. Poor old world, thought Hannie Richards.

Now it was an Irish Cardinal, Cardinal Riordan, who sat beside Bob on a well-upholstered, antique sofa in a small room in the Vatican. The walls were covered with florid paintings on religious and historical themes. Underneath sat a large number of people. There were many pairs of black, ecclesiastical boots on the marble floor. Hannie sat on Bob's other side. She had bought him an electronic toy earlier. He sat fighting an electronic battle and little bleeps came out of the machine, which he had refused to leave behind. Across the room Hannie saw Angelica and Father Martin sitting on another sofa, talking to each other, like patients in a dentist's waiting room.

Hannie, who had already told her tale, several times, to Cardinal Riordan, while a secretary took it down in shorthand, said to Bob, 'Are you looking forward to seeing the Pope?'

The boy went on pushing the buttons rapidly with his slender fingers and said, 'Like – you mean? I will like him?' He was still wearing the red robe.

'I'm sure you will,' she said. He had been abstracted today. She hoped that the shock of so many new scenes and events was not destroying his composure.

'I will like him,' said Bob. 'He will be my father.'

'That sounds nice,' Hannie said. She imagined they

would have to test him. He'd have to confound them, the way Jesus confounded the doctors in the temple. He might have to do a miracle. Poor Bob. The electronic toy let out a series of high-pitched bleeps. The crowd sat round the room, staring. A fly buzzed.

'How long do you think we'll have to wait?' Hannie asked the Cardinal. She felt Bob tugging at her sleeve.

'I'm sure he won't be long,' the Cardinal told her. He had a long face and an anxious expression. He had been kind to Bob, but withdrawn. The boy tugged at her sleeve again.

'Hannie,' he whispered. 'Outside.' He pointed at the imposing double doors.

'All right,' she said and got up. He rose too, still holding the toy.

'Where are you going?' asked the Cardinal in alarm.

'He wants to go outside,' said Hannie. 'I don't know why. But he isn't capricious or restless – if he wants to go out, he's got a reason.'

The Cardinal followed them into a large marble hall. Two Swiss guards stood on duty outside the double doors. At the end of the hall were more doors, more Swiss guards. Bob walked into the middle of the floor, looked back at the Cardinal, who was still trailing them, stopped and said, with a smile, 'I'm bleeding.'

'You're what?' said Hannie, but not loudly. 'Where? Where, Bob?'

He pointed between his legs and said, 'Bleeding,' in a reasonable way.

'Oh, God,' cried Hannie. Imagining some terrible complaint, she tried to tug up his red robe, but Bob, outraged, tried to tug it down again.

The Cardinal came up behind her. 'What on earth are you doing?' he asked.

Bob dragged Hannie a little farther off. 'Hannie,' he said earnestly. 'No, all right. I am a woman. I bleed. You do bleed, many times. I bleed now. Not before, but this time.'

She looked at him carefully now. It was true that he had been modest about his bodily functions while they had been travelling together. It was true that he had driven Angelica and her out of the bathroom at the Mission before he took his bath. For all she knew, he was a girl. Either that, or he was raving mad. She would have to find out.

The Cardinal had caught up with them again. She looked at Bob, who looked pleased. She had the idea he expected her to tell the Cardinal the joyful news now. The Cardinal said, 'You really must tell me what's going on. The Holy Father will be here at any moment.'

Hannie spread her hands helplessly. 'It's like this,' she said. 'Well – the truth is –' and she paused again. As she said afterwards, she had done some hard things in her time but probably the hardest ever was standing in the Vatican trying to explain to a Cardinal that the little African Messiah on whom all their hopes were pinned was also a girl, having her first period. She pulled herself together. 'Bob says he's bleeding,' she told Cardinal Riordan.

'Very good,' Bob interrupted.

Hannie could not help smiling. 'What he seems to be saying,' she continued, 'is that it's natural. He is, in short, a girl.'

The Cardinal's mouth dropped open, and his eyes widened. 'But this is very serious,' he said. 'Have you any reason to think he may not be male?'

'I don't know,' said Hannie.

'Mother say I must always be wearing boy's clothes,'

Bob said. 'Because bad men may rape me when I am not in the village.'

Hannie remembered his reluctance to put on the shorts Angelica had provided at the Mission until he was assured that they were boys' clothes.

'Would you get Angelica Simms?' Hannie asked the Cardinal. He seemed too stunned to move, so she opened the parlour door herself. 'Angelica!'

Responding to the urgency in Hannie's voice, Angelica came immediately.

'You speak Italian, don't you?' said Hannie. Angelica nodded.

'Well, you're not going to believe this one . . .' said Hannie.

After Hannie had told her, Angelica went immediately to the guards and asked them something in Italian. She went straight to Bob and took him by the hand. She led him through the next set of doors, down a corridor full of niches and statuary, through some more doors, through a small chapel, where two nuns were praying, through another door – finally she pushed open another door into a room with washbasins and two lavatory cubicles.

'Finding a Ladies in this place is like finding a needle in a haystack,' she remarked with Anglican disapproval.

Bob stood there smiling at them.

'Do congratulate her,' Hannie urged, 'I'm sure this is a cause for rejoicing among her people.'

'Better check first that it's true,' said Angelica.

'Now, darling,' Hannie urged. 'Let's just look.' They did. She and Angelica faced each other. 'What a turn-up for the Holy See,' said Hannie. She took some tissues from her handbag and gave them to Bob, who washed the blood from her narrow thighs.

144

Angelica said, 'I'll go and ask those nuns for some sanitary towels. Otherwise I'll have to go miles to a chemist.' She remembered Hannie's instructions, smiled at Bob and said, 'Bravo.' Then she disappeared. Hannie heard her outside saying, 'Yes, Cardinal Riordan. The child is a girl. Will you excuse me – I have an errand to do.'

Hannie put her head out of the door and said, 'Cardinal Riordan. We may have a long wait in here. Could you organize some chairs.'

'Mrs Richards –' he said imploringly, but she said, 'Please, Cardinal.'

'Of course,' he told her. 'I'll ask for chairs. But I must go and discuss this development.'

Bob said, 'Bleeding not nice? The Cardinal is unhappy?'

Hannie, looking down at the small figure, said firmly, 'I'm happy, and you're happy – that's what matters.'

Bob looked up at her and said, 'This place is strange.'

Hannie looked down at her and said, 'Perhaps you'd better change it.'

Bob said, 'Maybe.'

A nervous Swiss guard knocked on the door and handed Hannie two small, carved chairs. They sat down. A nun came in and was startled to find them sitting there. She used the lavatory and left quickly. Bob said, reflectively, 'There is much I do not understand. I have much work to do.' There was a knock on the door.

Cardinal Riordan whispered, 'Could you come out a moment, Mrs Richards?'

Hannie went out. He said, 'I have spoken in person to the Holy Father. He still wishes to see the child. Will you be long?'

145

'I'm waiting for Angelica,' said Hannie. 'She has things to get.'

'Oh – I see,' said Cardinal Riordan.

Hannie felt annoyed and said, 'You've had women saints. Jesus was born of a woman. I don't think this should upset you – you look as if you'd lost a shilling and found sixpence. What's wrong with women anyway? Half the world is women. Your position is – you want a Saviour, but only if he's a man, not a nasty, bleeding woman. You make me sick.' She went back inside the Ladies, thought of something else to say, put her head round the door and said it. 'Who told you God was a man anyway?'

Voices outside the door indicated that Angelica had returned. She came in saying, 'I had to send a man on a motor bike,' and put a package of sanitary towels on the edge of the washbasin. She added, 'The Cardinal's worried. He says you're behaving in a disruptive way.'

When they were ready to leave, Hannie bent and kissed Bob on the cheek. She said, 'I have to go now, Bob. I don't think we'll be seeing each other for a long time.'

'I know,' said the girl. 'Thank you, Hannie.'

'Oh no . . . Thank *you*, Bob,' said Hannie. As they walked through the chapel, she said quietly to the Cardinal, 'You know that if I hear anything's gone wrong with that child, I can blow the gaff.'

The Cardinal said, 'Yes.'

'You'd better make sure nothing goes wrong then, hadn't you?'

'Mrs Richards,' he told her. 'We know you helped save Bambarake's life, and we are grateful. But this does not give you the right to threaten us. I should advise you to go home quietly without saying any more.'

146

'I'm going to,' said Hannie. 'But I shall be keeping an eye on you.'

She watched them go off together, the small black girl and the tall red-clad figure. She had no doubt that in a short time Bob would be sitting opposite the Pope in a cosy room, talking and probably eating grapes. Sobered, she walked across the square, stopped by the fountain, looked at the water and began to laugh. It was a joke, she thought, to have driven all that way across the desert, to have fought with two sets of attackers, to have dragged the prize into the heart of the Vatican – and then to find that the eagerly anticipated Messiah was a teenage girl. All by herself, she watched the falling waters of the fountain and laughed and laughed. Then, catching a reflection beside her in the water, she turned. She faced the man she had seen on the beach, during the earthquake at St Colombe. Now she saw he had blue eyes, dark hair, a cheerful expression. He wore a dark jacket, a white shirt and a red tie. She gaped at him. Before she had time to speak, he smiled at her, strolled away and seemed to become part of a crowd of Japanese tourists who were clustered round a waving guide. She stared after him, into the group of tourists and around it. He was gone. Then she thought she could have seen him in Sydney, once, in the waterfront restaurant, by candlelight, at a table. Then, too, he had vanished.

Was it the same man? Probably not, she decided as she strolled along. He had looked amused. That was because she had been laughing. He was probably a hunter-down of wealthy tourist ladies and had changed his mind when he caught sight of her travel-torn shoes and broken nails. Then she thought again of Bob, wished her well, flagged a taxi and went straight to the airport.

147

Outside the Hope Club the Salvation Army band was playing 'Hark the Herald Angels Sing' when Hannie finished. 'So there you are – believe it or not,' she said.

Margaret Wilkinson said, 'It seems quite mad. How long ago did all this happen?'

'About a month,' said Hannie. 'It'll be kept dark, of course, either for ever or just for the time being. First they'll do the tests, you see. Then if they're convinced it's true, they'll groom poor old Bob for stardom – for example, in these image-conscious days you can't introduce a saint or a prophet who eats with her fingers. What worries me is what they'll do with her if she doesn't come up to scratch. I'm afraid they might stick her in a convent to moulder. That's why I said I'd keep on checking.'

'It had to be computer astrology,' Julie mused. 'They can run through the whole number in the time it took twenty wizards working all their lives to do it in the old days. That's what my mother said. "The next Saviour, he come out of Africa. It is the Bible, gal, you read it."'

'I think you half-believe all this, Julie,' Margaret said accusingly.

'It's good news for black women everywhere, if it's true,' Julie told her.

'The arrival of the daughter of God would be good for everybody,' said Elizabeth.

Margaret looked hard at both of them and said, 'Phooey.'

As the brass band outside played 'Good King Wenceslas', Hannie stood up and put on her cloak. She said, 'My only worry at the moment is whether it means that we have to celebrate two Christ-child's birthdays every year – Christmas and Bobmas?'

'That's a rotten thought,' Margaret said.

'Happy Christmas, girls,' Hannie called out as she left.

4. Christmas

Margaret Wilkinson, sitting in her study in St John's Wood, going through some papers, found even her formidable powers of concentration eroded by the footsteps, door-bangings and continual comings and goings of her own household. She tried again to read the statement of the private detective who, coming into the flat to find divorce evidence, found instead evidence of the murder of the lover in the case, by the husband or wife involved. The body lay, badly hacked by a teak-handled kitchen cleaver, on the bloodstained matrimonial bed, while downstairs in the dining room the husband was on the phone to his mother and, in the kitchen, the wife was making a cup of tea. What had been going on? Margaret's client, the wife, claimed she had known nothing. Margaret found she, too, knew nothing as she heard, simultaneously, the doorbell ring and a crash of crockery from the kitchen.

The nurse came into the room. 'Mrs Greensleeves is here,' she said. Lottie Greensleeves was the ex-wife of

Margaret's lover, Edward. She was now married to a banker. The two little boys, children of the marriage, were away at school and spent the holidays with their parents in rotation. Like all neat arrangements, this one broke down from time to time.

Lottie came in wearing a large fur coat. 'Margaret – this so sweet of you. It is dreadful. I'm frightfully grateful to you. I do hope you don't mind my coming to see the boys.'

'Of course not,' said Margaret, not getting up from the desk. 'The nurse will show you their room.'

'Well,' said Lottie, 'would you mind if I had a drink first? I started at six-thirty this morning. We had to drive through a blizzard to get to the airport. Scotland's a nightmare, isn't it?'

Margaret, surreptitiously looking at her watch, realized it was half-past twelve. That was it, then – lunchtime. She stood up and said, 'Yes, of course, and you must have some lunch.'

In the kitchen Mrs Harris, who had just broken two cereal bowls and a plate, was not encouraging when asked about lunch. She grumbled about the nurse. 'I'd like it,' she said, 'if she presented me with the boys' breakfast plates before midday. There's not much food I can call on at a moment's notice – I was thinking omelettes would do you.'

Knowing that she was being punished for Edward's children, who had developed serious cases of chickenpox over Christmas, Margaret said, 'I suppose there's some cheese?' She left the kitchen hastily before the discussion of the cheese began and went back into the sitting room to pour Lottie Greensleeves a drink.

For a little while it had looked as if it might be a pleasant Christmas. All had been perfect, from the

151

polish on the glasses to the well-stocked freezer to the tastefully wrapped gifts beneath the shapely tree. The household − Robert Wilkinson, his mother, Edward Thompson, Margaret's father and a couple of married friends − had been in good spirits. Over supper on Christmas Eve they had cracked jokes, chatted and got on like a house on fire. A peaceful family Christmas was beginning. Only Edward's two boys, aged eight and nine, had marred the occasion with displays of irritability and ingratitude, but this was put down to pre-Christmas tension. Even their fevers and nightmares that night were attributed to undue excitement about the imminent arrival of Father Christmas. Over Christmas lunch the first spots emerged − they were, in fact, quite seriously ill and could not be moved.

Margaret's mother-in-law, who, although she said nothing, knew of the unusual domestic arrangements between her son, Margaret and Edward Thompson, stayed on to help with the nursing of the two boys. She was not a friendly figure at their joint mealtimes. That Robert, Margaret's husband, was bi-sexual and had a young male lover in Bayswater was something Robert and Margaret had decided years before never to tell her. Margaret, therefore, bore most of the opprobrium for the *ménage à trois* but bore it philosophically. At times like this she reflected that there were two sides to every coin − here, after all, was Robert's mother stoically changing pyjamas and carrying up nourishing soups to the patients when, if she had continued with her plans, she could have been flying off to Barbados with a friend. In the meanwhile, the nurse had arrived the day before but got on with nobody, not even her little patients. And now, Margaret reflected, here was Lottie, drinking a martini and making a social occasion of the visit to her children, whose bedsides she was plainly not desperate to rush to. One stray germ, thought Margaret, and the best organized woman's life could become, instantly, like a Hogarth cartoon, with the staff quarrelling in the kitchen, pots and pans crashing down everywhere, the harlot drinking gin in the parlour and the children falling out of bed upstairs. Lottie asked her what she was working on at the moment. 'It's murder, actually,' Margaret told her.

Mrs Harris came in with the omelettes. There was a terrible expression on her face as she looked at the guest. 'The nurse is packing. Mrs Wilkinson is staying,' she said.

'Did the nurse and Mrs Wilkinson have a row?' asked Margaret.

'And a half,' said Mrs Harris with relish.

'I'll ring the agency for another nurse after lunch,' Margaret said and knew, for certain, that she would never get out of this place to her office at Lincoln's Inn. The pipes would burst, the sink would block, she would get chickenpox herself and Mrs Harris would leave. She would never defend a murderer again.

At almost precisely the same time, about one o'clock on 29 December, Julie St Just came back to her flat in Streatham, carrying a suitcase, walked into her sitting room, put the case on the floor and fell into a chair. Her younger son was watching Mary Poppins on TV.

'How's it been, Ma?' she asked a large, beautiful black woman in her late forties who was ironing in the middle of the room.

'Fine, Julie,' said the woman. 'You OK too? I don't know how you get these sheets the colour they was. They grey as a donkey's back when I come here.'

'I not plannin' to get marry in them, Ma,' Julie replied, in her Barbados voice. 'Jus' sleep, that's all. They clean, that's all that matter.'

'That remind me,' said Mrs St Just, 'that Raymond Genevieve come round yesterday night, lookin' for you. I tell him you out workin' and I try to make him realize how hard you work. I hope you don't ever have nothin' to do with him. He a bad boy, that one, you can see it. He tell me he got a father with a good grocery store back in Trinidad and he the only son. I think "You better off a grocer than a stickman, for that what you are." Out loud I tell him a pity he don't go back and help he father 'stead of hangin' aroun' here doin' nothin'. "They nothin' for you here," that what I tell him. I tell you Julie, they nothin' here but trouble and more trouble. You can't get no job or no decent place to live 'less you practically a millionaire. The children can't get a decent education where they learn. The teacher don't control them, they parent don't control them, they go wild. Here in London, I tell Raymond, no matter how you try, they catch you every way. They drive the heart and soul out of you. Here all you got is temptation. Ah, that remind me,' she said, 'that you John he go out yesterday and not been home since. "Where you goin' to?" I ask him. He say to me, his own grandmother, "Min' you business, there." I say, "I shock at you talking to you own grandmother in this way. I responsible to Julie, I should know where you goin' and who with," that what I tell him.'

'That's right,' said Julie. 'What did he do then?'

'I tell you what he do,' her mother said angrily. 'He say nothin'. He jus' go right outside the door and he bang it when he leave. Like I say, it not you fault Julie, how he is. It the place and the time. Everythin' against

154

you. You frien' Leona, she gone down to fin' him. Now then, you want some tea or coffee? You been workin' – you tire'.'

'That's right, Ma,' said Julie, standing up wearily. 'I'll get it.'

'No,' said her mother, pushing her back in the chair. 'I sorry to be talkin' on like this when you tire'. I make the coffee.' She went out into the small kitchen and went on speaking. 'No – I had a good time here, and it very generous and kind to send that fare. Cynthia she feel the same and even Sally please' though that baby she takin' all the life from her. They gone to see Buckingham Palace jus' now. It been a real pleasure to see you, and Thomas and John and the Tower of London and the TV and everythin'. I jus' saying' life here is hard for a family, and for a family with no father it worse somehow. You doin' well, though, gal, and we all proud of you. When I saw you at the big party on TV las' night I had tears in my eyes and runnin' down my face.'

'Good party we had on Christmas Day, though, Ma?' said Julie. 'I thought I'd never stop laughing when that boy came through the door with his long white beard, playing that drum, eh? Oh man, that was funny.'

'Good party,' agreed her mother. 'But I got to say I don't trust that Raymond Genevieve. But I suppose in you work you have to be friendly to all kind of people.'

'That's it, Ma,' Julie agreed hastily as her mother came in with the coffee. Her mother shot her a look. Julie said, 'What time did Leona go out?'

''Bout an hour ago,' said her mother. 'Thomas, will you turn down that TV, it deafenin' my ear.'

'I might get this new recording contract,' said Julie. 'If I do, I'm getting out of here, away from the action.

155

John's just fourteen – too young for all this.'

'This a nice flat,' said her mother, 'with a porter and everythin'. And I don't know there anywhere far enough away in this town for a black boy to keep out of trouble if he want to find it. He need a father to whip him.'

'Not over here,' said Julie.

'In Barbados, the father word, it law,' said her mother firmly.

'No law here,' said Julie.

'I been thinkin','' said Mrs St Just.

Julie flinched and said, 'No, Ma. No thinkin' please.'

'You hear me now, Julie,' her mother said. 'I right. You want me to take John back home with me when I go. He can come and live with me and his Uncle Peter, nice and easy. We won't be hard on him if he don't behave like we used to. But we make sure he go to school and learn somethin' and mix with decent friends we know.' Julie looked at her. Mrs St Just continued, 'It better, Julie. You know that. You got money, you can choose, not like the others. He can come back when he sixteen, seventeen year old, old enough to know what he doin'. The dangerous year he spend with me and Peter in Barbados. We love to have him.'

'It hard, Ma,' said Julie.

'Life hard, Julie,' said her mother. 'It best for the boy. You never regret it.'

The door opened with a crash, and Leona came in with a sulky boy, nearly six feet tall, beside her.

'I won't tell you where I find this boy or what is he doing when I find him,' the girl cried out. She was in her twenties and very thin. 'I won't tell, John St Just, because I don't want your mother and your grandmother to know because you so 'shamed you begged me not to say. At fourteen years of age. I don't believe it.' She shook him. 'You end up in prison if you go on this way. You know what that like – no light, no air, no fun, no music, just pushed around by people all day and all night. Sitting in a cell talking about Africa with your friends – you'll never see no Africa from the inside of a home for young offenders. You got us to thank you not there already.'

''Raas, man,' protested the boy. 'Lay off me. I done practically nothin'. I just go out to see some friends. What I suppose' to do – sit at home and watch TV all day long with Thomas? I got to go back to school next week. This is the holidays.'

'Where was he?' Julie asked Leona.

'Where you think – down a club in Railton Road, smokin' ganga with a crowd of big men and that not all,' said her friend. 'He didn't look like no schoolboy, I tell you that.'

Julie looked at her mother and then at John who stood there trying to look cool. 'You not going back to any school, boy,' she said, in a broad West Indian accent. 'You goin' back home.'

A big row followed this bit of news. Julie's aunt Cynthia, cousin Sally and the baby arrived not long after and were followed by, in rapid succession, Julie's agent, the drummer from her backing band, and the shifty Raymond Genevieve, who all joined in. This enabled the white neighbours in the smart block of flats in Streatham, delightedly, to call the police.

At this moment Elizabeth Lord was in her large Surrey garden, digging a hole by the Brussels sprouts. A dead marmalade cat lay on the garden path beside the hole.

'Why did Tomkins have to die, Mummy?' asked Elizabeth's daughter Amelia, for the ninth time.

'He took some turkey bones out of the dustbin and choked on one, you know that, darling,' said her mother patiently. 'I know it's sad, but he's dead and now we must give him a decent burial in his own garden. It's all we can do for him.'

Amelia sniffed. Her brother asked, 'Where's Daddy?'

'I told you, Roger, he's at the office,' said Elizabeth. 'A crisis happened in a foreign country. He had to cut his holiday short to go and help. And you know we can't keep Tomkins in the garden shed any longer. We have to bury him now, in daylight.' Some snowflakes fell on her glove as she dug. 'I'm sure Mrs Douglas will be pleased to let us have one of Tomkins' daughter's kittens, when they're born. One of them might look like Tomkins himself.'

'It wouldn't *be* Tomkins, though,' said Amelia.

'It might be nearly Tomkins,' said her brother, adding, 'Tomkins was just exactly the same age as me.'

'That's right,' said Elizabeth. 'Now, I'm going to put Tomkins in this hole and then put the earth over him. You don't have to look, but usually it's better if you do. When I was seven they took my old dog, Timmy, away and had him put down. He was ill. But because I never really saw what happened to him, I was never sure whether he was really dead or not. I used to go to bed every night and pretend he was alive and he'd be there in the morning. But another part of me knew he was really dead. So I think it's better to know the truth. Is anybody going inside?'

The children stood and stared at the hole in the ground, shaking their heads. 'Here goes, then,' said Elizabeth and, holding her breath, picked up the stiff body of the large marmalade cat and put it in its grave. The hole was too small. 'Damn,' she said, and pulled the cat out again, saying, in a practical voice, 'I'll have to make the hole bigger.' She glanced at the children. They were pale, but staunch. She brushed away a tear and, full of grief and horror, took ten more spadefuls out of the earth until the grave was large enough to take, she thought, the body of a labrador. Then she picked up the cat's body again and put it in. 'Right,' she said briskly. 'Now I'll put the earth in on top of him.' She flinched as clods of earth fell on the dead cat's face. Amelia and Roger clutched each other's hands. Elizabeth shovelled on until there was no more fur to be seen. Finally she patted the earth down on the little mound and, wiping her eyes, said, 'Now, as soon as I've put the spade away, we'll get straight in the car and go to see the new robot film. After that we're going to MacDonald's for a hamburger.'

She led the way down the garden path. 'Mummy,' said Amelia's voice from behind her, 'what's the oldest a cat's ever lived to?'

'I don't know,' said Elizabeth. 'You'll have to look it up in *The Guinness Book of Records* when we get home.'

It was hardly surprising after these Christmas cele-brations that later in the evening all the women drifted into the Hope Club. A sprinkling of women round the room indicated that the festival was wearing thin for others too. Elizabeth arrived first and sat down at the bar. She ordered a brandy from Mrs Knott's daughter, a drama student who was helping out until the barwoman came back. She drank that and ordered another. She was due to meet her husband, detained at the Foreign Office, for a late dinner at ten-thirty. She was sipping this second drink when Margaret came in, looking wearier by far than she ever did after a day in court.

She sat down, wordlessly, beside Elizabeth, who ordered her a double whisky without speaking. Her resolution had returned after yet another dinner with her husband, her lover and her mother-in-law. There had been tension at the table, and voices had been raised in the kitchen where the new nurse and the housekeeper were having their first engagement. She decided to spend the night with an old friend and go straight to work at Lincoln's Inn in the morning. Someone after all would have to pay for all the broken crockery. 'So much for your controlled Christmas,' Elizabeth remarked, not without satisfaction.

'Whether you win or lose, you've still got to try,' said Margaret grimly.

'Hullo, everybody,' said Julie from behind them. 'You both look relaxed after your holiday.'

'You too,' said Elizabeth. 'You may think I can't see dark shadows under your eyes, but I can spot them now I know your face so well.'

In fact, Julie had been obliged to leave the row in full swing to go and sing at a club. By that time it had begun to cool off, particularly after the police had come and gone. Leona had told Julie she would leave for good if John went to Barbados and Raymond Genevieve had come back from the off-licence with several bottles of champagne paid for by Julie. They all had a drink, relaxed, and it looked now as if John would stay in Streatham but change his school, and his habits, or be shipped off to Barbados. Nevertheless, Julie had given a bad performance at the club that night.

They were all talking when the door of the clubroom opened with a bang and Hannie Richards came in. She was wearing a long purple dress, muddy at the hem and torn at the shoulder. Her boots were covered in mud, her hair was rough and tangled; she wore no coat. She was very drunk.

Margaret got up. 'What's happened?' she asked and caught Hannie just as she swayed and half-collapsed. Elizabeth got the key to the new building from the back of the bar and opened up the double doors between the long room they were in and the new writing room. Hannie straightened up. 'I can walk by myself,' she said.

'Could you bring in some coffee?' Julie asked Mrs Knott's daughter.

'Pull up that chair by the wall,' said Margaret as Hannie swayed into the middle of the freshly painted room. 'Put a match to the fire, it's freezing. Hannie, sit here. What's happened? Have you been attacked?'

'That's quite right,' said Hannie in a slurred voice. 'That's true – I have been attacked.'

'What happened? Who did it?' asked Margaret.

But Julie shook her head. 'She doesn't mean what you mean,' she said.

'Flora and Fran can catch as they can and what will poor Robin do then, poor thing,' Hannie said clearly.

'Where have you been?' asked Margaret.

'I'm all right,' Hannie said. 'I'm quite all right. Don't worry. Just leave me alone.' She was shivering. Elizabeth went out and got her fur coat and covered her. She brought the coffee back with her. By now Hannie, lying back in the narrow chair, seemed to be asleep. She was very pale and had a bad cut over one eye. The blood had dried. Hannie groaned and said, 'I don't believe it. Is there a phone in this room? I must find a phone.' She started to struggle up. 'Must get the phone,' she repeated.

Julie pushed her down. 'The lead's too short from the bar,' she told her. 'You can phone later.'

161

To Elizabeth she said, in a mutter, 'That phone's just adrenalin – she doesn't need it – it'll make it worse.'

Elizabeth went up to Hannie with a tray and poured out some coffee. She handed her the cup and said, 'Drink this, Hannie. Then you can tell us who did this to you.'

'I thought Hannie was in the country with Adam and the children,' Margaret said.

Julie shrugged.

'I'm going to get an electric fire,' said Margaret. Meanwhile Hannie, like a cunning junkie, sat up in the chair with her coffee cup. Then she rose, the fur coat slipping to the floor and, walking carefully to the door, said, 'I'll be back. Just got a call to make.' She tried to open the doors leading to the bar. The coffee cup went sideways and the coffee spilt on the carpet.

'Sit down, Hannie,' said Julie. 'I'll get the phone.'

When she came back with the phone, Margaret was on her knees plugging in the electric fire. Julie put the phone in Hannie's lap. 'There you are,' she said. 'Make that call but don't blame me for what happens.' She turned to Margaret and Elizabeth. 'You two have got to go. You've got dates. I can wait here with Hannie. I can wait all night if I have to. My home will be calm in the morning. This is one woman's job, and I'm the woman. Hannie didn't get assaulted. Not that way. She's just been in some rough places, that's all. The thing is, why?'

Margaret said, 'What do you think?'

'I don't know,' Julie replied. 'What I have to do is try to stop her from making bad worse. You two go.'

Margaret scribbled two numbers on a piece of paper and said, 'Here you are – 'phone any time.'

Elizabeth pulled on her coat. 'All right,' she said, 'but

162

don't forget that there's a doctor in the house if you need one. Judy Brown's staying here overnight.'

'Before you go, ask Judy if she can give me a couple of powerful sleeping pills,' said Julie. 'That'll help a lot. I have to lay her out.' She nodded at Hannie. Hannie was holding the receiver of the telephone to her ear. She flung it down and pushed the phone off her lap. It fell on the carpet with a clang.

'All right,' said Elizabeth.

'And give me my coat, will you? It's the yellow one,' said Julie. She looked at Hannie, who was on her feet again. 'Oh, my,' she said, 'the times I been here. Sit down, Hannie!' she said. 'You ain't goin' nowhere. Get going,' she said to the other two. 'Just the coat and the pills, OK?' She went over to Hannie and said, 'Hannie, you're tired. Rest now. You can do what you have to do in the morning. It's late now.'

'I must go now,' said Hannie.

Julie forced her back into the chair. 'You can't drive in that condition,' she said.

'I'll get a cab,' Hannie said promptly.

'You made two long-distance calls,' said Julie. 'You were ringing Devon. You can't drive, and there are no more trains now.'

'I'll hire a car,' Hannie insisted.

'You'll get there at dawn, out of your skull,' Julie said. Hannie dropped on the floor, turned the telephone over and started dialling again.

'They won't answer this time, like they didn't the last time,' Julie told her.

'They're there,' Hannie told her desperately.

'Of course they're there,' said Julie. 'Only they won't answer. You rang too often before. You need some rest. Ring again in the morning. Go then.'

There was a long silence. Julie studied the pale face, the tangled hair and the bedraggled purple dress. Hannie looked back at her. She put the phone down and said, 'OK.'

'Want to go to bed?' asked Julie.

'I couldn't sleep,' said Hannie. The door opened and Elizabeth looked round. She handed the coat and an envelope to Julie and said, 'All right?'

'I don't know,' said Julie.

She tucked the envelope containing the sleeping pills into her pocket and said to Hannie as she walked back, 'I suppose the old man finally found himself another girl.' Hannie looked at her and nodded. Julie sat down in front of the fire. 'I'd like to say I'm surprised,' she said. 'Trouble is, I'm not.'

'That's what they all say,' Hannie said bitterly. 'You can't fucking win, can you? Why not?' she cried out. 'Why not? Why not – that's what I'm asking. Why can't you win? Why do you have to choose between life and men every fucking time? Why do they want everything? Why do they want to eat your life?'

'Don't know,' said Julie. 'Who's the woman?'

'Who do you bloody think?' asked Hannie. 'The girl next door, that's who. Victoria Hughes-Brown, aged twenty-eight, celebrated show jumper, housekeeper at Lanning Hall for her widowed father and dear old friend of the Richards family since the year dot. Sam Hughes-Brown's father and Adam's grandfather fought side by side at Mons. Adam remembers Victoria's christening. She was at Flo and Fran's christening. Good old Victoria,' Hannie said viciously, 'quite a figure in the county because of the show-jumping successes, works part-time at the local library, and her hobbies are helping out with the Brownie pack and knocking off the

164

neighbours' husbands. They very kindly didn't tell me until after Christmas – mustn't ruin Hannie's Christmas – but fucking Adam couldn't wait until I'd drunk my early morning tea on Boxing Day morning to tell me his little bit of news. My God, he was pleased. He looked like a dog with two tails.'

'What did you do?'

'Slung the lot at him – cup, saucer, milk jug,' teapot. Hit him three times out of four, got up, packed and got out,' Hannie said.

'So he's not the guy who tore the dress and brought up the bruises?' asked Julie.

'No,' Hannie told her. 'That was a later port of call.'

'I heard from friends you were at some clubs,' Julie said. 'But I said it wasn't you. I thought you were in the country.'

'You bet I was in some clubs,' Hannie declared.

'That help?' said Julie.

Hannie smiled and shook her head. She got up, walking quite steadily and went into the bar. She came back with a whisky bottle and two glasses. 'Want some?' she said. Julie nodded. Hannie handed her the glass. Julie went into the bar for a jug of water. She held it out to Hannie, who shook her head. She took a big gulp of neat whisky.

'Take it easy, Hannie,' said Julie.

'I took it easy,' said Hannie. 'I took it easy after I came back from Africa. And while I took it easy, like a stupid turd, thinking everything was all right – me, Hannie Richards, international smuggler extraordinaire – all this was going on under my nose between my husband and the lovely, well-bred Victoria Hughes-Brown – the funny phone calls, the peculiar disappearances. All the apparatus. All the usual. "I love you, but we must separate. She is, after all, my wife and the mother of my children." "Darling – I can't bear to lose you." "It's only fair to her to tell her as soon as possible." Like turning on the radio, and it's a play on BBC 4. Sounds of wind rising, horses' hooves on the turf – "We can't go on meeting like this, Victoria." Can you imagine it – the crumminess? And I never suspected a thing. Self-indulgent, fucking sods' – Hannie finished her whisky and poured herself some more – 'conducting their little deals in tweeds under the immemorial fucking oaks of their two fucking side-by-side estates. What do they know, the bastards? Suddenly it's love – the big L – an event, something happened, wow, amazing. What do they know, the sods? Sod all.'

Suddenly the phone rang beside her. She snatched it up, said, 'Hullo' in an eager voice. Then she said, 'Hullo, Margaret. I'm OK, thanks. Thanks – no – I'm all right. OK. Talk to you tomorrow.' She put the phone down. Her face was like a mask. Julie looked at her in despair. She was too strong, that was the problem. She couldn't collapse. She must have been days without sleep already. She would go on, and on and on, even though her best hope was to collapse, fall apart and start thinking. Now she said, 'So that's it. They have their big scene and tell me to bugger off. What about my children?'

'They can't tell you to do anything,' Julie said. 'Stand and fight.'

'I can't,' moaned Hannie. 'I can't do things like that.'

'Well, what will you do when you go there?' asked Julie. 'What do you want?'

'I want Adam to boot her out, tell me it was all a

mistake, say he loves me. That's what I want. It's all I can stand.'

'A lot of women would never have left,' said Julie.

'A lot wouldn't go back,' said Hannie grimly. 'Some would go back with a machine gun under their arms. I'm just a sentimental soul – all I want is what I had before. Given freely. I'm not fighting for Adam as if he was the last crust of bread in a concentration camp.'

'I don't know where you been all your life,' remarked Julie.

'You know where I've been, Julie,' said Hannie. 'All over the place, fighting.'

'Well – now you came back from the war, and there's another man's hat on the peg when you come in with your kitbag.' There was a pause.

Hannie said, 'It must have been like being married to a commando. What did it was the summer – he asked me to stay at home and have another child. I said not yet. In a year or two, I said, when I'd done a few more jobs, built up a reserve of cash. Like a gangster film, isn't it? The wife pleads with her husband to give up the game, and he says, "One more job, just one more. It'll set us up for life."'

'It's not natural – the woman going off into danger while the man stays home to mind the kids,' Julie said.

'No, Julie,' said Hannie. 'It's not natural unless it's convenient – then it's somehow right and proper. Adam always said it was all right by him if that was what I wanted. Then when the mortgage is paid off on the old family home, the farm's better equipped and better paying and there's a small reserve at the bank, the orders change. It's "Let's get down to the real business of life, and you stay home and bear a child" – no more plane tickets, scamming around the world – what's wanted now is a son to carry on the family name – this is serious. A son! I could have had five more daughters, one after the other. But orders are orders. First it's risk your neck for the firm, then it's give up this sordid business you've been engaged in, somehow without my knowledge, and become a proper woman. And let me tell you this,' Hannie said, 'it'll go on. There'll be more women keeping blokes from now on and getting wrong-footed the whole time because of it. Look at you – who stands out in front of the audience, who handles the agent, the record company and all that? And who stands around in a sharp suit looking cool and spending the money?'

'Name of Genevieve,' said Julie. 'But I'll say one thing for Raymond – you can see what he is. He's not trying to look respectable as well.'

Hannie shook her head wildly, trying to clear her brain, trying to shake away the thoughts. She said, 'I can't stand this. I can't stand it.' Then she said, 'I know what you're thinking. I know I've slept around like a salesman while I've been away. Now I come back and scream because Adam's done what I did. But it's different, what I did, Julie. What I do is different. I didn't damage anything. He's broken everything – everything. The whole thing.'

'That's what all the guys say, Hannie, when it happens,' murmured Julie. But Hannie was not listening.

Julie watched her as she dialled the number again. This time the telephone was answered. A woman's voice spoke sharply. It went on. Hannie grew even paler. She said, 'Vict –' and the receiver buzzed in her hand. 'She put the phone down. She told me I was disturbing them in the middle of the night – not to call again.'

168

'What's the number?' cried Julie. 'I'll tell her something. I'll come with you tomorrow and take her out. She'll find out not to mess with you.'

Hannie shook her head again, blurrily. She said, 'No, I'll do what she says. I won't call again. I'll leave.'

'You are mad,' said Julie emphatically. 'You take these –' and she held out the sleeping pills. 'Get some sleep. We'll talk in the morning. I'll come with you and sort out that bitch. She won't like me – I'm black, I'm nasty – we'll get it all straightened out, Hannie, I'm telling you, but,' and she held out the pills again, 'you must take these. Please, Hannie. Do it.'

Hannie took the pills and swallowed them. There were tears on her cheeks. She said, 'She talks to me like that. Adam lets her. They have my children there as hostages. What can I do? What can I do?'

Julie got her to her feet and hauled her into the next room, where she laid her on the sofa and covered her with the coat. Hannie went on crying. She sobbed, 'I tried. I tried. I only wanted a life away from the rain and the jam-making. Just something that would get money and so I wouldn't feel trapped. It just happened as it did. I would have stopped. I would have. It was the children's school fees. It was the sodding roof. My mother's in a private clinic with a bad back. Oh God, what a price to have to pay. What a price. It's ridiculous. I've been hauling round the world on my nerves for years and, now I look, I've been committing crime after crime to pay for shoes and clinics and roofs and ponies with dodgy fetlocks and sheep with foot-rot and now look, because I did it my husband's left me for the back end of a show-jumper, and he's got the children and I have nowhere to take them if I had them, and she won't even let me talk to them – she keeps on saying they're out, but they're not out. I can hear them. I heard Flo say, "Is that Mummy?" Oh, God, Julie, what am I going to do?' she cried.

And Julie, knuckling her weary eyes, said, 'It'll work out, Hannie' – and saw that Hannie was, suddenly and mysteriously, asleep on her sofa. Julie sat down in a chair thinking, She'll sleep for fourteen hours.

But it was early next morning when Julie awoke with a start. The lights were still burning, the fire was embers. Hannie was standing by the bar, and talking on the telephone. 'I'll be in Suffolk by midday. Thank you.'

Still half-stunned with sleep, Julie raised her head and mumbled, 'Hannie – what you doin'?'

'Fixed myself up with a job,' said Hannie. 'I just left a message on their answering machine to say I'm going down to check it out – got to keep on going, Julie.' Her voice was brisk and monotonous, as if it were being produced by a machine. That iron constitution again, Julie thought wearily, and that ability to keep on moving, no matter what. All the things which had kept her going as a successful smuggler were now operating against her. She had thrown off the effects of those two pills as if they were aspirin.

'You're making a big mistake,' Julie said. 'You're speeding. You're not responsible, you're going to get it all wrong. I know. We both know. This isn't brave. It's stupid.'

'I'm going to have a bath,' said Hannie. She turned in the doorway and said, in the same flat tone, 'I need the money, Julie.'

Julie hauled herself up and went to the door, yelling after Hannie, as she went up the stairs, 'Hannie! You don't need the money! That's your stupid excuse. That's not the reason. You're feeding your fucking pride! Let it go, man. Do this the ordinary way, like an ordinary person. Let go, Hannie; I'm going to stop you doing this!'

But Hannie Richards went round the bend in the stairs without a word or a sign to her friend. Julie, in a rage, hit her head on the doorpost, saying under her breath, 'Stupid – stupid –.' Then she went quickly to the bar and rang Margaret Wilkinson at Lincoln's Inn. The clerk told her Margaret was *en route*. Julie asked her to come straight to the Hope Club. She needed help. She decided not to ring Elizabeth, who was too far away to arrive in time.

Then she went downstairs and made some coffee, standing in the huge, empty kitchen surrounded by fridges and freezers and long shelves holding ranks of big aluminium saucepans.

Ten minutes later Hannie rushed in, still wearing the torn purple dress. In her hand she carried her boots. She started to wash off the mud, splashing the immaculate stainless steel sink, piling up soggy kitchen towels on the draining board.

'Have some coffee,' said Julie.

'In a minute,' said Hannie. 'I'll have to stop off on the way and buy some clothes, and a coat.'

'Shut up,' said Julie. 'You don't have to do this. Your judgement's right out. You're going to blow it. I've seen this before – I've done it. People in this state make mistakes. You'll get the wrong deal. You're trying to leave for a world where Adam hasn't got a new girl and nothing's happened. You can't do it.'

Hannie turned on her. 'Shut up!' she said. 'Just shut up, Julie! I don't care! I'm telling you I don't care. I'm going to take this job – whatever it is. I've got a reason.

The man's a multi-millionaire, and he's desperate about something, and when I find out what it is, I'm going to drive the price sky high. And why? Because I'm coming back rich, with enough money to set the girls and myself up properly. I'm going to claim my children from that bastard. He's ponced my earnings off me all these years – and now you think I should stay at home and mourn and fuck about with divorce settlements? I'm going to do it my way.'

'Yeah – the hysterical way,' shouted Julie. 'All I'm saying is, stop. Think. Decide later.'

'This is no time for thinking,' said Hannie, wrenching on a boot in the middle of the floor. 'This is time for doing.' And she pulled on the other boot.

'Hannie, it could be dangerous. You need your judgement,' Julie cried. She barred the door with her arm as Hannie tried to race through. Hannie pushed the arm away.

'Come back!' shouted Julie and heard Hannie's steps go through the restaurant, heard another door bang and then another. She smacked her hand against her head and stood in the silent kitchen, thinking, This looks a bad one, a really bad one this time.

Not long after, when Margaret arrived, she said, 'Sorry, I couldn't stop her.'

'Don't blame yourself,' said Margaret. 'I don't suppose anyone could have stopped her.' She added, 'Just prepare to pick up the pieces, that's all.'

Hannie stopped on her journey to buy herself a conventional skirt, jacket and jersey. She drove fast but carefully to Suffolk. She was conscious all the way that her brain seemed to have split into several parts, all doing different things. One part controlled the car, followed the traffic signs, even consulted the road map. The other seemed to be making calculations about what to do when she came back from her next job, whether it was this one or another. There would be a divorce, moves, money to be found and arrangements to be made. Another part of her head, compulsively, imagined Adam and Victoria and her children together. At other times she played over scenes of the past, finding all the clues that should have led her to know this was going to happen. A good part of her simply screamed, screamed with rage and pain, so loudly that from time to time she thought she could hear it echoing in the car. Sometimes she thought none of this had happened. Sometimes she thought she would be able, somehow, to recover what she had lost.

She drove on with concentration, understanding dimly that she was not thinking in an ordinary way but believing she was sufficiently in control to function normally.

In this state she arrived at the large gateway to Thrickston Manor, in Suffolk. The massive wrought-iron gates were firmly shut. Getting out of her car, she said into the speaker attached to the right-hand gate, 'It's Mrs Richards,' she said. 'I've come to see Sir Duncan Kyte.'

A security guard came out of a lodge on the other side of the gate. 'I'm afraid you have to leave your car outside, Mrs Richards,' he said through the bars.

'But that drive must be at least a quarter of a mile long,' she told him, pointing to the tree-lined avenue behind him.

'I shall be taking you in my vehicle,' he said. 'Would you park your car in that space over there . . .'

'Sir Duncan is obviously very security-conscious,' she remarked conversationally to the guard as they drove to the house. His coat was unbuttoned and he made no attempt to conceal the leather strap over his shirt which obviously supported a holster near his armpit.

'Better safe than sorry,' he told her.

'That's a fact,' she said. She did not like this surly guard. Ordinarily she would have treated the man as a clue. Ordinarily she studied the servant to find out what the master was like. But she was worn out and using too much energy to block off the thought of what had happened to her. The brain that is saying loudly to itself, 'Forget; it never happened,' is not alert, is not taking in the stray impressions which, in a trade like Hannie's, are often crucially important. Thus she discounted her surprise that Sir Duncan Kyte, the noted industrialist, needed a bully-boy to guard his gates. She ignored the gloomy impression made on her by the long, tree-dripping drive and did not particularly worry when two big Dobermans rushed across the lawn and barked viciously at the car as it passed. Her instincts, which she had relied on for so long, had failed. She had not guessed at her husband's discontent before she left for Chad. She had not spotted, when she returned, that he was having a love affair with a neighbour. All this had not only wounded her terribly, it had made her feel foolish and demoralized. And she was tired, seriously tired, but she did not realize that either.

At the front door of the large grey house she was handed over on the steps to a manservant. A glance passed between the two men which Hannie took to be one reassuring the other that she was unarmed and harmless. It must, she thought, be a dangerous world these days for multinational corporation bosses. Like their nineteenth-century equivalents, the Victorian mill and mine owners, facing the starving work-force from the steps of their mansions, these men must go in fear of enraged guerrillas furious at the political distortions created in their own countries by self-interested foreign capitalists. Or possibly maddened patriots angry about favours, like weapons, given to other countries. Sir Duncan must have enemies everywhere – or did he just imagine he had?

When she met him, after a long walk with the manservant through a hall hung with paintings, she decided that whatever else he was, Sir Duncan did not appear paranoid. He sat by a window which looked down over a long lawn to the river below. As Hannie came in he stood up – a tall, thickset man, around sixty, clean-shaven, with a great deal of well-cut grey hair. He was, she thought, not a fraction under six feet four inches, and was dressed in a tweed suit. As he came towards her, his face lighted up in a charming smile. 'My dear,' he said in a gallant tone, 'I've been so looking forward to your arrival.'

'I'm pleased to be here,' Hannie replied quietly. But there were too many large roses in the light, large room and the room itself was too hot. She felt slightly ill. She did not notice at that moment that Duncan Kyte's large, handsome and barely lined face bore, under its fading tan, an alarming pallor. She merely felt uneasy, as if all was not quite as it should be. She remembered that Duncan Kyte had won a VC during the Second World War, at the Normandy landings.

They sat down in two facing chairs by the window. Rain pelted down over the lawn and trees outside. He offered her a drink, and she asked for whisky. He sat looking at her closely, without speaking. He must, she thought, have disconcerted many an opponent that way. She said, 'Sir Duncan, if you're thinking that I look ill and tired, you are right. I've had some personal problems. But you'll have established my credentials, you know I'm reliable.'

He said, 'I have indeed. You're very candid. I'm sorry you have had difficulties, but this is not an easy task I have in mind. Can I take it the problems are over, as far as your work is concerned?'

'They had nothing to do with my work,' she said. 'Once I'm out of the country they won't even exist.'

There was a moment's silence, then he said, 'All right.'

'How did you hear of me?' she asked.

'Through Tom Dean. You helped him to get his family jewellery out of Rio, he told me. He was quite impressed.'

'I can't say it was a hard job,' said Hannie, recalling that all she had done was meet the jewel thief she had hired on a corner, take the package of jewellery and hand him his pay. She had smuggled the gems through in a false-bottomed suitcase, but that had been an unnecessary precaution. The likelihood of the twenty-two-year-old Mrs Dean the fourth reporting the theft was small. She had absconded with her husband's family jewellery, which was meant to be handed on intact from generation to generation, and either would not find out about the counter-theft in time, or would accept the loss philosophically. Hannie added, 'Mrs Dean was just a chancer.'

Kyte nodded. He said, 'What Tom Dean told me was that you were not the sort of person who aroused suspicion.' It was plain he was not prepared to discuss his business yet. Hannie hoped that the lines of fatigue,

176

over-tolerance, a kind of moral exhaustion which can give you away, had not started to appear on her face. She knew all that was in her brain, all right. But she needed this job badly.

They followed the manservant into a small dining room where oriental-style latticed windows hid the grey view from the diners. The table was set for three, but it was not until Hannie and Sir Duncan had finished their soup and begun on some veal cutlets that they were joined by a wispy girl in a blue kaftan. On her feet she wore sandals. Her blonde hair was frizzed out in a style reminiscent of some years earlier. This was obviously her at-home style, but it looked as if she had a strong attachment to the days of flower power or the *art nouveau* heroine. Hannie could not make up her mind if the girl was his daughter or his mistress. Whichever she was, a lot of Kyte's money was snorted up her *retroussé* nose and showed in her big, wandering blue eyes.

'Serena, did you have a good rest?' he enquired.

The girl nodded vaguely. She was shooing away the maid, who was trying to put a cutlet in front of her. Duncan Kyte was angry. 'It's about time someone in this household remembered – will you please go and grill some plaice,' he demanded. Serena, it turned out, was a vegetarian. The meal, fairly quiet till then, now became completely silent. Sir Duncan watched Serena. Hannie, who had never been able to understand the habit of leaving vital matters undiscussed until meals were over, became impatient. The topic hung across the table like a cloud of cigar smoke. At this point Serena complained about finding bones in her plaice. Kyte, fussing again, had it removed. Hannie decided Serena must be the girlfriend, not the daughter. In her experience even the most tender parent had no time for complaints about

177

fishbones. She was back on the subject she was trying to evade. When Serena began to give her lingering looks, she returned them, purely to take her mind off the subject of her children. Kyte, a stranger to these ways, saw nothing. Oh, is it worth it, thought Hannie, making eyes at Duncan Kyte's freaky girlfriend? Was anything worth it? Why didn't she get up and go away? Something was wrong here. She stared at her plate, feeling herself sliding down and down into the ashpit of depression she was trying to avoid. Pull yourself together, Hannie Richards, she told herself. You've got a living to earn.

'Do you know Kev Coleman?' Serena suddenly asked. Hannie looked up. Cocaine Sue here was no fool in her rodent-like way. Hannie said, 'I've met him,' in a neutral tone. Kevin Coleman, still in his twenties, was the vicious boss of a gang of vicious East End villains. If this girl had come within a mile's radius of Kevin Coleman and was also Kyte's girlfriend, then he, Kyte, was in trouble. No successful businessman, friend of banker and cabinet minister, an ex-son-in-law of a duke's brother and a man generally on nodding terms with the better end of the royal family could afford to have around anybody, man, woman or child, who even knew Kevin Coleman's name. This one not only knew his name but his address and telephone number as well. She even guessed why – Coleman had interests in pornographic video films, and Serena had the air of being a star from that stable. A child star, probably, Hannie thought gloomily. All she said was, 'He asked me to do a job for him once, but I didn't like the sound of it.'

Serena had left most of the second plaice. Hannie, still suffering as she thought from the days of excess, refused a dessert.

Sir Duncan stood up and said to Serena, 'We'll have coffee and a chat in the library.'

Serena nodded, helping herself to another portion of chocolate mousse. Hannie stood up. She went to the lavatory near the hall and was sick. She washed her face and hands and went to the library. On the way she passed the dining room and through the open door saw Serena, her blonde head well down over her plate, passionately shovelling in chocolate mousse.

In the library, where huge windows looked down towards the river, the manservant poured coffee and brandy. Hannie took both, hoping something would make her feel better. Sir Duncan said, 'Tell me what you think of Serena.' All Hannie thought was that if she spent too much longer in this house she might go mad. She also still felt sick. She would give the situation half an hour and then, job or no job, money or no money, she would leave. Her instincts were muddled, her head was unclear, but her body was sending plain enough messages.

She asked cautiously, 'Who is she, actually – Serena?'

'My girlfriend, obviously,' he said.

Hannie took a deep breath and said, 'I think that she might be dangerous for a man in your position. She may have awkward involvements and unpredictable friends – I hope you don't mind my saying so.'

'Not at all,' said Kyte. 'I thought you might say that. To a man like me the Serenas of this world are often fatal.' He paused for a long time. Then he said, 'They have undesirable friends collected during a past which hardly bears thinking about. They have bad habits and no standards worth mentioning. They would wrench the gold teeth from a dying man and think nothing of it afterwards. Unfortunately, their vicious little ways are appealing – irresistible.' The manservant had gone. Kyte walked to the table across the room and poured himself more brandy. As if in a dream, while he walked back and sat down, he said, 'The fact that they make no judgements, have no preconceived ideas about how anything should be makes them – relaxing.'

He seemed very tired. This room, like the others, was hot. Hannie said, 'The snag is that while you're relaxing, sometimes they're not. It's easy to come round and realize you weren't so much being relaxed as hypnotized.'

'You're very intelligent,' said the weary man. 'I suppose it's the fact that they are so weak that makes them so intriguing. Watching their little short-term plots, all those tiny, cunning manœuvres designed to purchase for them a moment's gratification, all those small greeds –' He put his glass on the table beside him and said, 'I'm sorry. This is of no interest to you. I saw the way you looked at Serena. I just wanted to talk about it for a moment. You see, ordinarily, someone like me steers clear of girls like her, with their low-life connections and their habit of gossip – now it doesn't really matter.'

'Why not?' asked Hannie.

'That's why you're here,' he said. 'I'm ill. Very ill. In fact I have cancer.'

Hannie was startled. 'I'm so sorry,' she said finally. There seemed nothing else to say. Of course that explained his pallor, his fatigue, the silent, over-heated rooms, the strange air which hung about the house.

'Is it Interferon you want?'

'Do you think I haven't obtained Interferon in sufficient quantities?' he said. 'You do me an injustice. It doesn't always help. In my case it hasn't. What I want is more difficult to get than that – far more difficult.'

What would that be – God's pardon, or the green eye of the little yellow god, Hannie wondered. All she said was, 'You look tired. Just go straight through it. Be brief, to spare yourself, and be completely frank. I'm utterly silent about these things, whether I take the job or not.'

'I had assured myself of that,' he murmured. 'But it's quite a long story and goes back into the past. I shall have to explain all that first.'

'All right,' said Hannie. 'I'm listening.'

Leaning back in his chair, looking like the sick and weakened man he really was, Duncan Kyte said, 'I have to start with my half-brother, Roderick Kyte. He's a biologist, well, more of a biochemist. He's the child of my father's first marriage. It was a bad marriage. He got out of it to marry my mother. Roderick never forgave my father, or my mother, or me for that matter – always felt his mother had been badly treated and that there was a family vendetta against her. There wasn't, of course. She was just rather a tedious woman who lived in a tedious suburb and never had the sense to make a new life for herself after the divorce. Of course, it can't be denied that I got the benefit of the old man's ever-increasing fortune, but Roderick didn't do too badly either – went up to Cambridge, got a good degree, did research, made a name for himself. Trouble is, wherever I was, there was the action – the good war, the spectacular marriages and so forth – and where old Roderick was there was a noteworthy lack of movement, if you know what I mean. His was the sturdily won scientific reputation, the decent marriage, but unfortunately his wife died – anyway, you can imagine the scenario.'

The scenario, as he described it, seemed to be reviving Duncan Kyte. As he spoke, he sat up straighter. His eyes brightened. Hannie had the idea that the ancient feud with his brother had always been stimulating, especially as he seemed always to have come out the winner. The way he spoke changed too, as he talked about it. He used the language of clubmen.

'About two years ago I got a press cutting, automatically, from my cuttings agency. It was extracts from a paper in a scientific journal by Roderick to do with his researches on various South American plants he'd collected on a trip he took there – about how the Indians in the Mato Grosso used them for contraceptives, insecticides, poisons and so forth. He'd been there in the sixties when the authorities decided to send a team out to collect stuff and generally examine the area before a big road was pushed through and the whole ecological balance changed.' He looked at Hannie. 'Are you with me so far?' he asked.

She nodded, 'I'm ahead of you. I read of the paper in a popular newspaper a few years ago when I was stranded in a snow-bound train. I can remember the headline – CURARE, CONTRACEPTIVES, A CURE FOR CANCER FROM THE JUNGLE. The journalist had done the usual thing – set to produce a story from the scientific papers, he'd gone over the top and said far more than the scientist really claimed. The scientist seems to have said, "Rubbish" when asked to comment. I suppose that was your brother?' Kyte nodded. 'Well,' said Hannie, 'how does the story go on? Did he really have a cancer cure? Is such a thing possible?'

'He'd been working on it,' said Kyte. 'I never saw the article you mention. Obviously there can't have been much to it or the other papers would have taken it up. The article I read was more sober. Roderick said he'd been working on plants collected from the Mato Grosso for twenty years. He'd found a narcotic, a poison and so forth. He mentioned he was hoping to prove that he'd got some results in checking cell damage and, in some cases, in stimulating the actual regeneration of cells. The word cancer was not mentioned, as befitted an article in a sober and reputable journal. Roderick must have been furious when some cheap journalist made that interpretation – it's exactly the sort of thing he'd most dislike. He's jealous of his reputation. Anyway, the main thing is that having glanced at the article, I forgot it. Six months later I found out I was ill and the whole subject became more important to me, as you can imagine. Then I remembered the article all right. On the other hand my relationship with Roderick was not exactly wonderful, so I didn't fancy going to him. I only did that when the operation failed to check the cancer and the Interferon did no good. I even tried a crank macrobiotic diet advised by a Japanese doctor. Well,' said Kyte, a kind of ruined pride in his grey, handsome face, 'after falling into the hands of the cranks, spooks and ghouls, the idea of approaching Roderick seemed less obnoxious. I thought I couldn't be made to feel any worse.' He looked at Hannie. 'Have you got any brothers and sisters?'

'One of each,' said Hannie. 'But we get on fairly well. I remember feeling the worst hatred for them I've ever felt for anybody, though, in childhood. I suppose that feeling can go on.'

'It does,' said Kyte grimly, but Hannie wondered if they were talking about the same thing. 'Those hatreds go deep – very deep. I could not have believed it myself if I hadn't experienced it. I went to see Roderick. I told him what was happening to me. I asked him if he would help. In the end I was almost begging, but he was quite determined. He would not help me. He just refused.'

'Didn't he give you an explanation? Even an excuse?' asked Hannie.

'Oh well,' said Kyte, 'he gave me an explanation. He said they were only just starting experiments on animals. They were by no means certain of the results. I pointed out to him that I was offering myself as a human subject – I had no future anyway. As I say, I begged him. It was no good. He said he didn't care who I was, he would not allow me to have the drug.'

'That must have been a bad blow,' said Hannie.

'No blow is that bad,' said Kyte, 'when you've been around as long as I have. What I intend to do now is secure the substance for myself. I have some papers of my brother's about the process. Unfortunately I was unable to secure the formula – the exact chemical breakdown of the plant he is working on. But I'm told there's enough information there to be going on with. All I need now is the plant.'

'The plant?' said Hannie.

'Well, what did you think I asked you here for?' Kyte demanded. 'I need someone to go to Brazil to get the plant. If you agree, I can get you in on an Anglo-Brazilian field trip to the area Roderick got his plants from. I've been told that with the papers I have of his, and the flowers of this tree he found, I can get the stuff synthesized and into assimilable form in a few weeks. You understand what that means?'

'I'd have thought it a lot easier to break into his laboratory and grab –' said Hannie. Then she realized. 'Oh – you did,' she said. 'Now he's got everything guarded.'

'And an injunction against me,' said Roderick Kyte's brother bitterly. 'The leader of the expedition is a Dr

Peter Davis. His deputy and the head of the botany section is Dr Joe Spinelli. The fee for getting those plants is £100,000.'

Hannie flinched. It was a lot of money for what might turn out to be a fairly easy task. To give herself time to think she said, 'I can't see Joe Spinelli taking me on.'

'I heard he always liked you,' said Sir Duncan. He knew a great deal about her then, thought Hannie. And was not surprised.

'He liked me,' Hannie said, 'as a girlfriend. But not as a scientist.'

'Let's be perfectly frank,' said Kyte. 'There is very little chance of your ever being selected, on the strength of a third class degree in biology, as a member of this team. I have made a very useful donation to the expedition.'

Hannie thought quickly. He must have given the expedition at least as much as he was offering her. That was quite a big stake. But not very much in exchange for his life – not very much to him, that is.

'£100,000 isn't enough,' she said flatly. 'I'd need double.'

Sir Duncan Kyte's face went rigid. He detested her, as the rich will, for wanting his money. It was not so much the bargain he resented as the fact that she was in a position to bargain at all. Hannie knew he needed her. The problem was that men like Kyte will do almost anything rather than be bullied. For almost a quarter of a million pounds he could bribe Joe Spinelli to get the plants for him. Hannie knew that Joe would have done it for five hundred and a pint of beer, but she gambled on the fact that Kyte would not suspect that Spinelli's well-earned scientific reputation was paired with a lack of personal integrity so marked that his nickname for years had been 'Pig' Spinelli. And if Kyte made an offer and was refused, his position would be worse than before. Even at her inflated price she was a better and a safer proposition. Also, Kyte was in a hurry, the biggest hurry a man could be in. As the two of them stared each other in the eye, Serena came in. 'All settled?' she asked.

Kyte, still looking at Hannie, said, 'Yes. All settled.'

'Good,' said Serena. She came in lightly and poured herself a drink. She looked more cheerful than she had at lunch. Hannie, sagging in her chair, thought that whatever Serena had in her bathroom worked wonders on the human spirit. At the back of her mind a voice was saying, 'You got it. You got it. You got the money. You get a fresh start.' She also heard Julie's voice behind her, shouting for her to come back. I'm tired, she thought. I need some rest. I got it, that's all that matters.

Meanwhile the bright-eyed Serena stood behind Duncan Kyte's chair with bare white arms round his neck. She whispered in his ear. A smile crossed his tired face. From behind the chair Serena looked up, gave Hannie a quick smile of complicity, as if congratulating her on joining the gang and getting her share of Kyte's money. Hannie was feeling sick again. She barely heard Kyte saying, 'I propose to pay a third of the money directly to your bank and I'll lodge the remainder in the form of a post-dated cheque at my solicitor's. The expedition leaves in nine days. You could be back in under three weeks. I'll date the deposited cheque for thirty-one days from now. If you are not back, or fail in the mission, I shall cancel the cheque.'

'Fine,' said Hannie. She felt slightly dizzy now and

stood up. 'I'll go back and make some preparations. Thank you for the nice lunch. I'm reasonably hopeful about this – if the plants are there I'll get something, anyway.'

Serena was still whispering to Kyte. He got a peculiar kind of peace from the girl, some kind of release from his fear, perhaps from the burden of his past. In his attitude she suddenly saw something of her own weary gratitude to Adam when she arrived back from her trips. She shrugged off the thought. Kyte looked at her and said, 'Can you do something else while you're *en route*? It's a contract I don't want to put in the mail. Can you deliver it to some associates of mine in New York? That's all – they'll arrange a courier for the return trip.'

'Of course,' said Hannie. He went to the desk, put some papers into an envelope and wrote an address on it. As she took it from him, he gazed at her imploringly. He said, 'You will be quick, won't you?'

'Yes,' said Hannie. 'As fast as I can.'

Already Serena was at Kyte's shoulder, her hand on his arm, her face upturned, seeking to divert his attention from his own fears to herself.

Hannie said goodbye and in the doorway she turned again, seeing the tableau of the girl clutching the sick man.

She was happy to find herself on the steps with the manservant. The wind buffeted her and the rain hit her face. She felt better to be out of the heat of the house. She told the manservant to telephone the lodge that she was coming on foot and walked down the drive under lashing trees, taking deep breaths. By the time she got to the bottom she could hardly believe how ill she had felt.

In the evening she rang her husband from the Hope Club. 'Adam,' she said, 'I thought I'd just tell you – I'm going to South America. I expect to be back in a few weeks.'

He said uncomfortably, 'I expect that's a good idea, Hannie. I hope it goes well for you.'

'Thanks, Adam,' she said. 'Give my love to Flo and Fran, tell them I'll see them soon.'

'Will do,' he said.

There was a pause.

She said, 'We'll have to talk about all this when I get back.'

He said, 'Yes, yes.' He sounded nervous. Nothing else – just nervous.

'Well,' she said, 'goodbye.'

As she put the receiver down, Elizabeth, who had come in quietly without knocking, said, 'What a fool – sorry, Hannie, but you are. You're going away for weeks – they'll just settle in with the children and put up the sandbags.'

'They can do what they like for three weeks,' said Hannie. 'I'll be off earning £200,000. When I come back, I make the terms, that's what.'

'You're entitled –' said Elizabeth.

'To half the house,' agreed Hannie. 'But only if I'm prepared to hang around for a divorce. Then I sell Adam's family home and take away the place my children have grown up in – where their roots are.'

'I ask myself,' said Elizabeth, 'if a woman can afford to be so gentlemanly. Off to shoot tigers, are you? You won't stand and fight for your husband, just like all the other women?'

'No,' said Hannie. 'As a matter of fact, I won't.'

'I wish you would,' said Elizabeth sadly. 'If you go

away now you might lose him for good.'

'I'm not hanging about making him feel guilty with a load of scent behind my ears in case he changes his mind,' Hannie said. At the same time she was heaving herself into a pair of tight leather trousers. 'No, he's in love with her, not me. That's the long and short of it.' She put on a maroon silk shirt, leather top and flung a long, matching silk scarf with a fringe around her neck.

'I'm off to the Hunt Ball, Elizabeth,' she said and left the precincts of the Hope Club for another kind of club in North London. This was dark with flickering strobe lights, and all the clients were women. A women's band played, and the women danced to it. Hannie leaned against the bar, looking round. Through the darkness came a glittering figure in a shiny green-blue dress. The blonde hair on either side of the pale face was frizzed out. Hannie straightened up and kissed the girl on the mouth. 'Serena,' she said, 'I thought you'd make it.' Serena giggled. 'I thought you could do with some fun,' she said, 'before you went off on the big adventure to find a cure for death.'

5. The Adventure to Find a Cure for Death

Breathing was like taking in air from the spout of a boiling kettle when the steam is filled with tiny insects. They should, Hannie thought, be wearing oxygen masks. Something bit her on her already-bitten cheek. She was too tired to raise a hand to hit it. They should also, she reflected, putting one foot after another on the uncertain carpeting of leaves, vines and decaying vegetable matter, be covered in sterile gauze bandages from their toes to the crowns of their heads with little holes just for their eyes. Over those they'd wear goggles, she decided, as another wave of tiny fruit flies hit her eyeballs and made her eyes stream with tears again. Better than that, they should be wearing space suits, with cooling systems. Then she tripped, recovered and put her booted foot into a large mound, from which a string of two-inch ants began to pour. She said to Joe Spinelli, who was walking behind her, 'We should have space suits.'

He said, 'I should have been booked into a mental

home before I left. Don't they call this "The Green Hell"?'

'Depends what paper you take,' Hannie said, 'The *Guardian* calls it the Brazilian bit of the Mato Grosso.'

'Shut up, smart-arse, and check the compass,' said Spinelli.

Hannie checked and found that her usually accurate sense of direction had again betrayed her. It was easy to avoid a vine here and a fallen log there and end up going miles off course. All around were curtains of thick, green vegetation on either side of the narrow, overgrown trail they followed. The high trees met overhead, blotting out the light. Nets of thick vines ran up, down and across. Hannie, hacking at a thick stem of liana which made a trip wire across the trail, said, 'People nurture things like this in England. They get upset if they die.' The stem gave, and she straightened up.

'Want a rest?' asked Joe Spinelli.

'Standing up with sweat pouring off us – no thanks. Let's push on to the *campo*.'

They were only four miles from the base camp, and it was still early morning, but an hour and a half of plodding over stems of vine, cutting back vegetation and stumbling over fallen trees, all in a sauna bath laden with insects, made the day seem farther advanced than it was. The heat was intensifying, even now, although only occasional patches of light came through the tangle of leaves and vines overhead. They went on.

'Space suits would tear,' came Joe's voice from behind her.

'Well, it's an experience,' said Hannie.

'Ain't no more cane on the brazou,' came Joe's wailing song from behind. 'It's all been ground up to molasses –' Hannie bore the singing with fortitude. After all, Joe had taken her presence on the team in good part, even though she was not well enough qualified. He had made it easy for her. As it happened, she had suddenly become useful when his real assistant, incautiously reaching up a tree trunk for a botanical specimen, had disturbed a nest of the notorious Afro-Brazilian bees, which can kill a horse. Dragged away, still indignantly saying that the bees should not have been found in that spot in the first place, he was nevertheless severely stung. She had stepped in to help Joe while Paul was recovering back at the camp, although her hastily boned-up knowledge of Brazilian flora and fauna was not really adequate.

As she went, she looked round and up continually for the flower-bearing tree, the plant she was looking for. According to the rough map in Roderick Kyte's notes – which, she was now sure, must have been obtained by breaking into his laboratory – he had found the original tree some twelve miles from where she and Spinelli were. It had been discovered at this time of year, which helped. The bad news was that there were rumours of an extreme Protestant sect which had bought land near the area involved and was rapidly burning off the jungle to make arable land. There were also tales of a diamond find in the same area. If any of these tales were true it could mean encounters with religious fanatics or even arriving unexpectedly in a diamond boom town full of shanties with a rough air strip and rougher bars. Worse than that, she might meet no one but the Indians each of these groups had antagonized. And they still killed people, she'd learned.

As she looked from side to side, checking for the tree, she felt discouraged. Her reading had not prepared her for the sheer abundance of the vegetation or its variety. Of course, she was sceptical about the efficacy of the plant and always had been. There was something so basically improbable about a cancer-cure found in the jungle that it was hard to take seriously. On the other hand, the basis for the contraceptive pill had been a Mexican cactus, and from Kyte's original scientific paper she knew that he at least claimed to have discovered a narcotic drug, an effective antiseptic and a useful insecticide among the plants he had collected on the same trip.

It was an extraordinary tale he told. He had, waking up in the Indian village which he and another member of the team were staying in, found the village deserted except for the very young and the very old. After a search they discovered every able-bodied Indian from the village in a clearing, tearing purple flowers from two trees and throwing them to the ground. Others dug frantically at the roots of the same tree with their knives. When he tried to find out what they were doing, and why, they had been secretive. He had finally got something out of an old woman. She seemed to be saying that, pounded together, root and flower had some effect on tumours. Of course he had snatched the substance, analysed it and tried the mix in various combinations on experimental animals. At this point, to Hannie's annoyance, the purloined scientific notes gave out.

At this point she rang Duncan Kyte and told him that she had looked at the papers. She had no doubt that if his brother had come up with anything that seemed even halfway promising to the government, the drug firms and the research departments of universities would have given him no peace until he handed over the information. These experiments, she said, had been conducted in the middle of the 1960s. If Roderick Kyte's results had been any good, the papers would not have been standing about for the last fifteen years, and he would not have been experimenting in his own laboratory, and seemingly in his own time, in a small provincial university not renowned for its Department of Biology. She said she thought she would be going to the Mato Grosso on a wild goose chase. But, as she spoke, she knew he would not hear of her turning back. Her main aim had been to cover herself, in case she failed. She really needed the money. Her one worry as she spoke was that Duncan Kyte would die before she got back to England and that would put a stop on the post-dated cheques awaiting her at her solicitor's office.

What she did find out from Roderick Kyte's work was something about the man himself. At the end of a scribbled note suggesting as a working hypothesis that the substance he was using might make cell changes possible by inhibiting or stimulating hormones, possibly in the pituitary, he added, to himself evidently, 'Courage, Kyte. Courage.' At the end of one of the earlier experiments, carelessly conducted when he thought results would come quickly, he was left with what had once been two baby rabbits, which had rapidly grown to the size of Yorkshire terriers and then died. After stating that one had died of an embolism and the other of no cause he could determine, he wrote, 'Evidently these experiments were conducted without the proper earlier procedures being carried out. There will be no more.'

And for a long time there were not. He had worked on the structure of the plant patiently from then on. Experiments had been done on tissue after that, not on living creatures. In the margin of one paper Hannie read, 'We are dealing here with two sets of ignorant people – the Indians, who know nothing, except by trial and error, and the endocrinologists, who know nothing by scientific methods.' Poor, patient, frustrated Roderick Kyte, Hannie thought. He really did not seem like the kind of man who would deny his brother life.

Meanwhile, she and Spinelli lunged on until, suddenly breaking through the humid darkness, they left the forest and found themselves on the edge of a natural clearing of grass and fern. The bright light made them blink. They dropped their rucksacks on the ground and took out the jars for the specimens. In the centre of the clearing Hannie arranged several knives, some heaps of beads and two shirts. They had no way of telling if there were any Indians in the vicinity or what their previous contacts with white people had been like. The gifts were a sign of friendship. The shirts were in sterilized packages. It was easy to infect a whole group with a germ or virus which could kill.

'Come on, Hannie,' shouted Spinelli from the forest edge, 'bring me the pointed trowel.'

She sweated over with it and began to help him dig at a huge yellow mushroom the size of a dinner plate. 'What the hell do you think you're doing?' he said crossly. 'I want it all.' Hannie started patiently digging near the base, thinking that she would have to carry it back undamaged through the forest. 'Get on with it,' he said. 'I want several of these. And I want to hurry – they could go off fast. I wish fucking Paul was on his feet again.'

All right, Joe Spinelli, thought Hannie, but the next time I hear something prowling round my hammock at night I'll assume it's a jaguar and shoot it. He shook his head. Huge blobs of sweat flew off. Hannie's clothes felt like damp towels. He brushed her aside to complete the uprooting. 'Better do this bit myself,' he muttered.

She had loved him wildly for three months, Hannie thought as he eased up the mushroom and handed it to her, saying, 'Wrap it in a bit of polythene and don't damage a hair of its lovely head, or else.' That was in the days when he still had some hair. Suddenly it began to rain, and she laughed. Joe's head was like a billiard ball under a tap. Grey battering water came down. Spinelli straightened up and said, 'Let's get that mushroom under cover, shall we? It could get damaged.' They got under the thick trees, and Spinelli said, 'Nip back for the gifts, Han. Those shirts will get soaked.' So Hannie ran through the downpour and picked up the gifts. Under the trees Spinelli was looking fondly at his mushroom. 'I knew we'd get one if we came out between rains,' he said. 'I've always wanted to come here in the rainy season.'

Hannie, dripping, stared out at the sheets of rain and then glanced back into the green interior. She wondered if there were any Indians about. Some of the groups in this choked forest were even now unknown and unrecorded. They were invisible, moving like spirits through the trees and creepers. There was no sound but the heavy drumming of the rain. A bird shrieked. And yet, she thought, it was no more savage here than parts of New York. Just different.

'Let's eat,' she said. 'If it stops, we can see what comes up after, and how long it takes.'

'I think this one's keeping off the worst of these insects,' said Spinelli. 'Remind me not to tell Paul. I can't stand his homeopathic medicine rubbish.'

They made big pads of leaves to sit on. They dug in

their rucksacks. Spinelli poured coffee from a flask and said, 'A picnic. I keep thinking of you and me, in the lab, in the old days.' He gazed romantically at her. Hannie, blowing a drip from her nose and eating some nuts, remembered just how unsentimental Joe Spinelli was. And neither of them had, at the time, thought much about his wife, stranded outside Cambridge in a small house with two children, where people would drop in to tell her about her husband's affair with his wild, twenty-year-old, red-headed student. They hadn't thought about her, that is, until she'd tried to kill herself. Even then Spinelli had remarked, with his usual humanity, 'Take no notice. She's done it before. She only does it to get attention.'

Meanwhile, he said, pouring himself more coffee from the flask, 'Eh?' He must want some reaction before this evening's prowl round the hammocks, thought Hannie. She said, 'Mm. Fifteen years ago, that was. A lot of water's come down over the Mato Grosso since then.' She was thinking about several things at once, and none of them was Joe Spinelli. She remembered his wife falling down in the court at King's College, lying flagrantly on the lawn on which only fellows of the college were supposed to tread. And she was wondering whether, in the New York jungle, any of the local Indians had got into her hotel room, and if so, why? There had been no signs that anyone had been there, and yet it suddenly occurred to her that she had had the sensation the room had been entered while she was out. What was it? A smell she was not even conscious of, or tiny trackmarks she, like an Indian herself, had noticed without really recording? She had delivered Duncan Kyte's letter to his associate, a well-tanned businessman with an open-air face and executioner's eyes. She had lunched with a former enemy from the CIA. The lunch had turned itself into an afternoon in a cocktail bar and a long evening at a party. She had come back to her room to pack and leave for the airport, and that was the point when she felt, without taking much notice of the thought, that someone had been in the room before her. In the flurry of departure, the flight to Rio, the plane hops and final helicopter trip to the base camp she had not worried about it. Now she was wondering. And all the time came the barely suppressed thoughts of Adam and her children and the shocking fact of the supplanter in her home. She stared at the teeming rain and imagined Victoria bringing home a labrador puppy to make her children's lives complete. She sighed. Joe Spinelli was saying, 'I remember your wedding. You had this big maroon hat on. I wanted to stand up and shout at the registrar. I wanted to call out, "This woman's mine, really. Tell that man to go away."'

'Rain's stopping,' said Hannie. 'We might as well dash out and get another mushroom.'

'Come on, Hannie,' said Spinelli acutely. 'We've all had marriage problems. No need to let it get you down. I never have.'

'How many is it now?' asked Hannie.

'Three,' he told her. 'But there's always room for one more.'

They went back to the spot in the clearing where they had found the mushroom. Spinelli dug up earth and put it into little plastic bags Hannie held out. He dug up another mushroom. Then he started to take more samples of earth and grass. It began to rain heavily again, and when the little bags Hannie held out began to get more water in them than earth or specimens they decided to leave.

Later they were talking at supper time at the long table outside the huts which served as accommodation and work places. It was dark. The generator had failed again, and while it was being repaired they had lamps, which threw pools of light over the bags set on the table. All the biologists were sitting together, including Spinelli's assistant, Paul, whose face was still like a purple cauliflower.

'Shut up, Paul,' said Spinelli. 'I don't want to hear any of your old hippie folk-medicine ideas. We're supposed to be here doing growth cycles, looking at the flora and fauna, not interviewing witch doctors.'

'That mushroom's keeping the insects off, isn't it?' said Paul. 'What are you going to do about it? Ignore it?' It was true that the large mushroom, now lying rotting under the lamp, was deterring the worst of the insects that plagued them. Lower down the table, where it was less effective, plans were being made to grow the mushroom from spore if necessary in order to be free of the constant irritation of bites and stings.

'I say we've lost our own herbalism,' said Spinelli. 'Let's not rush around trying to grab everyone else's. Let's just turn to science and let folk wisdom rot, like that confounded mushroom.'

'We can easily spend ten years developing an insect repellent like that,' said Hannie. 'It's not economical to waste information.'

She was hoping to persuade Spinelli to give a little of the team's time to hunting for therapeutic plants. That way she might get hold of some of the purple flowers Kyte wanted. Her ruse failed. Spinelli burst out, 'Yes, start thinking like that, making a few experiments on the side into interesting phenomena of that kind and you wind up getting obsessed, like poor old Roderick

Kyte. He's spent near on twenty years on his wonder cure, the magic mixture which is supposed to cure cancer, abolish evil and solve the problem of Britain's poor rate of industrial growth. That idiot was a serious scientist once with a solid reputation. Have you ever read the papers he wrote on mosses in the fifties before he came here and became a crank? Did you know he did all the preliminary work on the Hardiman-Baker stuff about that disease in rice which was wiping out harvest after harvest? He'd have made the Royal Society by now, no question about it, if only he'd kept his head down and not spent his life on phoney cancer cures. What did he get? The largest rabbit in the world – and lost his scientific reputation completely. They wouldn't let him sweep up in the Royal Society now. He's wasted his training, his life and from what I hear he's never without some poor dying bugger, pleading for help. All this is a dangerous path to take, Paul, and since I'm in charge of this section and I say what goes, I say you work on the project, the whole project and nothing but the project. If you stray one iota from the brief, if you totter off the trail for a quarter of a second to pick the celebrated Wicki-Wocki headache cure, I'll have you on the 'copter and back in Rio with a bad reference before you can say mumbo-jumbo. I do not want anyone here to discover anything – all they ever find is two undetectable poisons and twenty things which make you high if you chew them, smoke them or stuff them in your ears. The world doesn't need any more poisons or any more narcotics or hallucinogenics. We can manage quite well with what we've got, thanks very much. All this is the Third World's Revenge – we give them VD and typhoid, grab their territory, force them into towns where they hang around getting drunk. They retaliate by handing on their age-old secrets – poisons, dope and the magic plant that drives sane scientists to their ruin. One bud, one stalk, one spore, Paul, with anything like that in mind, and you're out on your ear. That's my final word.'

'You're insane on this subject,' said Paul. 'All I can say is that if you'd spent a week drinking through a straw, in pain all over, you'd be more interested in local cures.'

'The local cure for what you've got,' Spinelli said savagely, 'is not stuffing your hand in a bloody bees' nest in the first place.'

Paul stood up. At first Hannie thought he was going to hit his boss. Then he said, 'I'm going to bed.'

There was a silence. Hannie felt depressed. After Spinelli's tirade there seemed little chance of getting official support for her quest for Kyte's plant. Spinelli muttered, 'It's like El Dorado, that's what it is. Instead of an instant fortune in gold they want an instant scientific reputation. Let's go for a walk.'

'All right,' said Hannie. She stood up. She knew now she would have to go and get the flowers by herself, on the sly. If Spinelli found out what she was doing, she would be sent packing straight away. As they walked in darkness towards the camp's perimeter, towards the curtains of vines, the tall, staggering trees, the sharp points of the thorns, the snakes, she said, 'Joe, even the Indians don't wander about in the forest at night.'

'I just wanted to get you round the back of the water tank,' he said, grasping her by the hand and drawing her along the edge of the forest to the back of the camp. Uncharacteristically, she thought that she had loved him once and perhaps could again. Perhaps Spinelli could take away the sharp pain and anxiety she lived with all the time now that she knew her husband loved another woman and her children were threatened. That was what she thought that night.

In the morning, as she stolidly stumped along the track out of the camp at dawn, she felt confused and unhappy. Sex behind the water tank, on ground which poked and, worse still, actually bit her back was bad enough. But sex anywhere, when you wanted it to give you love, or security, or a brand new life was even worse than that. She, Hannie Richards, had been silly enough to make that mistake. Probably Spinelli had the same idea, she thought, slogging on through the heat, then changing direction onto an even narrower trail. He had probably hoped for something that would make him want to marry for the fourth time. Their joint hopes had been dashed, come to nothing behind the water tank.

And she'd come out worst. Her sweaty back, on which she carried a pack, was still stinging and aching, thanks to the missionary position. After a restless night in her hammock she had thrown back her mosquito netting and got up to go and find the tree. Perhaps, she thought, sweating gloomily in the green sauna of the jungle, it was just another example of what Julie and Elizabeth had, in their different ways, complained about. She would not sit still in hard times, would not accept depression and sadness, would not deal with normal things in a normal way. Sir Walter Raleigh, she knew, had done the same thing in this land of high hopes and bitter endings. He hadn't sat still in the Tower, asking James I for pardon. He'd set off for El Dorado and come back empty-handed, without his son, who had died on the venture, and had been executed anyway. She stumbled, tripped into an ant heap, fell

202

over and rose quickly, dashing scurrying ants from her face and hands. She heard Julie's voice crying out, 'Hannie – you're feeding your fucking pride!' Like Sir Walter Raleigh, she thought, and slogged on. She was obstinately set on walking sixteen miles from base camp, all alone, along a track which might have disappeared, and which, if it were still there, might be open only because Indians were using it. Indians or mad sectarians or possibly diamond hunters. At least she hadn't been completely irresponsible. She had made a note of her direction and departure time in the book under the plastic cover outside the expedition leader's hut. Presumably, if she did not return next day, they would come looking for her or, she thought gloomily, what was left of her.

She bent down and scratched furiously behind her knee, where an insect had crawled between her trouser leg and her boots, or down her neck. There wouldn't be much left, she thought, once the ants got at her. She checked her compass, checked Roderick Kyte's map of the area, hoped his compass bearings were as good as her ability to follow them, and carried on.

Three hours later, because of the meandering trail and the impossibility of making any speed over the tangled vines and through the hanging, often spiky branches on the trail, she straightened up and checked her bearings again. She had come only seven miles as the crow flies. She might have to camp overnight in the jungle. She went on.

She glimpsed a vast red snake, lying over her head along a branch. She hacked continually at the vegetation growing across the trail, made detours to avoid trees which had grown up on it or fallen across it, had often to search for the marks of where it had once been. Each venture into the solid jungle alarmed her. Snakes rustled near her feet. Every leaf she brushed had the power to bite or sting.

She could hear nothing in front of her and nothing behind, only the birds, the odd, weird scream of a monkey, the rustlings and scratchings from either side. She could turn back, but she was determined not to. 'I'll go on,' she thought to herself. 'I'll find that tree. I'll get a bit of root from it, whatever happens. I won't turn back.' She remembered Duncan Kyte's face and the healthy skin with the underlying, wasted look. She remembered the distanced, creepy girl, Serena, whose eyes, even in bed, had the same blank, frightening expression they had had at the lunch table and when she looked up at her employer and lover in the library in Suffolk. They were uncommunicative eyes, eyes that did not respond but instead looked into people to discover their hopes, their fears and their hidden beliefs so that the owner of the eyes could profit by them. Serena was afraid, thought Hannie. She was always afraid. That was why she had to use people. To protect herself. And it was for this little set-up – Kyte, the rich man in his rich house, terrified of death, and Serena, his vampire – that she was sweating through this dark, green place which smelled of vegetation and rot.

Not long after, just as she was thinking she would have to stop soon to rest and eat, she noticed a slight thinning out of the trees and a small increase of light and realized she must be coming to a clearing. There, she thought, she would take a break, out in the reassuring openness. As she pushed through the last of the vines and stared into the blinding light, she saw an Indian village. To the right lay the river, broad and sluggish. In the centre of the encampment stood a long hut. There were other, smaller huts dotted about. A fire smoked in the middle of the clearing, which was about 200 metres wide. But there was no one there. She stood in the shadows of the jungle, knowing that she must have been trailed for many miles by the Indians, moving like ghosts through their own underworld, and that now, as she stood there, feeling alone, she must be watched by many eyes. Even the women and children had been cleared out. They suspected her.

And, across the clearing, on the other fringe of forest, there was the tree, tall and spindly, reaching for the light, dark-leaved and covered with the purple flowers she was seeking. She almost laughed as she stood there, expecting an arrow to hit her, or a body holding a knife to hurl itself at her at any moment. Then, knowing that in doubtful situations unambiguous actions are best, she took a few deep breaths and walked into the centre of the clearing, dropped her pack near the fire, knelt down, unbuckled it and began to take out the gifts. Perhaps greed, or sheer curiosity, would draw the Indians to her. It might hang on whether they had contacted white people before and what those contacts had been like. Just as she was taking out a bundle of knives from the pack, her left arm leaped. Putting the knives on the grass she looked down slowly at the arm. A flightless arrow, just a stick of wood, jutted from the back of the arm, a little above the elbow. She waited, expecting more arrows to follow, or a crowd to come out of the forest behind her. She said to herself, 'Oh, God. Don't let me die here, now.' She saw her children's faces clearly, even Fran's grin and the missing top front tooth. Then, because nothing happened, she twisted her right arm, set her teeth and pulled. The arrow eased slowly out through the flesh. A gush of blood stained her jacket. Some trickled down her arm. She put the bloody arrow carefully on the ground. She thought that it could be poisoned. That would be why no one had emerged and no further arrows had been fired. They would stay under cover, watching her until she dropped.

Then the noise began. It was a gentle clatter, which grew slowly louder. Still on her knees in the grass, she watched a stream of ants heading towards the blood on the arrow in front of her and thought, they're banging on their shields to work themselves up. When the noise gets loud enough, they'll rush me and kill me. She knelt there, breathing shallowly, waiting for the end. The noise increased and increased.

It was only when she saw the grass in front of her rising and swishing to and fro that she realized the noise had become far too loud for the sound of club on shield. Even then it took her some time to work out what it was. Slowly, she looked up and around. The helicopter came low across the river and landed near the bank, not far from the forest edge. The rotation of the propellers stopped. The noise died away. She looked at the purple flowers swinging on the branches of the tree opposite her. Then, slowly, she stood up, clutching the bleeding wound in her arm with her right hand and walked towards the helicopter. As she went the blood dripped through her fingers to the ground. She was not curious as to who was in the helicopter, or why. She merely saw it as safety. She was therefore unsurprised when an elderly man with a shock of white hair stepped out of the door. He gave her a hostile stare and shouted back, 'Martin – chuck the stuff out quickly!' He said to Hannie, 'Are you alone?' She nodded.

At that moment a plastic-covered bundle, the size of

a small suitcase, landed beside him. Someone in the helicopter was content to push things out but not so keen to come into the doorway of the machine. The man said to Hannie, 'More fool you. I suppose you're with Davis's party?'

She nodded again as another bale landed on the ground outside the helicopter.

'That's enough, Martin,' said the man. To Hannie he said, 'Can you get hold of that one with your good hand and follow me?'

Hannie reluctantly picked up one of the plastic-covered packages with her right hand. He picked up the other and she followed him to the middle of the clearing, where they set the parcels down next to her abandoned haversack. He said, nodding at the scattered knives and the blood-stained arrow, 'Well, you tried.'

Hannie said, 'What makes you think they won't start shooting again?'

He called out something in a guttural tongue and said, 'I'm known to them, through their parents. I was here before.'

'Is it the same lot?' Hannie asked.

'I've checked,' he told her. 'I'm not as stupid as Dr Davis.'

'Davis didn't send me here,' she said sulkily.

He was opening the packages with a sharp penknife. He produced three machetes, some knives, some packages of beads and some clothing. He turned a torch on and off. Hannie stood clutching her wound and watching.

He said, 'Go back to the 'copter and get Martin to look at that arm. He's got a first aid kit in there.'

She said, 'Do you think it was poisoned?'

He shook his head. 'You'd be dead by now. It's the

germs which'll get you. I should clear off – these Indians are a chancy lot. There's always a risk, and I hear they've run up against some religious fanatics who've tried to convert them to a fire and brimstone form of Christianity – been rushing them with Bibles and trousers and trying to point out the errors of their ways. That sort of thing causes confusion in the primitive mind and confusion, I always say, is dangerous.'

'I think they're coming out of the forest,' Hannie said nervously.

Her companion looked round. 'Ah well,' he said. 'you'd better stay by me.' Hannie watched the village, naked men, women and children emerging from the thick, green cover of the forest. They were very small, only a little over five feet. They were naked and their thick, dark hair was cut pudding-bowl style, framing dark faces and slightly slanted, very black eyes. The men, she was relieved to see, dropped their bows to their sides as they advanced.

The old man picked up a machete and held it out to the man who headed the main party of Indians. He took it, as about thirty men and women converged from all sides of the clearing and stood round her and the old man, crowding closer and closer to see what was available. A man pointed at the old man's hat. He lifted it from his white hair, sprayed it with a small aerosol can he took from his back pocket, and handed it to the Indian, who put it on. As the Indians drifted slowly off with their gifts – the old man, like some peculiar Santa at a Christmas party, had managed to make sure everyone had something – Hannie heard him say in a low voice, 'All right. You can get back to the 'copter now.'

'I came here for something,' she said. 'It's that tree,

over there.' She nodded towards the tree bearing the purple flowers.

'Ha!' he said, not troubling to keep his voice down, 'So after all he's said, Davis has decided to take an interest in it, has he?'

Hannie turned to face him. 'I told you, Davis didn't send me. Who are you?'

He dropped his voice again. 'More for me to ask who you are, I think. As it happens, my name is Kyte – Roderick Kyte.'

'Good God,' said Hannie. She stared at him in amazement, then remembered herself and said, 'I'm Hannie Richards.'

'That tells me little,' he said. 'What do you want with that tree?'

'I heard of your work on it,' she told him. 'My boss, immediate boss, that is, won't hear of anything like that. I decided to come and collect some samples on my own.'

'Foolhardy,' said Roderick Kyte. 'But I suppose I have no exclusive right to the flowers – there's plenty for everybody. Since you're here, you might as well help. The sooner we're out of here the better.'

As they crossed the clearing towards the tree the Indians did not look up. They were grouped around the big hut. One hacked at a stump with his new machete. Two traded sets of beads. The children were passing Kyte's hat from hand to hand, head to head. None of them apparently even watched the man in the helicopter, Martin, as he slowly and nervously crossed the *campo* to join Kyte and Hannie. He carried a small revolver in his hand.

'We won't stop too long, Martin,' Kyte told him, as they all walked towards the tree. 'They could turn nasty after the horrible time they've had with those Christians – and we could be carrying a germ which will wipe them out. The less we get involved, the better for all concerned, I think.'

They paused right under the spindly, thick-leaved tree. The purple flowers, fleshy and bell-shaped, hung over them. Several lay on the ground. Some had turned completely brown, others were withering.

'I'll have to go back for my pack,' Hannie said. 'All my jars are in there.'

'Walk slowly and look at ease,' advised Kyte. Turning to Martin he said, 'Up you go, laddie.' As Hannie went back for the pack she saw the Indians still occupied with their new things. She picked up the bundle containing her specimen jars and plastic packs and carried it back to the tree. Her left arm was now throbbing and useless, even though the bleeding had ceased. When she got back, Martin was seated on a low branch, shaking the branch above him to dislodge the flowers, which began to rain down. Two lodged in Kyte's snow-white hair, giving him an oddly festive look. Hannie dropped her pack on the ground and took out a plastic jar. With only one arm she was awkward. The map she had been using, the one purloined from Kyte's laboratory, came out of the pack with the jar. It fell on the ground. Although it was crumpled up and sweat-stained, she guessed that if Kyte saw it he might recognize it. She picked it up and tried to push it back into the rucksack. But Kyte had leaned over and grabbed it. He straightened up and smoothed it out. He looked at it for several seconds. Hannie, like a child, stood by and said nothing. There was nothing to say.

Then Kyte said, perfectly gently, 'You got this from my brother, Duncan?'

210

Hannie said, 'Yes.'

Roderick Kyte nodded resignedly. Hannie said, 'Dr Davis isn't responsible. I was hired by your brother to get the flowers and roots of this tree. Will it really cure him?'

Kyte said in the same gentle tone, 'He's a fool. I told him it would do him no good in its present form. What do you think I'm doing here – a man of over sixty, standing in a clearing full of Indians of uncertain temperament? I need fresh plants in order to make a fresh synthesis. Last time, I was foolish. I relied on my own analysis of the plants and let the plants themselves go hang. This time I shall start all over again with the chemistry, and this time I shall try to grow fresh plants also. That way I can go back to the source. What I have can sometimes correct cell malfunction – I've seen it restore damaged tissue – but the effects are arbitrary and often grotesque. I have to go back and start again – resynthesize from the original plants, make fresh compounds, test every possibility again and again in a variety of ways. I've no idea how it works. It may trigger immunities through the gland system but that doesn't explain how it can restore tissue, if it does. I've discovered to my cost, that what works, seemingly permanently, on one animal can produce a horrible escalation of the disease, with side-effects, on another. And if it works here, among the Indians, it may be due to exterior factors – diet, other immunities they've built up, anything. If you want to know, I'm not here because I've found a cure for cancer but because several months ago I gave up trying. I was bitter because of the uncertain nature of the results. They weren't results – just a stray collection of phenomena. I was tired of being a crank scientist, always derided, without any professional standing. I thought I'd let it alone and die in peace. Then I found I couldn't. So I came here, at my own expense, to collect more specimens and start again from scratch. I might,' he said wearily, 'find something which will be of value to others who come after me. That's all I hope for now.'

Hannie looked at the old man with the flowers in his hair. She plucked the blooms from his head and looked at them. She said briskly, 'Well, your brother paid me to come here and get these flowers. I'll do it.'

'I can't stop you,' said Kyte. 'But while you're here you can help. Start digging around to find the roots of the tree. We'll need them.'

Martin, now down from the tree, Kyte and Hannie started digging in the hard ground to find the roots. Hannie's arm ached badly now. She found one of the roots of the tree about a foot below the ground and began to follow it out to where it was thinnest. Two feet away Kyte was doing the same. He grunted. He said, 'This isn't going to help him, you know. He's going to need a big team to get any results. He'll probably die a very horrible death.'

'His choice,' said Hannie shortly.

'If he manages to save his life, with your help,' Kyte said conversationally, while hacking at a root, 'do remember how he got the money. He controls companies everywhere in the world there's labour to be underfed and exploited. South American mines, tea plantations – men, women and plenty of children, too, have died to feed Duncan Kyte. If he does recover, it'll be in order to go on doing the same. It's odd, don't you think, that these people whose ambition is to eat up the world are always the most reluctant to slacken their greedy grip when the Reaper comes to call? Or maybe it's not odd at all.'

Hannie said nothing. She was in pain. And everything Kyte was saying rang true. She had no defence. I don't need to defend myself, she thought fiercely. I'm doing a job for money. What's wrong with that? Meanwhile Kyte, still on his knees probing for fresh roots, said in the same calm tone, 'You might recall the Bocca Island affair. It was on TV about a year ago. Remember the islanders sitting around outside their huts, all swollen up, with vacant expressions on their faces – questions in Parliament, neatly evaded, but someone at the Ministry of Health had to resign? That was Duncan, you know. They had a one-crop economy on Bocca Island, and a subsidiary of Duncan's bought the crop. Just them and nobody else. Obviously, they ran the island. Then, as it happened, another company Duncan had an interest in wanted to test a new psychiatric drug they've developed. There was one hospital on the island, part-funded by Duncan Kyte, masquerading as the XYZ Banana Company or something similar, and one drug company, in which this same Duncan Kyte is a heavy shareholder, wanting to conduct tests on a new drug. There were a few words in the club and in the City, a persuadable doctor on Bocca Island and – bingo – the tests get organized, the adult population of Bocca played human guinea pig, the effects turned them into zombies with very unpleasant personal appearance – goodbye Bocca, goodbye people. Do you know what he's doing now?'

'No,' said Hannie, without looking up from her trowel.

'He's importing a fresh population. Best part of the work force is no good now, you see. And if the work force can't work what about the bananas and, therefore, what about Duncan Kyte's investment and profits? That's the man you're digging away to save. You'd be doing more good to the world if you were digging his grave.'

Hannie looked up and said, 'Please be quiet. I'm here now. I've got a job to do. Just let me do it.'

'They drove my mother off like a starving dog, you know,' Kyte told her remorselessly. 'It broke her heart. His second wife killed herself – Duncan's, I mean. You've got to hand it to him, his public life and his private life have always matched. He wrecks and exploits wherever he is. His third wife was in and out of the bin most of the time during the marriage. He's got two boys. One lives on an ashram in South India. The other's as bad as his father. He's corrupt as hell – goes for little girls. Not Duncan's kind of little girls but real little girls, the ones in Brownie uniforms. He stinks. Duncan stinks.'

Hannie stood up. By now she had filled a long plastic box with enough of the root of the tree to provide a proper sample and taken some earth samples. She began to cram the jars with purple flowers. She could hardly bear the sound of Roderick Kyte's voice, dinning into her ears the kind of information about her employer she did not want to hear. She reminded herself that she was working for him because of Adam, the new house, the children. She screwed the cap on the jar and said, 'Suppose he gets someone on the job who actually can use this stuff to cure him. That would upset you, wouldn't it? Because you want to do it yourself. But just supposing he does it – think of all the other people who would be helped by it.'

'Estimate the probabilities,' said Kyte. 'He's got six, possibly nine months to live. Do you think any reputable scientist or even a team of them can come up with results in that time? And test them properly before risking the stuff on the boss? What'll happen is that Duncan will get the samples. Then he'll drive the team mad with demands for results. After all, his life is on the line. Finally, he'll drive the better ones away. He'll be left with the weak men, who will allow themselves to be persuaded into doing what he wants out of fear or greed. And what he will want is to use the substance they produce. And there's every chance that if he does he'll die anyway, and probably far more horribly than he would have done.'

Kyte stood there in the clearing, looking at her. 'You see what that means? If my brother dies unnaturally, in a terrible way, there'll be publicity. Difficult to avoid an inquest, for example. A famous multi-millionaire industrialist dies because of a substance his own brother has been working on unsuccessfully for years. Imagine what that will look like. My university is trying to make cuts – how long do you think I'd last if they had a cast-iron excuse like that?'

Martin was saying at Kyte's elbow, 'They're looking at us, doctor. We'd better go.'

Hannie and Roderick Kyte both turned and looked at the Indians. Four of the men were staring incuriously at the party of Europeans near the edge of the forest. Kyte nodded. 'We've done what we came for,' he said. 'Let's just walk quietly back to the helicopter. You'd better come with us,' he told Hannie. 'It might be unsafe to set off back through the jungle.'

And so they walked across the clearing, past the fire, the groups of Indians and the long hut. As they went, Kyte, evidently in no mood to let Hannie off the hook, continued, 'I want to go on with my work. You can't help my brother. Can I persuade you to return without the plants, tell him you couldn't find them?'

And Hannie, without hesitation, replied, 'I can't do what you ask. I see no reason to fail in my job because of what you think might happen if I return with the specimens.'

Kyte sighed. 'Very well,' he said. 'I suppose I was foolish to think that I might get a decent response from anyone hired by my brother.'

'Is there any chance you could drop down on our camp so that I can pick up my stuff and then take me on to somewhere I can get transport in the direction of Rio?' Hannie asked bluntly.

'Your interest in science has ended now that you have the plants?' Kyte suggested.

'That's right,' said Hannie.

She got into the helicopter and sat on the floor. Her arm felt as if it were on fire. She thought, Sod Spinelli and sod you, specially, Roderick Kyte. I've got the flowers and the roots, and I'm getting out of here.

In the co-pilot's seat Roderick Kyte turned round and looked at her. Hannie stared at the floor.

6. The Luck Runs Out

'You want it. Come on, you know you want it,' came the voice again. Hannie wrenched away across the bed. A dozen floors below this room, she knew, tanned bodies lay idly on the sand of Copacabana beach. She could not believe the life of Rio was going on outside this hotel room while inside four walls this grotesque event was taking place.

'Bloody get back!' she cried and tried to slip off the bed. The huge blond-haired hand held her down, pressing into the small of her back. She turned her head. She saw he had raised the heavy belt of his uniform again. He swung it down. She buried her head in the pillow in case it hit her face. It hit her buttocks for the second time. She screamed and, while he was off balance, turned over and kicked him under the chin. Then she jumped off the bed. He was large, heavy and he must have been six feet four inches tall. The kick under the chin meant nothing to him. He reached over and grabbed her by her left shoulder, which was still painful, and shoved her down on the bed again. Pushing her into the mattress, his hand still on her shoulder, the man, Tomas Green, laughed at her, saying, 'I like them like this – a little trouble, a little fire. More fun, eh?' He had rather small, red-rimmed blue eyes.

Oh God, thought Hannie, why did I tell him the name of my hotel? Because he looked all right last night, in the bar. Why did I let him in? He didn't look all right this morning. Why did I let him in? She was saying, 'Tomas, I'm well connected. I have a cousin at the Embassy. You could lose your job.'

She felt him rip away her nightdress. He said, 'For a little fun. Don't tell me you don't like it.' She shut her eyes as the belt came down again. It lashed round her hips. The buckle tore her side.

She forced herself to speak calmly. 'Tomas, it hurts too much. You must stop.'

'Stop?' he said quite reasonably, as if talking to a child, 'but we've only just begun.' The huge hand moved from her shoulder to her rib-cage, driving all the breath out of her. She gasped, 'Let me get up! Let me get up!' He dropped the belt on the carpet and pulled back his other hand, balled up into a fist.

'No!' she gasped. 'No!' Then he smashed his fist into her face. For a time she felt no pain, only shock, and as she lay there, staring up at him, he turned her over like a fish in a frying pan. Then perhaps the worst part of the pain began. He held her down with one hand and she heard him unzipping his trousers. Tears ran from her eyes as he forced his prick into her anus and began, violently and methodically, to bugger her. Hannie, desperate, could not even feel the pain of her bruised face for the agony of this rough entry and of the terrible, heavy onslaught. She was afraid he was tearing her open. She tried to make herself relax, knowing that if she did not the pain might be worse and the injuries dangerous. She told herself it would soon be over, but Tomas Green took a long time and, as he went on longer, his thrusts became more violent, more rapid and deeper. Sometimes there was pain. Sometimes all she could feel were the buttons of his tunic biting into her back. Hannie, her teeth clamped to her lower lip, prayed she might faint, and did not. Finally, with one long, agonizing thrust, he finished. She lay still, not daring to breathe, with his heavy weight on her. She moaned softly and was still again. In the silence that followed he got off her. She heard him pull on his trousers and zip them. She heard the clatter of his belt buckle hitting a button as he put it on. She heard him open the door. He said, 'Goodbye', and she heard the door close. She lay there with her eyes shut for a moment, too weak to rise. Then she got up cautiously and crept, doubled up, to the door. She locked it and, still bent double, went back to the bed. She lay down and wept, saying to herself over and over again, 'Did it have to get like this? Did it have to get like this?' and then, suddenly, she was asleep.

An instinct awoke her an hour before her flight was due to leave for London. Her face, where he had hit her, throbbed. She hoped her nose was not broken. Her back, where he had hit her with the belt, was agonizing. Her anus hurt excruciatingly. She dared not move but raised her arm to look at her watch. For a moment she thought of cancelling the flight and staying where she was until the next one was due. But she knew that if she stayed she would feel worse. She had to get up, and out, somehow. So she got up and hobbled painfully to the bathroom. While the bath ran she looked in the glass. There was a huge mark on her cheekbone which would shortly turn into a large bruise, but she must have turned her head as his fist smashed into her face. He had missed her nose and her eyes were all right. She pulled her nightdress off painfully, for the belt had gashed her and it was stuck to her back with blood. She got in the bath and thought that she never wanted to get out. He had not, she thought, made any tears in her anus, and that was lucky. She made herself get out of the bath, dried herself carefully and automatically put on a white dress, a black jacket, in case any more blood leaked through from her back, a black hat with a floppy brim, to hide her face, and dark glasses. She did all this quite numbly as if her brain had stopped working properly because she could not bear to think any more. The porter came for her bags. She followed him downstairs, paid her bill and got into a taxi.

It was in the taxi, for a fundamentally robust mind and body will not stay numb for long, that she found herself gasping, in a kind of hysteria. Her brain began to replay the scene at the hotel over and over again, from the knock on the door as she sat eating a late breakfast, through the peculiar conversation which had preceded his assault, the lashing with the belt, the gasping breaths as he laboured over her, tearing at her, rending her, as it seemed, in two. As she sat in the taxi she thought she could smell his hair oil, his sweat, the semen which had leaked from her as she crossed the door to fasten it behind him. She became, in the heat of the vehicle, very cold.

At the customs desk her face, even with the worst of the damage hidden, must have looked strange and pale. It could have been the pallor, it could have been her shakiness of manner, it could have been some smell, like that of a beaten animal, which she gave off. Perhaps it was just sheer bad luck – but the official gazed at her curiously and, as she was about to board the flight, two uniformed airport officials came up to her and pulled her out of the line. She went off between them, anxious about the possibility of missing the flight but knowing that this time, for once, she was in the clear. Her suitcase contained only clothing. Her hand luggage, a shoulder bag, contained only a wallet, a passport, a make-up bag, a copy of Speedwell's *South American Flora and Fauna*. She imagined the complication could be connected with the plant specimens, which she had taken to the airport and arranged to despatch separately to London, refrigerated and covered by arrangements made with the expedition some months ago. It should take no time to sort out, she thought, and the likelihood was that she would get her flight.

In the office sat two policemen, one a short dark, tubby man and the other, Tomas Green. He was still in his uniform, wearing his cap. Around his waist was the belt. Hannie's eyes moved to it automatically. When they returned to his face she saw that he was sweating. She was terrified; the sight of him made her flesh crawl. And then she had a sudden, sick knowledge that something else was horribly wrong.

'Follow me, please,' said the airport official. They went through the door of the small office into a larger one. The two policemen and the other airport official came after. Hannie stared at the desk. On it lay her suitcase. The contents, clothes, her jungle boots, a pair of shoes, underwear, were placed neatly to one side. The case itself lay open. It was a blue case with a red quilted lining. It was the case she took with her on family holidays. The airport official said, 'May I see your passport, please?' Hannie gave it to him. It was her own passport, not one of those she obtained by scouring graveyards for little girls who had died when she herself was a child and claiming passports in their names. It was the passport she took with her when she and Adam and the girls went to Spain in the summer, or to Austria skiing in the winter. He looked at it and put it to one side, on one of the piles of her clothes.

Hannie, conditioned by years of guilt, realized that a normal person would here utter a complaint. But inside she had a bad feeling that for some reason it was pointless. She was also afraid. The official stood behind the desk, guarding her clothes, her passport, her perfectly innocent suitcase. Green stood behind her, where she could not see him. Nevertheless she said, 'I don't understand this. Is there something you think is wrong? I shall be too late for my flight in five minutes.'

'This is your case?' asked the official.

Hannie said, 'Yes. It is.'

The airport official beckoned. Green stepped from behind her. He stood behind the desk. He did not like it. He glanced sideways at the heap of her clothes. Hannie stared at him.

'Show her,' said the airport man. 'Step closer, Mrs Richards.'

The atmosphere had turned bad. Hannie moved towards the desk and looked at the case. She saw now that the lining of the corner closest to her had been slightly unpicked. She could see that the small, cut threads were black.

The man pulled back the flap of red quilted material. Underneath was a cellophane packet, about three inches wide. It was filled with white powder.

Hannie closed her eyes, then opened them again. It

must be heroin, or cocaine. It had been planted on her.

The airport official said, 'I propose to cut out the entire lining, in front of these witnesses and in front of you.' At this point a small man, carrying a briefcase and wearing a business suit, hurried in. He said, 'Luis, Mrs Richards has admitted to being the owner of the case.' He said to Hannie, 'This gentleman is a lawyer. We like to have him present because in the past airport staff have been accused by passengers of tampering with their luggage in order to smuggle goods into other countries.'

'I understand,' said Hannie wearily. 'You'd better get on with it. But please note that I deny any knowledge of whatever it is.' She scarcely knew what she was saying. She knew only, as the airport official, scrutinized by Green and the lawyer, carefully cut the stitches which held the lining in place, that she was being caught red-handed for something she had not done. Indeed, she thought sourly, if she had done it, she would have been more careful not to have been caught. Gloomily she watched them peel back the whole lining. The little plastic or cellophane packets, full of white powder, covered the whole of the bottom of the case. If it is cocaine, she thought, at about forty dollars a snort, the powder represented about £50,000. If it was heroin, less. She was not absolutely sure of current prices. She did not really care. What was certain was that she had been caught with prohibited drugs in quantity. It was her case all right. She recognized the stain made by a piece of chewing gum when she had put the bag down at Heathrow. She had scraped off the gum, but the mark remained. She stared at the round brown mark at the edge of the case. The man in charge said, 'We're going to open one of the packets.'

She said, 'Very well. But I don't know anything about all this.'

He said, as he stripped off the slip of scotch tape holding the flap of the packet down, 'We found this during a routine search.'

Hannie nodded. She could almost believe it. All they had to do was feel the bottom of the case. Their experienced fingertips would tell them all they needed to know. She wondered how she had not noticed. Perhaps the airport staff had planted the stuff. But she had arrived so late at the airport she had barely had time to get her case to the check-in. One lot would have had to slit the lining of the case completely, plant the stuff and sew it up again, and another lot would have had to inspect the baggage and find out what the first lot had done, all within the space of ten minutes to a quarter of an hour – it did not make sense. But if they had not done it, then who had? Meanwhile, the man had tipped some of the white powder into his palm. He smelt it, sniffed it carefully, licked his finger, picked some of it up on his fingertip, tasted it and said, 'Cocaine. We shall have to analyse it, but there can be little doubt. I shall have to arrest you, Mrs Richards.'

'That's right,' said Hannie.

Hannie lay on her bunk in her very clean cell, staring mindlessly at the ceiling. She had gone through her trial merely denying her responsibility for the hidden packages. There was no point in defending herself further. The Brazilian government had no tolerance for drug smugglers, and she was given eight years. She did not care. There was nothing she could do except sit in her rather comfortable little cell with its white paint and crucifix and think. It was peaceful in her cell, but she could not do very much thinking. She felt she was going mad.

She had, however, more or less worked out when the plant must have been made. It could have happened while she was out for a walk on the night in Rio when she had met Green. But anyone who had planted the drugs on a total stranger in a Rio hotel would have to reclaim them when the carrier got to the other end, in London. They would have to orchestrate a very ingenious luggage switch at the airport or else rob her later when, for all they knew, she might be met by two brothers in the CID or whisked off to a castle in Scotland. It was too chancy for the sort of drug operators who got the stuff up professionally in little New York-style plastic packets. There was no chance that the cocaine had been planted by a dedicated scientist in the middle of the Mato Grosso. This took the whole thing back to New York, and she knew, logically and instinctively, that the plant had been made there. Her hotel room had been entered while she was out. The man to whom she had delivered Duncan Kyte's message had the healthy, corrupted, white, Anglo-Saxon Protestant appearance of a man with bad connections. It had been done in New York all right, but she could not work out why. And although she tried to blame Duncan Kyte, she knew that there was no reason for a man desperate for the delivery of items which might save his life to complicate matters for the bearer of those goods.

Her lawyer had urged her to make representations to the embassy, to her family, to friends in Britain. But Hannie had broken. She did not care. 'Your husband?' the lawyer had said urgently. 'Surely he will come and help you.' Hannie felt that she would rather face the electric chair than Adam's reluctant assistance. She laughed at the lawyer and said, 'The biggest favour I can do him is go to gaol.'

Now she lay there in her little white room muttering, 'I went to gaol. I went directly to gaol. I did not pass Go. I did not collect £200.' So it goes, so it goes, so it goes, she thought to herself. She lay on her bunk, absolutely numb. Under her pillow was a letter she had just received from Duncan Kyte. He was plainly desperate. He told her that he had discovered that the plant specimens were at Heathrow but could not be released without her signature, and he implored her to write a letter authorizing him to collect them. He added that he was making efforts to secure her release, that he would not cancel the post-dated cheques awaiting her at her solicitor's, but that he must have the plants as soon as possible.

Hannie, on her bunk, thought vaguely that she must write to Heathrow to save Kyte's life or something, but then she started thinking about the other Kyte, with the blossoms from what she now saw as a poison-plant in his hair. All plants, in this business, she thought to herself and laughed. The fat wardress, the nice one, came in and looked at her strangely. Hannie stopped laughing and tried to seem ordinary. She knew enough to work out that she was all right where she was and that if she behaved too oddly they might take her out of her little room and make her go somewhere else. She did not want to leave the little room, ever. These rooms, she guessed, were where they put the women who were a cut above the others. Judging from the noise below, in the compound where the other women talked or laughed or suddenly started screaming and fighting, there was a rough end of town, even in a gaol, and she was not part of it. Down there were the prostitutes and thieves, the Brazilians. They had noisy quarrels about who had stolen a pair of shoes, or a man. They wept for their children. They pulled each other's hair. Hannie did not want to have to live with them, or anybody else. She did not want to go to a mental institution either. She wanted to stay where she was.

The only thing she hated was the half-hour exercise each day. Every afternoon, the compound was cleared of its seething crowd of women, and they pulled her out of her little room to go and walk about with the other four women who were too good for the gaol. There was the tall, thin, repressed one she called the Governess, and the young woman with the raven hair and the huge dark eyes, the Beauty. The other two were German girls who wore sneakers and jeans. Hannie called them the Valkyries. There were no particular rules against talking to the others, but Hannie, who felt threatened by the sky, so brilliantly blue above her, stood by the wall as much as possible. Sometimes she made herself walk about the yard a bit or went and stood and looked through the barbed wire to the perimeter beyond. One day she found a tortoiseshell comb on the ground and handed it back to the guard. She hoped there would not be a row later on about which of the other women it belonged to. Sometimes she could not help standing in the yard and weeping, although she did not know why. She seldom cried in her little room. When they took her back, she was comforted by the sound of the door banging and the key turning in the lock. Then she was at peace again and could lie down on her bunk and rest some more. There was another bunk in the room, opposite her own, but she never used it or even sat on

227

it. It was not hers. She kept all her things, such as her toothbrush and her spare dress, on her own side of the cell.

Now she looked around her room and thought that, although she had not wanted to come here before, she was pleased. Later they brought her some food – beans and meat – and she ate a little of it, for she was cunning enough to know that if she ate nothing at all they would take her away for forced feeding or might even make her leave her little room for good. After she had swallowed the food she remembered that she was thirty-four and would be forty-two when she came out of gaol. Then she lay down and dozed. She woke up thinking uneasily about the letter under her pillow. Kyte was stupid.

His letter was like someone nagging at her. He said she should never have risked his plants to try to make extra money by bringing drugs into the country. That was stupid. She had not. Kyte was stupid and so was his brother. She would have had a good rest, she thought, when they released her.

Later the cell was dark. She said into the darkness, 'Bye, Baby Bunting/Mummy's gone a-hunting/Gone to get a rabbit skin/To wrap the Baby Bunting in.' She sang, 'Bye, Baby Bunting,' and tears came to her eyes. She brushed them away and said aloud, 'When Adam delved and Hannie span, who was then the gentleman?' She laughed and said it a few times more until the thin wardress, the nasty one, came and told her to stop. So she did stop. She lay there having a nice rest and thinking, I'll feel better when I'm more rested. She was careful not to say this aloud. She went to sleep then, but had bad dreams and woke up screaming.

One day she heard them discussing her outside her

door at dawn. She thought they thought she was asleep. They also thought she knew very little Spanish. That way did not have to talk much to them. One said, 'She's getting weaker. We'll have to inform the Governor.' The other said, 'She'll come round, they always do. She needs a firm hand.' This was the thin one who did not like Hannie. She thought Hannie was proud. She herself was in love with someone who was not in love with her. She thought Hannie did not know, but she did. Meanwhile Hannie thought of nice things – a field, a tree, a herd of gazelles running, ice skaters dancing, a pattern made by a kaleidoscope. She tried not to dream, for when she did she sometimes dreamed of bad things like puppets coming to life in horrible ways, or spooky houses full of horrors which never quite emerged, or people following her. Once she dreamed she was on a boat on a sea which never moved and where there was no wind. Just occasionally she had good dreams about rivers, or that she was walking along with someone she loved who loved her. But often she dreamed she was being left behind at a station or an airport.

She did not know it, but she had been in gaol for five weeks.

One afternoon when she was taking exercise with the four other women, a storm broke. The leaden air moved. Wind lashed her. There was thunder. Lightning flashes illuminated the dark compound. Rain began to pour down. Hannie backed along the wall of the prison until she got to the corner. Then she slipped down the wall and sat crouched there with her hands over her ears and her eyes shut. The kind, fat guard led her inside. Once the door was locked she lay down and slept. Later she awoke. The storm had ended, the other women were back in the compound. A terrible fight broke out. Hannie lay there, afraid, with her fingers in her ears. Then there was silence. A woman called, 'What is it?' Another called, 'Rosalia! Your child is dead!' The air was pierced by a howl, like that of an animal. And then came the wailing of the women, all the women, as if they had all lost a child, as if all their children were dead. It went on and on. The guards tried to stop it half-heartedly but failed. Even they, Hannie thought, could not deny this awful sound. She fell asleep with this noise in her ears.

Now she dreamed of Angelina's bare feet on the dry track on Beauregard, saw a scramble of half-clad black children outside the shacks on St Colombe. She dreamed of a column of women – mother and daughter and daughter's daughter, carrying waterpots on their heads through the desert in the Republic of Chad.

She dreamed of the half-Indian woman she had seen as she came into Rio in a taxi, walking between some huts beside her husband, who carried a lidded cardboard box, a little larger than a shoe-box. The woman's face betrayed nothing, nor did the man's, but a child tagging along behind them in the dust had been crying. The taxi driver, a cigarette between his lips, said, 'It could be a dead baby – they go to bury it. Too many children, you see.' Then, in her dream, as if a camera back-tracked, she saw a great vista of the women she had seen. They bent over their crops, hoeing, weeding and planting.

They carried burdens – babies, water, vegetables, piles of laundry. She saw them tending their young, their old, their sick and their dying. She woke with a sense of the everlasting patience of the women, patience wide as the sea, fathomless, without borders or boundaries, patience as old as mankind itself, which has kept children alive and men on their feet for the next hard day and the next since the beginning of human history.

Well, well, Hannie Richards, said a voice in the cell, you never noticed the background to the main event, the big performance, did you? Never noticed all this for what it was, while you waltzed your superstar personality through the landscape, carrying a faked passport, a little well-tooled luggage and a small consignment of this, that and the other? You've been like a kind of upper servant at the court of Marie Antoinette, doing nicely on the perks, a bottle of wine here and a golden louis there, while all the time the people producing that wealth were standing about starving in the streets. The voice stopped.

She woke up properly, seeing the ceiling of her cell as if for the first time. The wailing of the women had stopped. They were talking now. Hannie Richards, gaunt, grey, thin as a skeleton, lay on her bunk. Her mind was clear.

She did not notice the sound of feet coming up the corridor outside her cell, nor hear the voices. She was not even particularly aware of her cell door opening.

Then, 'Hannie,' said the voice of her fellow-pirate, the tall man who had dragged her down the hillside during the earthquake, who was at the fountain in Rome. 'Hannie. Your friends have sent me. You're free now.'

She turned her head and saw the man she knew. A shorter, fat man stood behind him. She recognized the governor of the prison.

'You are released, Mrs Richards,' he said in Spanish.

'Thank you,' she said. She could not understand what was happening, but she knew something was expected of her. She stood up, feeling suddenly dizzy. 'Who are you?' she asked the tall man.

'James Carter,' he said. 'You don't know me. Your friends asked me to come and collect you.'

She distantly recognized the old world of evasions, concealed instructions and half truths. He meant she did know him. He meant her to ask no more questions in front of the Governor. He held out her shoulder bag and said, 'Put your things in here. We can leave straight away. We're booked on a flight to London in a few hours' time.'

The old world came back hot and strong. Fumblingly she collected her toothbrush, washing things and a pair of shoes and put them in the bag. She picked up the white dress, black jacket and white hat and handed them to the kind guard, who stood behind the Governor.

Not long afterwards she and James Carter walked out of the prison into bright sunshine. Traffic whizzed by, startling Hannie. He helped her into a car and said, 'I've booked a hotel room. We can go there. You can eat and then rest until it's time to go to the airport.'

She said, 'I'd like to go straight to the airport. I don't mind waiting a long time.'

He gave her a shrewd look and told her, 'We could go to the cinema. To pass the time.'

'All right,' she said.

'*Butch Cassidy and the Sundance Kid*,' he said. 'English sub-titles – that OK?'

'Yes,' she said gravely.

'You'll have to wait outside in the cab while I go to the hotel and pick up my luggage,' he said.

Hannie sat in the corner of the cab watching the busy streets, the street vendors, the avenues of trees. She saw

no women, no man with a cardboard box containing a dead baby and no snivelling child dragging
behind, but she knew they were there. They were
somewhere and always would be.

James Carter got his bag from the hotel while
Hannie, the door of the cab slightly ajar, waited
outside. She was taking no chances. As the car took off,
she became nervous again.

He said to her, 'Your friends' names are Julie St Just,
Elizabeth Lord and Margaret Wilkinson. These are the
tickets for the plane back to London.' And he showed
her two airline tickets.

She must have felt reassured, for she fell asleep for
most of the film and almost missed the end, the final
shoot-out in Bolivia.

'At least you're getting out alive,' James Carter
remarked as they left the cinema. 'Now it's time for
dinner.' In the restaurant a band played mechanical
Latin American music. The players wore bright
costumes. It was early, but a few parties of prosperous
diners sat at the tables. Hannie, still in the flowered
dress she had been wearing in prison, felt uncomfortable, and said so.

'You'll feel better when you've had something to eat,'
said James. As she picked up her spoon to eat the soup
he had insisted on ordering for her she noticed her own
hands. They were very thin and pale. She had not seen
herself in the mirror since she left the hotel. 'I bet I
look awful,' she said to him.

'I've seen you looking better,' he told her.

'That was you, then,' she said, 'in those other places?
St Colombe?'

'Australia, Italy,' he said. 'I get about a lot. I've been
interested in you for years. Like a groupie, really.'

'Who are you?' she asked.

'Well,' he said, 'I'm in the same game as you, in a way. Weapons.'

'You mean an arms trader?' Hannie said.

'I've been described as that – in the *Daily Mirror*. But eat your soup and don't make faces at me. In any case,' he said with some regret, 'I've got to face the fact that the game's over. So you can spare me your criminal-style snobberies, bank robbers looking down on house-breakers, muggers bashing ponces in prison because they despise men who live off women. All that. Anyway I'm thirty-two, and it's a cut-off point. The fun's disappearing and the grot's getting worse. They're all getting into nukes now. I don't like it – too indiscriminate.'

'It can't have been the playing fields of Eton up to now,' Hannie said.

'Come off it,' he said. 'Do you know what percentage of weapons are supplied by independent arms traders, these days? About five per cent or less. The rest is one government selling arms to another, for profit or politics or both. And the more sophisticated the technology gets, the more difficult it becomes for the independent operator. It's a dying trade, has been since the thirties. The fact of the matter is I'm fascinated by weapons, weapons technology, that sort of thing. But I'm getting too old to continue with my boyhood enthusiasm. And either the clients are looking grimier or I am beginning to see how grimy they are. Five years ago I thought I was selling to gallant patriots – now half of them look like bloodthirsty maniacs. They don't want guns any more. They're all itching to get their hands on an H-bomb so they can hold the world to ransom from a suite in a Hilton hotel somewhere.'

How romance dies,' Hannie said thoughtfully.

234

He grinned at her. 'In that area,' he said, 'when one door closes, another one opens.'

'I hope you're wrong,' she said.

'Come on, Hannie Richards,' he said, 'nothing's worse than a man with a hangover who's sworn off the stuff – not when he goes round and makes a fuss about his auntie's small dry sherry before dinner. You got burned, that's all that happened. It's a miracle you got away with it for so long.'

'Yes,' she said soberly. She stared round the restaurant, looked at the small musicians with their Indio faces, churning out their colourless version of their own music to make a background for the wealthy diners. She studied the heavy male faces at the tables, and the faces of their womenfolk. She stared at their make-up, their clothes, their jewellery. They must be among the most beautiful, the most extravagant, the best-dressed and looked-after women in the world, she thought. They were like queens.

'A touch of the green monster?' James asked tastelessly.

Hannie shook her head. 'Women don't always look at other women in that way. Sometimes they're just wondering who they are, not where they got their shoes or if they had a nose job – I had a dream in prison about the women I've seen. Poor women.'

'There aren't many of those here,' he said.

He had a rather long, pale face and a long, undistinguished nose. His hair was dark but not black and a little long. Perhaps because of that he had the look of one of those conventional portraits of the soldiers of a particular family – the cousin who fought with Wellington at Corunna or the great-uncle who died at Ypres. The only strange features in this conventional,

235

restrained face, the kind of face usually found in England or Scotland, were a full and mobile mouth and the very bright blue eyes. He poured her some wine and said, 'I do know what you're talking about. But eat now, and have some wine.' He poured her a glass. He cut some veal from his own piece and held it out to her on the end of his fork. 'You can't help them here, if anyone can ever help them. Nibble a bit.'

Hannie, distracted, took the titbit in her mouth, but her eyes watched the slender white hands of the woman at a table opposite her. They glittered with fine diamonds as she toyed, conscious of the effect, with the stem of her glass, or gestured at her companion.

'Those hands could save a thousand lives, we know,' James remarked, as if reading her thoughts. 'And she wouldn't have to lift a finger – except to take the rings off.' He turned and said, 'Keep eating. You're slacking.'

'All right,' she said. 'While I eat, tell me how you found me.'

'I didn't find you,' he said. 'Your friends started the hue and cry. Julie had a bad instinct when you left. She said she'd had a row with you. She started ringing your husband about three weeks after you'd left. He had no word of you and was embarrassed about the whole thing. A bit more time went by and your friend Margaret got on to him and made him ring the Foreign Office. The Foreign Office had no word. Then they really got to work. They put ads in the papers as well. They got hold of Davis and Spinelli as soon as they got back. From Spinelli they heard about you coming back to the camp with Kyte. They got on to Kyte, who told them his part of the story. At that point I came in. Among other things, they'd used *The Times*. There was a piece in it about you, a member of the British-Brazilian scientific expedition, being missing. I read it in Hong Kong, and I thought, Well, if my favourite star Hannie Richards is doing scientific research, then I'm a Dutchman. I got back a fortnight later and got in touch with *The Times*, which led me to your friends. By that time they were trying in vain to contact Duncan Kyte, who was trying equally hard to evade them.'

'He knew where I was,' Hannie said.

'So it turned out,' James said. 'But there it was – Duncan Kyte had fled into paranoia and, quite honestly, his brother wasn't much better. Truth is, they're both peculiar. Roderick's the good guy, but he's obsessed with these flaming plants and all he could think about was how disobliging you'd been to him when you refused to withhold the plants from Duncan. Duncan's obsessed by his rotten wealth and his rotten health and by these same utterly stinking plants, and, of course, they hate each other, which doesn't help. Meanwhile, the Foreign Office, true to form, has lost all the papers due to Julian Critchley-Smith-Jones being off at an elderly aunt's bedside or due to not wanting to imperil at that time a valuable trade deal between us and the Brazilians. Of course, nobody loves a drug-dealer; most governments won't chuck themselves about to help one.'

'I never did that, you know,' said Hannie, through a mouthful of veal.

'I thought not,' he said promptly. 'It didn't seem like your style. Anyway, at this stage none of us knew where you were or even if you were still alive. Your friends asked me to come here and try to find some traces of you. I agreed, willingly. I told them I'd seen you around from time to time and would like to help.'

'Did you tell them what you are?' Hannie interrupted.

'I told them what I had been,' he said. 'They didn't

237

care. They wanted to find you and they knew I had a better chance of helping than most – women are far more pragmatic than men in a crisis, I've noticed. But obviously I wasn't going to set off for Brazil without any background. And we all knew that if Duncan Kyte had not been returning calls left on his answer-phone and was instructing his manservant to turn enquirers from the door, then it was likely he knew something. So I went down to his place late at night, entered his house and went upstairs and found him in bed, watching video with that corroded little blonde. I took a big shooter, to cut down on the time involved. It was faster than it would have been because the blonde told me everything straight away. God knows why he'd stopped anybody knowing where you were.'

'He thought I'd sign the specimens over to him faster if he promised me release,' Hannie told him. 'I don't think people like that can refuse the chance to use leverage. Threats and promises get to be a habit. He wrote to me, but I was too far gone by then to reply.'

'Over-calculation, that's always a pitfall,' James said.

'Hadn't we better start for the airport?' Hannie asked.

'Only if you want to be nearly an hour and a half early,' replied James. 'But I can see you don't like this restaurant so –' He signalled for the bill.

'I don't like Brazil,' said Hannie.

'Pity,' said James. 'It's a wonderful country. I shall try to spend holidays here when I'm respectably settled in life.'

As they left the restaurant, he tipped the leader of the band, remarking, 'Poor bastard. Fancy having to do that all day long.'

In the cab Hannie asked, 'What will you do – if you're getting out of trouble, so to speak?'

238

'I don't know,' he told her. 'My family's mostly in the army, thus the fascination with weapons. That's why I never felt too bad about my filthy trade, I dare say. What's the difference between taking pay for selling them and taking pay for using them? With one you stand the risk of going to gaol and with the other you get knighted on the battlefield. Well, I'm just the classic sixties drop-out child of the respectable middle classes. When it comes down to it, I've got no qualifications and no training. I'm just fit to run a fairground shooting range.'

'Travel agent,' suggested Hannie.

'Don't laugh,' said James Carter. 'I suspect you're out of a job, too. For one thing your face is getting too well known.'

'And my nerve's gone,' Hannie said truthfully.

'It sometimes comes back,' he told her.

'Can't do it any more anyway,' she said. 'This was meant to be the last time, just to get a lot of money to take care of my children. I'll be staying at home for a while. I won't be able to shoot off at a moment's notice and risk never coming back, or never coming back for eight years. That's all over.' She suddenly felt depressed.

'What a pity,' he said. 'I didn't half enjoy you – never knew where you'd pop up next or what you'd be up to. We'd have made a wonderful team. Like Butch Cassidy and the Sundance Kid.'

'Bonnie and Clyde,' said Hannie.

'Laurel and Hardy,' he said. 'Ah well, here we are.'

In the airport she said, 'I'm sorry to have brought us here so early.'

'Don't worry,' he said. 'Let's have some final Brazilian coffee. It's like nothing else in the world.'

As they drank the hot black sweet coffee she said,

'Why did they release me?'

James's blue eyes sparkled. He said with enjoyment, 'Insanity. Your friend Elizabeth did something terrible. You must never tell a living soul – a professional man's reputation is totally in your hands.'

'Go on,' said Hannie.

'Well,' he said. 'She had this analyst – right? Couldn't get out of bed to do the housework so her husband found a shrink?'

'Right,' said Hannie. 'You're a terrible gossip. I can't believe in you as constructor of secret deals. I should think everyone in the world would know if you sold a peashooter.'

'Gossips hear a lot as well as telling a lot,' James said. 'But you've got a great deal to thank Elizabeth Lord for, and you must never do it. She's embarrassed and doesn't want it mentioned. She didn't tell me about this, but Julie did.'

'There you go again,' said Hannie. 'Gossip, gossip, gossip.' She peered at him. 'What did she do?'

'We had to produce a reason, if only a formal one, for why the authorities in Brazil should voluntarily release you. We were all sitting around in the Hope Club one night –'

'You got into the Hope Club?' said Hannie.

'Through the back door. It was an emergency,' he said gravely. 'It's a lot better than the men's clubs. However, there we sat, trying to figure out a reason for them to let you go, and Margaret came up with the idea of insanity. If you're mad you're not culpable. And a lot of governments don't like the idea of keeping mad foreigners, particularly women, in the gaols. The notion offends them. So that was fine – you were supposed to be mad. But we needed documentary proof, dating back over the years, to show that you had a history of serious mental illness. So Elizabeth – wait for it – compromised the quack.'

'She what?' cried Hannie. 'Compromised the doctor – Elizabeth? How?'

'How do you usually get compromised?' demanded James. 'I'm telling you, she compromised him sexually.'

'Elizabeth?' said Hannie. 'I don't believe it.'

'Well, she did,' James said. 'Never underestimate a friend. Once she had – well – compromised him, as it were, she put it to him that she needed his help over a document saying that you had been his patient for many years, and he had no hesitation in stating that in his medical opinion you were right round the bend. And it was dangerous to keep you locked up without proper attention.'

'Poor Elizabeth,' said Hannie. 'How awful for her.'

'She didn't mind,' James asserted. 'Honestly, she laughed about it. You see, women are pragmatic.'

'Well, I'll be damned,' said Hannie. 'Fancy Elizabeth doing that for me.'

'She didn't do it for herself, that's for sure,' James said. 'Nor is her account of it is to be trusted. On the other hand,' he continued cheerfully, 'perhaps she did get something out of it for herself. Harmless revenge. From what I gather her husband, a perfectly nice man and naturally desperate for a clean shirt and a wife who doesn't keep on crying all the time, sent her to this analyst to sort her out. And the analyst, who saw the thing in much the same terms as the husband, tried to make her into a good wife and a happy woman, without spotting that she needed more than that. And she, confused by then, felt more confused and also guilty, because she couldn't manage to meet the demand. Also her husband was paying for the results he wasn't getting. After that she managed to put herself together all by herself and realized they'd been wasting her time and energy and making her feel worse by sheer stupidity – perhaps she didn't really mind making fools of both of them, briefly. They'd told her a lie, after all – that she was a poodle and all she had to do was get adjusted to a poodle's life – so she probably felt better when she tricked them in return.'

'Does he mind – Elizabeth's husband – now she's doing all this work at the Club?' Hannie asked.

'Not so far,' James said. 'It seems like voluntary work to him. And it seems practical. He can still be the family brain. But wait till he finds out how far it's gone. There may be a ruckus then.'

'What's gone far?' asked Hannie. 'Is it the Club?'

'I'll leave them to tell you,' he said. 'They want to talk to you about it all.' He lit a cheroot. Hannie put out her hand for it, and he gave it to her, then lit another for himself. 'Brandy?' he asked. She nodded. They were very confidential now. Hannie stared at him. He stared back. The blue eyes were blank in his long, ordinary face.

'How do you know all this?' she asked.

He shrugged. 'They told me,' he said.

'I know,' she said. 'But why? They've confided in you like the district nurse – Julie said this and Elizabeth said that and you tell me what Elizabeth thought about the analyst –'

'You mean I became one of the girls?' he said. He looked around the room and said, 'You're right. There's a lot men and women only talk about to members of their own sex. It's partly trade secrets the opposition's not supposed to know. And partly that there are things

242

men just don't understand about women and vice versa. No point in talking to someone who doesn't understand the language. But I've got four older sisters. My parents were after a boy – for the army, you see. I've been a disappointment. I was meant from an early age to become some corner of a foreign field that would be for ever England. Anyway, I suppose four sisters are an education in themselves. You pick up a lot of information.' He paused, thinking, then said, 'I suppose a Freudian would say that's why I became an arms trader – to prove I wasn't a girl. Although living with them was like training with the SAS. Or it could have been my father making me learn to strip down and reassemble machine guns when I was five.'

'Certainly looks as if you were predestined, one way or the other,' Hannie said.

'So what turned you into a smuggler?' he asked.

'I don't know,' Hannie said. 'I wondered about it while I was mad in gaol. "Where did all this begin?" – that sort of thing. My mother's always been ill. I think that had something to do with it. And then I found I was a pregnant woman, waiting for my husband to come home all the time. I couldn't bear being that woman, hanging about, trying to make ends meet, keeping a candle in the window. We were short of money.

'It started when I suggested we take our boat across the Channel and pick up some wine and brandy like classic British smugglers. It was sort of adventurous in a thoroughly traditional way – watch the wall my darling while the gentlemen go by. The next thing was that someone in the district said that some friends of theirs had taken their cat to France in a boat, but the boat had packed up. They had to come back by train and, obviously, they couldn't bring the cat back without having to put it in quarantine for six months. This would break the cat's heart, the children's hearts and so on and so forth. Of course, I shouldn't have done it in case the cat had rabies, but in that part of the country, especially among boat-owners, the regulations get bent. After that there was another call, and another, and another. I got connections, trade built – that explains how I came to do it. It may not explain why. Why don't you tell me how you got the authorities to release me? Did they just accept the certificate of madness for which Elizabeth traded her virtue?'

'No,' he said, glancing at his watch. 'I'll make it brief. We'll have to start boarding soon. By the way, what was your husband doing while you stood at the helm of a storm-tossed craft?'

'Sometimes he was with me,' Hannie said defensively. 'Sometimes he was busy with the farm.'

James said nothing about this. As they drifted slowly to the barrier, he remarked cheerfully, 'Yes, the business of you being mad – well, obviously in these situations you should never use one angle when two would be better. Luckily, I had some connections.' Standing in the queue, he said, 'Nice to be here with nothing on our minds, eh?' Then, in a lower voice, 'So, with my certificate in one hand and a nasty little photo in the other, I went to see an influential friend at the Ministry of the Interior. The photo, I'm sorry to say, showed a young man in a peaked hat and very shiny boots giving the order for some soldiers to fire at some scruffy-looking characters lined up facing a wall. Jews, in short, in Warsaw, forty years ago. The photo's in a book, in fact. As you probably know, Brazil's run partly on medieval lines, under the surface. There are a few very powerful and influential families, interconnected and very rich.

The man I saw was a member of one of those families, married to a beautiful wife, whom he loves dearly. Her father lives on the family *estancia*, a dear old white-haired gentleman, very fond of his grandchildren but, unfortunately, the former Oberstleutnant Bremmer, a famous name in the Warsaw Ghetto, so long ago. Naturally the wife, her husband and the rest of the family have forgotten all this. They certainly don't feel they want any interfering person informing the Jewish Agency in Vienna about the whereabouts of this desirable person. Or Jewish agents turning up and kidnapping him or killing him. I'd saved up this item of information in case I ever needed help at a later date.'

As they walked across the tarmac, he said philo-sophically, 'I have a feeling there won't be many more later dates. Anyway, a few hints about the earlier career of the father-in-law and the production of a document stating that you were mad but otherwise blameless, and the authorities decided, with creditable speed, that it would be nothing short of inhumane to keep you banged up like that. It's a pity really. I was quite looking foward to being out of the game, in no need of blackmail weapons, and shopping the old Nazi.'

'You still could,' Hannie said.

'You know better than that,' he said. 'Information should only be used once, like teabags.'

They sat in a corner. She breathed more freely after take-off. They were travelling first class. 'What did it cost to bail me out?'

'Nothing on my side,' he said. 'I'll stand the cost of the odd plane fare for the fun of it. I've been fascinated and entertained by you for years. "How does she get away with it?" I used to ask myself.'

'But they hired you?' she said.

245

'I did it as a friendly act,' he told her. 'And as an act of solidarity. The truth is you'd flown one mission too many. We've all done that. Slight fatigue, followed by slip-up, followed by the consequences – it's just the sort of thing I know about. Occupational hazard caused by living off their wits for too long. Like a window cleaner falling off his ladder.'

'All I can say,' said Hannie, 'is thanks.'

'Think nothing of it,' he said. 'You're serious about those drugs being planted?'

'Why would I lie?' Hannie asked.

'No idea at all who did it?'

'No,' she told him. 'I think it must have been when I was in New York. It's annoying – all those years of successful operations and then I get caught for what I didn't do.'

'Part of the game,' he said. 'I still think you'd had enough.'

'And the domestic problems,' she said.

'Julie said something about that,' he admitted. 'Actually, she started shouting. I suppose you'll have to sort it all out when you get back.'

'I shall,' she said. The lively blue eyes met hers directly. He said, 'I'll be there.' Without waiting for a reply he told her, 'Go to sleep, now. If you stay awake any longer, they might give you an airline meal.'

She woke up two hours later to the sound of a cork popping beside her ear. There was a fizzing sound and James Carter handed her a foaming glass of champagne. She laughed. 'I fancied some champagne,' he said. She drank the champagne and wondered about him. Behind the kindness – was it the kindness of the little brother, she wondered? – behind the chatty gossip, even the silliness, she felt a hard, cutting edge. And what, really,

246

did he mean by saying he had been watching her for years? What was that all about? She heard him saying, 'I suppose you'll be going to the Hope Club when we arrive?'

'Yes,' she said, thinking how often she had sat in planes like this, on the way home, looking forward to her return to Devon, anticipating the reunion with Adam and the children.

'I'll be able to find you, then,' he said. 'It's my idea we should see more of each other in future.'

'Well, yes,' she said. 'Yes, of course we should.' Suddenly it seemed obvious that she did not want to lose James Carter in the crowd or the darkness as she had on other occasions. But at the same time she felt defensive. She had taken a beating. She had taken a series of beatings. She was frightened, she told herself. James Carter might be serious business. And she was very weak, she told herself sombrely. Physically weak after the long period in gaol, and psychologically weak because of the failures, the self-doubt and the batterings she had sustained. Perhaps she was in a state where anyone would do. Having reflected on all this, she leaned over to him in the seat and kissed him, the kiss intended as a pact-kiss, an assurance that some day, when she had washed her hair, got back on the tracks, bought a pair of shoes, kissed her children, she would be ready for him, perhaps. In fact the kiss went on and on. They ended uneasily entwined across the seats until he drew back and said, 'You'll love me soon,' and she, a little frightened, said, as if reading out the paper after a peculiar game of consequences, 'I'm going back to sleep now.'

'You're not,' he told her. She shut her eyes, but not for long. They talked throughout the journey. They said they would rather be in bed together.

At the airport in London, after a long embrace, Hannie said hopefully, 'I don't really *need* to go to the Hope Club. What about – ?' but he pecked her on the cheek and said, 'I've got some things to sort out. I'll be back.' Then he gave her a hug and disappeared, as usual, into the crowd. One minute the tall, thin figure was there, and the next it was not.

'Oh, sod,' said Hannie, standing there holding her bag, wearing battered boots and the same floral dress in which she had left gaol. She was cold, full of misery and rage. If it's going to be like this, Carter, forget it, she said to herself.

She pulled herself together and went to release Kyte's flowers from cool storage at the airport. The official was happy to see her. 'I've had Sir Duncan Kyte, I've had a Dr Davis – I've had dozens of them in here. I couldn't do anything. I had to have your authority. I'm glad to get rid of them.'

'I bet you've had a break-in, too,' Hannie said.

He looked at her curiously. 'Attempted break-in,' he said.

'I don't suppose there'll be another,' she said and went off to phone a safe courier who would take the plants from her at the Hope Club and ferry them down to Duncan Kyte's home in Suffolk straight away. Not that they would do him much good, she suspected. The plastic bags containing the roots and jar containing the flowers, now mauve-brown, lay beside her on the seat of the cab as she rode into London. They disgusted her. These few stale specimens seemed to sum up all the troubles she had left behind and to which she was returning. She thought again of her lost husband, whom she still loved, and of her children, and of her home – all barred to her. As she approached London she saw

February had struck the London streets. There were little piles of dirty snow along the edges of the pavements. There was a transport strike. Pinched people hung round bus stops hoping a bus would come. It was in a gloomy mood that she returned to the Hope Club. The new façade, with the long windows outside and the fresh green and cream paint impressed her. She walked into the new hall and said to the woman in the little glass-fronted porter's lodge, 'Hullo, Mrs Knott.'

'Mrs Richards,' said Mrs Knott. 'You've caught us hopping. We thought you'd be here tomorrow. You're too early for your celebration.'

'This is enough of a celebration,' said Hannie.

'Oh, you'll have to have your coming-out party,' said Mrs Knott. 'Here's your key – suite 12 – very posh now. Here's a few letters, and there's a courier waiting for you over there.'

Hannie thanked her and carded quickly through the letters and phone messages as she walked over to the courier. There was nothing from Adam. There was no note from her children. She gave the plants to the courier and told him how to get to Duncan Kyte's house. She went slowly upstairs to the grandly named suite 12. It was small, but there was no denying it was a suite. There was a big vase of flowers on the table with a card from Elizabeth. She turned on the television and fell asleep in a chair, dreaming briefly of a long, dry plain across which women of all ages carried pots of water.

She woke up because Elizabeth was hugging her. 'Oh,' she said, 'I'm so relieved to see you. You look so tired. I really shouldn't have woken you.'

'Very inconsiderate,' said Hannie. 'First you help get me out of a Brazilian gaol, then you make it worse by waking me up. Elizabeth – I can't thank you all enough.'

'We can get some tea sent up,' said Elizabeth.

'This is very posh, now it's room service. Will it make ends meet?'

'It's a long financial story,' said Elizabeth. 'I've brought you some clothes – thick tights and a skirt and jumpers. They're mine. I'm afraid you'll look a bit Home Counties. I was just dropping them in. I thought you were coming tomorrow.'

'I'll have a shower,' said Hannie. 'Thanks.'

From the shower she shouted, trying to sound normal, 'Any word from Adam?'

Elizabeth shouted back, 'We told him you were safe.'

'Oh, never mind the tact,' cried Hannie. 'What happened?'

'He said, "Good",' Elizabeth called back. 'He asked if you faced charges over here. I said no.'

Hannie came out of the shower in a towel and sat down to comb her hair. 'So that's that,' she said. 'He still doesn't care – just as long as I'm not had up at the Old Bailey in a blaze of publicity. I didn't do it, you know. Someone planted those drugs – I don't know who. I hope you'll believe me, but I suppose I can't really expect you to.'

'James and Julie said you didn't,' Elizabeth told her. 'I'm afraid I thought you'd lost your head and were trying to get a lot of money because – because of what happened. It would have been understandable.'

Hannie looked through the mirror at her friend and saw she was trying to believe her. She dropped the subject. She put on the warm clothes and tights. Then a small Chinese girl brought in the tea, on a tray. She moved the flowers to the window sill and put the tray carefully on the table, but something reminded Hannie

250

of the load-bearing women she thought about so often. 'What do you get paid?' she asked.

The girl said, 'Seventy pounds a week. I'm part-time.'

Elizabeth said, in a tight voice, 'Mary's Mr Lee's daughter. You know Mr Lee. He owns a restaurant.'

The girl said, 'I'm a student at LSE. The hours fit in with the course.'

After the door had shut Elizabeth said, 'Really, Hannie. Do you need to sit there and imply that I'm exploiting the staff – while they're in the room?'

'Oh, don't be so snobbish,' said Hannie. 'Oh – I'm sorry. I'm rattled. I must have been on the verge of a breakdown in that gaol.'

'My analyst used to say that sometimes that is the first stage of a reappraisal and readjustment. I never got past it myself.'

Hannie looked at her and could not help laughing, even though James had told her not to reveal that she knew of Elizabeth's sexual blackmail of her analyst. Elizabeth laughed too. 'I told him not to tell anyone,' she spluttered.

When they'd stopped laughing, Elizabeth said, 'You know, James Carter's a very nice man.'

'Really, Elizabeth,' Hannie said disapprovingly, 'you're going from bad to worse.'

7. The New Hope Club

Hannie spent the following week at the Hope Club, gradually regaining her strength but waiting for James Carter to get in touch with her.

It was not a situation she enjoyed. During her affair with Spinelli, she had spent three months pinned in her lodgings, unable to contact him at home in case his wife found out, and waiting for his secret calls from phone boxes or his unexpected arrivals at her door. She had resolved never to assent to a situation like that again, and on the whole, never had. Now she felt inhibited about even ringing Adam, too tired somehow to take the initiative. She thought despondently, Let him have it his way as long as he looks after Flo and Fran properly. She also very much wanted to see James Carter. One night she dreamed he came, suddenly, into a landscape of rocks and dust, carrying the branch of a tree covered in leaves.

In the meantime she was waiting for two men to get in touch with her and did not know whether the fact that there were two made things better or worse. The waiting woman was a Victorian luxury: these days, while woman wait, they have to keep up with the pace set by the world. One of the matters claiming Hannie's attention was the Hope Club. She had been alarmed when Elizabeth had told her there was a long financial story concerning the Club. She feared the worst. It was a relief when Elizabeth suggested that she, Margaret and Julie should all find a free evening and meet for dinner and a chat.

The dinner itself was a brisk affair and business was not discussed. Afterwards they had coffee in the little writing room, served by the Chinese girl, who, as she put the tray down, looked nervously at Hannie as if she feared another sharp enquiry concerning her wages and working conditions. Elizabeth, with her feet tucked up on the sofa, pulled her blue stole around her shoulders, remarking, 'I haven't quite worked out the heating yet.' Julie was cross-legged in front of the fire, rolling a joint, and she said, 'It's OK.' Hannie, who was bundled up in a cream robe with fringes, said, 'Come on, let's get on with it.' She felt worried. The Hope Club was, if temporarily, her only home now. She did not relish the idea of its being threatened. She suspected they might all have to work out a way of bailing it out of financial trouble. At this point Margaret came back into the room and said, 'I've spoken to Tracey Burrows. She's getting promoted to the Grosvenor branch of the bank. She's agreed to take over the account. Might as well keep it all in the family. She understands the problem.'

'Can she come and explain it to us?' asked Hannie.

'She's just left,' said Margaret. 'Elizabeth, you do it.'

'Well,' said Elizabeth, 'obviously, the expansion meant I had to study the books of the Club in a way I suspect no one has done since 1945. The problem's been that running as a co-operative means nobody takes full responsibility. As long as the bills get paid, everybody's satisfied. And that's what Mr and Mrs Knott had been doing all this time.'

'The fact is,' added Margaret, 'that the Knotts have been running this place – money, administration, everything – for thirty years. But we can't organize on that basis any more. We have to elect a management committee and try to sort it out.'

Hannie shifted uneasily. 'Bang goes freedom,' she remarked.

'You're on it,' Margaret told her.

Hannie nodded glumly. 'First it's prison, then it's a committee,' she said. 'Things are changing.'

'That's settled, then,' said Margaret. 'We all stand for the committee.'

'Come on, St Theodosia's,' said Hannie.

Elizabeth looked at her. 'Decisions have to be made,' she said.

'Tell us about the bad news first,' Julie said. Plainly she had been at meetings like this before. 'Tell us what we owe.'

'We don't owe anything,' said Elizabeth. 'We're rich.'

'What?' Hannie said. 'I thought we were going to have to pass the hat round.'

'Me, too,' said Julie. 'What's the problem then?'

'The percentages of income our members are likely to give to the Club over the next year,' Elizabeth said, 'are over £200,000 – that's a rough figure. Only a half to a third of that will go on running costs. The situation is that we either decide to scale down the percentages, so as to continue on a non-profit-making basis, or go on as we are, making a profit and getting richer and richer. I don't need to tell you that £100,000 per annum,

254

invested, can provide a million in seven or eight years. When I examined the accounts at the bank, I also found a stray £250,000 which had accumulated over the years of the Club's existence. The old building was run on a shoestring by the Knotts – the surplus left over from members' fees just sat on deposit at the bank gaining interest over nearly forty years. As I say, we're rich. What are we going to do about it?'

'Say the rest,' Margaret urged.

'I went mad and had a flutter in the futures market. I just got £25,000 on a cotton harvest,' said Elizabeth.

Julie said, 'Babylon.'

'What?' asked Elizabeth.

'Babylon's the City, the white man's cash, the power,' Julie told her. 'That's where we are. I'm not complaining. Just I never thought to be there.'

'Babylon's what it's all about,' said Margaret.

'It's Duncan Kyte,' said Hannie. 'Why can't we leave the money where it is?'

'Oh,' said Elizabeth. 'You don't mind fighting guerillas or pushing on through the steaming jungle and so on and so forth. But when it comes to the stink of money, your courage fails, you draw back in ladylike disdain – that it, Hannie?'

'Elizabeth!' protested Hannie. 'I'm not used to all this stuff. All right – I don't like it. But why can't we leave the money there and cut the membership rates? Anything over can just stay in the bank in case we want to open a new building or something.'

'Listen,' said Elizabeth, 'money you leave in the bank isn't just kept there in a locked box with your name painted on the front, you know. They don't just brush the cobwebs off the box, unlock it and give it to you when you want it. What banks do is lend your money to

255

people like Duncan Kyte – that's what they do. They buy shares in profitable firms with very little regard to the form of business engaged in. And a lot of the bank profits are coming from investment in the Third World. It's their duty to make money. You don't even know what that money's going into. The only way you can evade the responsibility for money is by turning it into gold or burying it under the hearthstones.'

Hannie said nothing. The she looked at Elizabeth. 'I've had a revelation,' she said. 'Or rather, it's something I've been thinking of for a while. Listen to me, here it comes, begun in a Rio gaol and ending in London. Tell me what you think. Because I think that you and I and the other members, between us, can make it work.'

She began by relating her imaginings about the women she had met on her journeys in India, in Africa, in Latin America. She said, 'We know that for every poor woman, there's a poor man and poor children. But the aid almost always goes to the men. It doesn't work for the women, often not for the men in the long run. Half the time the men go for cash. They say they want a sawmill so they can cut down the lumber – that means the women have to walk five miles farther to get the wood to cook the family food. No one notices the women with bundles of wood – until suddenly the trees are gone and the land's eroded. Or the men get a big irrigation system and start growing cash crops. The landlord comes past, gets jealous and takes back the land. All the time the women are still carrying water to grow their own small crops – the crops that feed the family. The water supply is too far from the houses so the children are still dying of dysentery. Half the people in hospital in the world are there because of water-related diseases. While the money goes to the men, the answer to women's problems always seems to be contraception and sterilization. Everybody knows that people have too many children when they're afraid their children will die. Every time a child dies somewhere with a high death rate, the parents respond by having two or three more children – just in case. Sometimes I think all this carrying on about contraception stems from misunderstanding. We all know, because we're women, that no woman, however simple and uneducated, wants to be pregnant all the time, wants to have children she can't feed or wants to watch them die. Men talk about traditions of child-bearing as if they were fixed and unalterable. We all know that if you give a woman a way of not having so many children – and some reason to think she'll rear the children she does have – then she'll cut the number in the family. We know that because our grandmothers did it.

'The women should have small industries, maybe, so they can use their own skills, and a way of growing their crops and a way of making their lives and their children's easier and safer.

'Do you see what I mean?' she appealed. 'If men are handing out money to other men, let's give ours to the women. It would take so little. Small industries. Standpipes so that crops could be grown more easily, children surviving because they had water that wasn't polluted, women living longer because they weren't so overburdened. Wouldn't that be enough for a start? I could go there and find out what they wanted. You could handle the money. I could take it there if I had to – that's the kind of thing I know how to do. We'd get contributions, I'm sure, if we asked. We've all lived off rotten money, in our different ways, at some stage in our lives. Speaking for myself, my moral character is certainly not all it should be. But at least, this way, we'd be handing something back.'

There was a silence. Then Julie said loudly, 'You got it. Hannie, you got it!'

Elizabeth said, 'It's workable.'

They all looked at Margaret, who said, 'They started Oxfam in one house in Oxford. Now it's our turn.'

'What if the men take the money?' Julie said. 'That's the usual thing.'

'The person with the purse,' said Hannie, 'is the person with the power. If we supply small looms so that women can make more cloth, we'll expect to find them there when we get back – right? It won't take the men long to find out what we're doing, for the women will help everybody.'

There was another silence. Hannie stood up and went into the long room. It was full of women. She crossed over to the bar and said to Mrs Knott, 'Champagne?'

'Of course, Mrs Richards,' Mrs Knott said. 'Celebrating?'

'Hope so,' said Hannie and took the tray and carried it back to the others.

'Well,' said Margaret with a grin, raising her glass, 'to Womanfam, or something like that.'

'And Hannie, smuggling for a good cause,' Julie added.

They all raised their glasses.

The next day Hannie telephoned the house in Devon and spoke to her husband. She said that she must come down soon to see the children and to talk to him. Sounding nervous, he suggested he bring the children to London to see her. She told him firmly that she was coming that day and he had better make up his mind to it. She set off immediately.

The door was opened by Victoria Hughes-Brown. Hannie, looking briefly at the face of her erstwhile friend and neighbour, realized that while she felt nervous, Victoria was as determined, and as desperate, as any of the people she had met on her adventures. She thought suddenly, My God, it's like a jungle – and then stepped inside saying, 'I don't intend to have a row. I hope you don't either.'

Victoria, who was tall and fresh-faced with long, dark brown hair, said, 'Of course not,' but Hannie was not sure. Her children, she discovered, were out riding. She walked ahead of Victoria into the sitting room. The furniture had been rearranged, and in one corner there stood a small cabinet of china she recognized as having come from one of the rooms at Lanning Hall, where Victoria had lived with her father.

Adam stood by the fireplace, where a log fire burned. He said, 'Hullo, Hannie.'

Victoria advanced into the room, poked the logs in the fireplace a little, added another log, and sat down. Hannie, still standing, said, 'Hullo, Adam. I came because I thought we had a few things to sort out. Sooner the better. Would it be too much to ask if we could talk in private?'

'Victoria has said she would like to be here,' Adam said. 'She is involved, after all.' He was very embarrassed.

'Oh,' Hannie said. 'I should have liked to see Flo and Fran when I arrived,' she added.

'They'll be back in an hour,' he said.

'They've arranged to have lunch at the Woodalls',' Victoria said. At this, Adam looked even more embarrassed.

259

'Oh, sod you, Adam,' Hannie said, forgetting she had meant to be cool and sensible. 'Did you have to do all this, Adam – have Victoria around stressing her ownership of my poker, hiding the children? This makes me feel sick. It's disgusting.'

Adam said nothing. Victoria said, 'Adam offered to meet you in London, to spare you the upset of coming here. If you had agreed to that, of course the children would have been there. They're not simply because we thought you might get upset and upset them.'

'Shut up, Victoria,' Hannie said. 'You're here in my house, with my husband and my children. You're lucky I didn't come here earlier, with friends, to disrupt the atmosphere. As for you, Adam, you might as well not be here. All you're doing is standing commandingly by the fireplace, doing nothing.'

He said, 'You can't imagine how much I hate this, Hannie.'

'That,' Hannie said, 'is a very weak remark. I've protected you too long, Adam Richards.'

Victoria said, 'I told you she'd become abusive.'

Hannie said, 'I think I'll pour myself a drink. Don't worry – I know where it's kept.' She poured herself some whisky at the sideboard and asked, 'Anybody else? No? I'll just say what I've come to say, after which you, Victoria, can just telephone the Woodalls and say there's been a mistake and will Flo and Fran come home to see their mother. When I've seen them, I shall leave. So, here goes. I want the children to live with me in London and come here for holidays. I want a divorce, simple and straightforward with no complications. If you like, Adam, I'll divorce you for adultery quickly. I'll make no financial claims on you. You can sit here and fester like gentlepeople in this nice house in this nice part of the country for as long as you like.'

'You can't do that, Hannie,' said Adam. 'They don't want to live in London.'

'I can,' said Hannie. 'Or you can fight a long, unrewarding and expensive custody case for them if you want to – you'll only disturb them in the process. Plenty of children live in London and like it – they're getting older. It wouldn't be long before they started yelling for excitement and saving up to run away to the city.'

'You can't get away with it, Hannie,' said Victoria. 'We can prove you've been in gaol on a drug-smuggling charge and only got out because of a history of mental illness. You'll never get those children.'

Hannie had been afraid of this argument. She finished her whisky and said, 'If you go to court. But is it worth it? You don't really want another woman's children hanging about, Victoria. At the moment they're a way of anchoring Adam to you here, but as soon as you've got your own child, you won't need them. They'll be second-class citizens once you've got a brace of sons. I'm not going to stand by watching Flo and Fran picking up the toys of the son and heir. They'll be better off with me. If you impulsively go to court and prove me an unfit mother, I shall have nothing to lose. I can go to the police and confess to everything I've done – to re-surface the tennis court, to buy the ketch in the harbour and the bull in the field. The stink will go on for ever. Then what price your landed-gentry act? You'll be sunk – and the place will probably go under the hammer. It's a Mexican stand-off. If anybody pulls the trigger, we both die. Think about it, and while you're thinking, phone the Woodalls. I want to see the children before I go. I'll just go out for a walk for the moment.'

She went out of the back of the house and crossed the wintry lawn. There was going to be little argument about terms, she thought. Victoria needed a good excuse not to have the children there permanently. Without them she would feel less secure with Adam, but as long as Hannie agreed to a speedy divorce she could soon marry Adam and turn to and have children of her own. Safe at last, Victoria Hughes-Brown, she thought. Or will you ever feel really safe now?

She ducked under the swing, walked across the tennis court, into the orchard. A freezing wind came off the sea. There was nothing here which did not remind her of the past. On the lawn Flo and Fran had staggered and toppled as they learned to walk. She had pushed them on that swing. There, she had caught Flo as she fell off a branch of the tree. Under the oak she and Adam had sat up, all one midsummer night, talking. Just here, in the orchard, where the trees were black and twisted and the grass stood up in frozen spikes, was where she and Adam had walked after dinner, in summer, on the day she had come down for the first time to meet his parents.

It's all gone now, for you, she thought to herself. Flo and Fran would have it temporarily, for a while, in the holidays, sharing it with little half-brothers and -sisters until they were old enough to sulk, resent the situation, feel bored and refuse to come. What a mess, she thought. What a horrible series of mistakes. Perhaps, she thought, I should have stayed at home, entertained the neighbours and made jam with Victoria in the summer. Perhaps I should have guarded my threshold the way other women do. Perhaps I should have, she said to herself, but I'd have sulked and had to open a pottery shop for summer visitors in Porthtrevanion. Swallowing the lump in her throat, she leaned against the grainy trunk of the big, twisted apple tree, the early one, whose blossom always came out first. She felt very bleak under the bare, rattling branches, twisted together like a vast cat's cradle gone wrong above her. She brushed tears from her eyes and sniffed. She looked up. There, on the black and knotted branches, were the first, faint green swellings which meant the buds were coming. She stared intently at them.

She was being hailed — 'Hannie!' from across the orchard. She couldn't believe her eyes. It was James Carter, plunging across the grass towards her in a huge, flapping coat and long scarf. Her joy and relief were enormous. It seemed too good to be true. She rushed to him and embraced him. They kissed, frozen lip to frozen lip until the warmth came to their faces. 'Oh, my God, am I pleased to see you,' Hannie burst out. 'Oh, James. I'm so miserable in this dump.'

'They told me at the Hope Club you'd come down,' he said. 'I thought you might be annoyed I'd followed you.'

'Annoyed!' she said. 'I've never felt so rotten, till you came.'

'I thought you might need some assistance,' he said. 'Anyway, my excuse was that I wanted to tell you who planted those drugs.'

They started to walk round the orchard. 'Well, I wouldn't mind knowing,' said Hannie.

'I'm sorry I disappeared for so long,' he told her. 'I had some things to sort out — deals to conclude, explanations to make — you know the idea. Mine's not a trade you can just walk out of, not unless you want to bump into somebody nasty on a dark night later on. Basically, that's how I got on to who did it to you. Not the Rio police or Duncan Kyte the wicked industrialist

– nothing like that. No, it was just Kyte's druggie little girlfriend – Serafina – Serena?'

Hannie started to laugh, 'Serena. Of course, why didn't I think of Serena?'

'The story is that she's been having it away with Kevin Coleman. He was, or still is, the lover and the dealer, so he's got a double hold over her. He gives her love and drugs. Also money. Also, she's afraid of him, which is hardly surprising because everybody's afraid of him. She was chatting to him and mentioned what you were up to and that you were going to New York. Coleman couldn't resist the idea of using you to bring in a few drugs –'

'He got vindictive when I refused to work for him once,' Hannie interrupted. 'He told me he'd do me a mischief one day. I thought it was bluster.'

'Well, it wasn't – though I don't suppose he wanted to get you caught out and the stuff confiscated. Anyway, there it is. Serena innocently finds out from Kyte who you're going to see and where you'll be staying. There you are, covered by superior credentials as a member of a scientific expedition. All he has to do is get friends in New York to plant the cocaine while you're out of your hotel room, and everybody wins. That spot-check on the luggage at Rio was pure bad luck.'

'Serena,' Hannie said thoughtfully. 'I ought to have known. Still, all's well that ends well, that's what I always say.'

'Quite right,' said James gravely. 'I hear you've got a new job, smuggling alms. Will you be needing any help?'

'Oh, yes,' Hannie replied. 'Lots.' She added, 'Lots and lots of help.'

'Good,' he said. 'First things first, then. I suggest we go back to the house, talk to the delightful couple in there and wait for the children. Then we can go back to London for a very long, nice time together, which we deserve.'

They were standing under the old apple tree. Hannie said, 'Good.' But she still wasn't sure. James looked up into the branches and said, 'Look – the buds are coming.'

'I know,' said Hannie. And just then her daughters, wellingtons scudding and flame-red pigtails flying, came rushing across the grass to meet her.

So here ends the story of Hannie Richards and the Hope Club. Hannie has her work and her children and, probably, love. The Hope Club has its own premises where women can meet and talk and relax, and now its other purpose, which is to foster the kind of organization for which women run jumble sales and children go out singing carols – all proceeds to other women and children.

So all ends well for the time being, although there are, as we all know, no final answers for women or anyone else in this world, except those found by courage, effort, love and, of course, hope.